OUR CHOICE

OUR CHOICE

Jeannette Krupa Amanfo

OUR CHOICE

iUniverse books may be ordered through booksellers or by contacting:

iUniverse
1663 Liberty Drive
Bloomington, IN 47403
www.iuniverse.com
1-800-Authors (1-800-288-4677)

Because of the dynamic nature of the Internet, any web addresses or links contained in
this book may have changed since publication and may no longer be valid. The views
expressed in this work are solely those of the author and do not necessarily reflect the
views of the publisher, and the publisher hereby disclaims any responsibility for them.

Any people depicted in stock imagery provided by Getty Images are models,
and such images are being used for illustrative purposes only.
Certain stock imagery © Getty Images.

ISBN: 978-1-5320-6706-8 (sc)
ISBN: 978-1-5320-6707-5 (e)

Library of Congress Control Number: 2019900939

Print information available on the last page.

iUniverse rev. date: 01/24/209

I'd like to dedicate my book to my, loving husband Kenneth Amanfo Jr.. Knowing it was God that brought the two of us together, it shall keep us together. With God all things are possible.

1

Levi Ubani, is a thirty three year old man, and one of great authority, what Levi wanted is what Levi usually got. It wasn't always this way for him coming from an African back ground. He remembered there were times as a child in school, that he was laughed at, and called names, and told that he was a nobody. He couldn't understand it because, living in Detroit, was full of people with a colored background. He had a lot to overcome when it came time for his race. Having a large law firm in Michigan, came at a price, some not always a respectable one. There were times that he would have a person paid off, to keep his client from being found guilty, when they indeed were guilty of the crime they were being accused of. He was not a man to take *no* for an answer. There were many times, when he heard someone tell him, that something couldn't be done the way that he wanted it done, he would go through any length, to get just what he wanted. But this gave him a strong reputation of being the best law firm of winning all his cases. This brought in cliental, and anything that would bring that, is what he was after.

One evening coming home from a sports club bar he was a mem-ber of for the last ten years, he was driving along the interstate 1-94. When he noticed a parked car on the right side of the road. Before he knew what was happening, the car pulled right out in front of him. He didn't have enough time to swerve, he hit right into the little yellow car. He sat there for a minute trying to gain his wits, then after gaining his composer, he got out to check on the other driver. He walked slowly as he tried not to stumble and fall, he was shaken up a bit from the impact of the accident. As he approached the car, now all smashed on the driver side door, he wanted to see if the driver was alright. It was a young woman that lay there bleeding from behind the wheel. He was unable to see just where she was bleeding from, although it did look as though it was her head bleeding. Quite possible from hitting the steering wheel. There were cars going by slowly, gazing at the two wrecked vehicles.

One man stopped, and called the authorities. Another pulled over, and jumped out, to see if anyone needed help. Levi and another man, was looking through the window, of the car. But couldn't tell if the young woman was breathing or not.

Levi tried to open the door, but it would not open for. He knew it would take the Jaws of Life, to get her out. They walked around to the other side of the car, but the passenger door was pushed up against the railing so tight, they were unable to open that door too. For the first time in his life, he felt like he had no control over the situation. He was lost, he stood outside the smashed car yelling, and tapping on the window trying to get movement from the woman.

"Ma'am, can you hear me ma'am?"

Levi could hear the ambulance sirens getting closer. By now there was quite a crowd gathering close to see just what had happened. He would look down the road, telling folks that were driving to slow. "Move ahead can you hurry! Get past so the ambulance, and the rescue team could get in here to help this woman." He didn't know if the woman that lay in the front seat was alive or not, because she hasn't moved since the accident. But what he did know is he needed to get help to her. He stood there waving for the ambulance, and the workers to get in close, so they could get to the woman that lay there so lifeless. He wanted to know her name, and if she was married, and if she had any children. He just wanted to know something about this woman that pulled right out in front of him. And why she didn't seem to have noticed, that he was fast approaching. His mind was now racing in all sorts of directions. *What was she thinking, pulling out in front of me like that? Did she not see me, was she trying to kill herself?* He stood as close as the workers would allow him to stand, without getting in their way. He watched as the door was being sawed and ripped away, from the car. He seen where cops were looking inside of his car. At this time Levi didn't care what they were looking for, he was sure they were looking to see if there was any sign of alcohol that could have been a factor that led to the accident. He watched as a man checked the woman for her vital signs. It seemed like hours were just slipping by and they still never got the woman out. Now all nervous, and pacing as his mind was racing, he heard the answer he waited to hear.

"She breathing!" the voice came loud and clear, from one of the rescue workers that was checking her vitals. "Let's get her out of here: He yelled to the other workers, as he cut the seat belt off of her.

Levi was very happy to hear this woman was alive, even though he didn't know how much alive. He knew she was alive, and he needed answers, to why she pulled out in front of him.

Does she even know what's going on right now, is she aware that she been in a car accident? He thought.

"Is she going to be alright?" he asked one of the workers there.

There was man that was looking inside the car, it appeared he was looking to see if she might have been drinking and driving. He approached Levi. "Who are you sir?"

"I'm the man she pulled out in front of. My name is Levi Ubani."

The man stood there, looking at him for a minute. Are you the Levi Ubani Law firm?"

"Yes, that's me. Is she going to be alright?" He asked trying to get the man back to the issue of what was going on.

"Do you know who this lady is?"

"No, I don't, is she going to be alright?" Levi asked again.

"All I can tell you is that her vitals are good, they seem to be strong. I think she's going to be just fine. They will be taking her to Beaumont hospital, if you would like to go there."

"Yes, I would, I want to know if she's going to be okay. I need to know why she pull right out in front of me, it was if she didn't even see me coming down the road."

"I think that it will be awhile, before you get all your answers that you're looking for. This woman is hurt pretty bad." The man spoke, while heading to the ambulance.

"I thought that you just said that she will be fine." Levi commented.

The man looked at Levi. "Yes, I do believe she will be fine, but when one is hit this hard, sometimes it takes awhile to get back to your old self.

It can be weeks before she feels up to answering any questions. And then at times from the impact, some folks never remember what happened. Head injury is not so good."

"But you're sure she will be alright?" Levi asks the man while the following him to the ambulance.

"That is not for me to say, that is something I leave up to God. Would you like me to take a look at you? You look like you're in need of help yourself."

"No, I'm fine, I'm just wondering if this lady has any family that I can call?"

"Their putting her in the ambulance now, you might want to check with an officer to see what you can find out about her." The man informed Levi, and then patted him on the arm as he was getting into the ambulance.

Levi stood there watching the cops look at the woman's car, he walked over towards them, to see if they could give him any information about the woman.

"Officer, Officer!" he called out.

"Yes!" A short young cop answered, while holding a camera in his hand. "How may I help you?"

"Could you tell me, if anyone has found out this woman's name, or anything at all about her?"

"And who are you? Did you see the accident?" the officer asked.

"I am the man that she pulled out in front of. That's my car right over there." He pointed towards his car with a smashed front end.

The officer then reached into his pocket and pulled out a pad of paper and an ink pen. He took down all of Levi's information that he needed, and then he told him the ladies name was Yvonne McAlester.

Without really thinking about what he was saying, Levi heard himself say the words aloud. "Jesus please help this woman to be alright."

Levi was not a praying man, although he had a grandma that he heard pray many times, in his life, when he was a young boy.

Another officer came up to him, and began to ask him questions.

"I understand that you're the gentleman that was driving the blue corvette? I'd like to ask you some questions." asked the officer.

Levi looked at him, and began to shake his head. Trying to find the right words, but not wanting to tell the same thing he just did to another officer. "I just told that officer everything that happened. He pointed in the direction of the other officer. I'd like to get to the hospital to see if she is alright if you don't mind."

"If I have any more questions, I'll get a hold of you then."

Levi jumped in the second ambulance that was at the site, to get a ride to the hospital. On his way there, the driver asked him the same questions that the cop had already ask. He told him all that he could remember.

Then the driver began to talk to him about God. Levi could hear the man talk, but what he heard was words; it didn't mean anything to him now He heard this rugged looking man which seemed to be in his mid-forties, say how God loved him, and spared his life today. Even though back at the car he asked the Lord to help the woman, he was in no way wanting to hear this stranger, talk to him about God. Levi was mad, how could he say that God loved him, when there was a woman that just got hit by him, and might not make it. What kind of a God does that to someone?

"Do you know that the Lord cares for you?" The driver asked.

Levi looked at this man, without saying a word. If the truth be told, he wanted the man to just get him to the hospital and leave him alone. He had nothing of any meaningful words for him, his words sounded powerless. Levi sat there trying to close out, the words that this stranger was sharing with him. Then he heard the words he heard as a little boy, when his grandma took him to Sunday school. John 3:16 For God so loved the world that he gave His only begotten Son, that whosoever believeth on Him shall not perish but have everlasting life. Those words pierced his heart, like none other that the man spoke. He couldn't believe that he remembers those very words when he was just a boy. After his grandma died when he was only six years old, he never went back to church. His parents never took him, nor did they believe in Jesus. Not long after his grandma died, his father left him and his mother. At first it seemed as though his dad would stay in contact with him, but after several months went by, his father was never to be seen again. His mother never married again, she lived her life for helping Levi stay in school, and out of trouble. Holding down two jobs, then starting her own house cleaning business, to where she was able to hire others to clean homes for her. She was able to put him through school, so his life would be greater than she had while raising him. The man looked over at Levi, and seen a tear come down his cheek. Not knowing it was the words he spoke to him, that caused the tears to fall, he reached out his kind hand; and gripped Levi's shoulder. "I prayed for this young woman and I believe that she will be just fine."

"Thank you for your prayers, I sure hope that she will be. I found out her name is Yvonne McAlester, she is twenty-eight years old. No one could tell me, if she is married or has a family."

"The hospital has a way of finding all that information out. They may already know the answer by the time we get there." replied the driver.

Levi sat quietly the rest of the way to the hospital; all he could think about is if this lady by whom he recently learned of her name is alright. Is she alive, or did this car accident take her life. Finally, the time came were they arrived at the hospital, he could hardly wait before the ambulance came to a stop, he had the door opened, before it came to a stop, when the driver slammed on the brakes.

"Thank you, I got to go." With those words Levi was gone walking up to the hospital door. He could hardly wait, to get inside, to see if Yvonne was still alive.

"Can you help me?" Levi asked, as he approached the nurses' station.

A nurse turned to see who it was calling for help, then noticing a handsome black man, with muscles that stuck of his shirt in all the right places. "I can try" replied a nurse with long blond hair pulled back in a ponytail. "How can I help you?"

"A young woman was just brought in here today, about an hour ago she was in a bad car accident. Can you tell me anything about her? Is she okay, I mean is she alive?" Levi asked, as he stood there looking down the hallway, as if to see her come walk up to him.

"Do you have the name of this person, that you are talking about" asked the nurse.

"Her name is Yvonne McAlester."

"We are not allowed to give out any information on anyone that's not family. Are you her family?" Asked the nurse.

As he was talking, a doctor came down the hallway, and noticed him talking to the nurse.

"Hello, I am the doctor on call when they brought your wife in today. Please follow me, she will want to see a friendly face when she wake's up."

Levi didn't know why the doctor called him her husband. He wasn't going to tell him any difference at this time. Expecially after the nurse told him that no one outside of family can know anything about her.

Levi followed close behind him, in hopes that someone there would not recognize who he was and let the truth come out about him not having a wife.

She is in room two seventeen, second bed. Just down this hallway." He said while pointing down the hallway.

Levi thanked the doctor after he was told him she was going to be just fine, he continued to Yvonne's room.

2

Levi was not one to like being at hospitals, he remembered when his grandma got sick and was in the hospital. Although very young, he never forgot the time and hours that was spent waiting to see if she would ever come home. After several weeks of not getting any better she died. Ever since her death, he hasn't spent much time at any hospital.

He approached the door, and quietly he began to open it. As he walked to the second bed to see this woman that lay there, that could have died just hours earlier, he didn't know what to say. Her eyes were closed, when he walked over to the bedside. *What a beautiful woman* he thought. She had long brown hair that wrapped around her shoulders; she looked as if to have some kind of Indian in her. Although she was covered up, he could tell that she was a petite woman. She looked so small and frail, it's of wonder she came through the accident alive. *I wonder if she's already asleep, did I get in here too late.* Levi stood there looking down at her, thinking she was asleep. Just when he was ready to turn and walk away, he heard her ask him a question.

"Are you in the right room?"

Levi was shocked to hear her ask him that question.

"Yes ma'am, I am, do you remember anything?" he asked her.

"Not really, but the doctor told me that I pulled out in front of someone. Would that someone be you?" she asked.

Before he could answer her question, the doctor walked into her room.

"Well I see your talking, it's good to see your husband I bet huh dear? Let me check on you later, I'll leave you be."

"My husband! What is he talking about? Did we get married and I not remember it?"

"No, not at all. I really can't say why the doctor thought that I was your husband. But when he called me him, I never let him know any different because I would not have been able to come in to see you or know if you are okay."

"Are you that man that I pulled out in front of?"

"Yes, that would be me."

I figured since I didn't know who you are, that it just might be you. I am very glad that you are okay. I would have felt so bad if anything would have happened to you. I mean I already feel terrible, and I just want to say that I'm so sorry. I don't know what happened, why I didn't see you."

Levi had thought that he might get a little angry with the woman, once he found out that she was going to make it and not die. But after hearing her kind words towards him, he moved with compassion. "I don't want you to worry about that right now, you need to just get yourself better." he replied, all the while thinking at least she wasn't trying to kill herself.

"I looked and didn't see a thing, I just thank God that you were not hurt. You're not, are you?" she asked.

"No ma'am I'm not, I was a little shaken up. But I think the biggest reason for that was because I was so worried about you."

Yvonne managed to bring such a beautiful smile across her face, that Levi thought it lit up the whole room. She thought to herself, this man is quite handsome, and a body that built fits his good looks.

"Do you have any family that you would like me to call for you?" ask Levi.

"Only my son Van, he will be worried about me. But I think the hospital may have called him at school already. My parents live in Florida, I really don't want to alarm them."

"Would you like me to go and check for you, if they were able to get a hold of your son?"

Before she answered him, she looked at him into his eyes. "I'm not sure, maybe I can find someone that I know that can pick him up at the school. I don't even know what your name is, and where you live."

"I see, would this be anything to do with me being a black man?"

"No, it would not, I have lots of friends that are African-American. But my son doesn't know who you are and I'm sure he will not want to go anywhere with you, rather white or black."

"Okay, I understand that. My name is Levi Ubani, and I live here in Detroit."

"Thank you for letting me know that. If you wouldn't mind, I was laying here trying not to fall asleep until I hear from him. I was beginning to think that maybe they never did get a hold of him, because I haven't heard anything yet.'

"I'll go down to the nurses' station, and ask someone if they were able to contact your son. How old is he?"

"He is eight years old, but he thinks since he is the man of the house that he is twenty."

"Oh yeah I was for my mom when I was just a young one too."

"I hope my son won't be afraid to come with you. I so much want to see him tonight before I go back to sleep."

"Well can I call someone else to get him them? I don't want to scare you and you son."

"Oh that's okay, I know I have some bumps and burses, on my face but I really feel fine. I think the doctor should just let me go home. I hate hospitals; we've never gotten along so well."

"You're funny." Levi spoke liking the humor of this beautiful lady. "I think that the doctor might need to keep you for a few days, just to keep a close eye on you. You know we don't want you to get out to soon, then something go wrong."

"We!" thought Yvonne. "**I** need to get out to care for my son, he will be waiting at my home now all by himself right now He's probably very scared, sitting alone."

"I'm sorry, I'll go to the nurses' station now. To find out if they got a hold of him."

Levi left the room to find out about Yvonne's son, but to his dismay they were unable to contact the young boy. Levi knew that if she didn't have any family that lived in the Detroit area, she would need to get someone to get a hold of him. Although to him, it really was none of his business, one way or the other. He could see that she was going to be okay, and that's what he needed to know. But for some reason he felt like it was his job to help out this woman, he knew nothing about. But why should I worry, I have so many things going for me right now, I don't have time for this. Then to his surprise, as he was walking back to **tell her that the hospital staff** was unable-to contact her son, he had compassion fall all over him. What was this, it was not like him to feel this way. Yes, he did a lot of things to make himself look good to the public. Like giving to the poor, so others could see. But this was different, there was no one there to impress. It was up to him to go get the boy, and bring him back to the hospital, to see his mother.

Levi walked back to let her know that they were unable to get in touch with him. Then he asked if she would like for him, to go get her son. He knew that his corvette was wrecked, but he had many cars at his home. He would have to call a cab, to take him back to his house so he could go pick up the young boy, if she agreed to him going.

"Why would you do this for me, when I'm the one that caused this terrible accident in the first place?" She had tears falling down her cheeks.

"You said you have no family here but your son. If you would rather someone else go get him, and then I will call them for you." Levi stated.

"I don't mean to sound ungrateful to you, I mean it's very nice for you to offer; but I don't even know you. I don't know if Van would even get in the car with you.

I just wish that they would let me out of here so I can get home to him."

"I understand how you feel, is there anyone that you can think of, that I can call for you to go pick up your son. I just don't feel right about leaving, knowing he's there waiting and you not being able to get to him."

"My parents are too far away, to come get him. My husband died two years ago, and it's been just Van and I ever since Yvonne put her hands over her face and began to cry hard. "I want to trust you, but I don't know you. I mean you can be anyone, and Van is all I have."

Levi felt for this woman, he could feel for her pain. He didn't know what to say, and then he thought of something that might make her feel more at ease.

"Yvonne I can let you hold my wallet for me, I will only take my driver's license, so I can pick him up."

Levi took out his wallet from his back pocket, to hand it to her, then he held back to get his license out.

"As you can see I have lots of money in there, and credit cards. Oh, I will need money to pay the cab driver, to take me to pick up another car, so I can go get your son. Look I stayed around here to make sure that you were going to be okay. That's got to count for something." Before he could finish the words what he was saying. Yvonne agreed to let him go get Van. She wrote her address down for him.

"Please hurry back, so I don't lay here and worry. He's all I have, please bring him back." She asked while putting her hands over her mouth, like she knew that what she was saying was not really believing that Levi was a good man.

"I'll leave you my cell phone number, that way you can call me at any time. I will be back as soon as I can. Matter of fact when I see Van, I'll call you here so he can talk to you."

"Thank you that will be great. I think that I will take a little nap, while I wait for your phone call. I can barely keep my eyes open; I think they gave me something to relax me before you came here."

Levi walked out the door, with one thing on his mind. He knew that he needed to get home, and grab a car, so he could get to the other side of town to pick her son up.

After Levi arrived at the woman's home, he saw a young boy sitting on the front porch. He knew just by the look of the home, that they didn't have much. The home although kept up neat from the outside, was very tiny. He could see there were flowers planted, on both sides of the sidewalk leading up to the house. He wanted to approach the young boy with caution; he knew that it would be hard for the boy to trust a perfect stranger.

"Hi, is your name Van?" He asked as he walked slowly towards him.

The boy looked up at him, with a fear in his eyes. He stood up as if he was getting ready to run.

"It's okay son, you don't have to be afraid. Your mom sent me over here to come pick you up." Levi reached in his jacket and took out his phone.

"Where is my mom at?"

"Van my name is Levi Ubani, I'm kind of your mother's friend."

"I don't remember seeing you before, how do you know my mom? He asked while his fingers were in his mouth, which looked to Levi like the young boy was chewing his nails.

"I told your mom that when I got here, I would call her up so you could talk to her; would you like that?"

Levi sat down on the porch, so the boy would feel more comfortable with him.

"Yes, but where is my mom? She's usually here when I get home."

"Well I'm sure she would be now, if she could. But we will call your mom up so she can explain what happened, to why she's not here. Does that sound okay with you?"

"Ahah" Van replied shaking his head up and down.

Levi called the hospital, and asks for room two seventeen bed two.

Van's eyes opened wide, like he knew then, that something had happened to his mother.

"Hi Yvonne, it's me Levi Ubani, I'm here at your house with your son Van. I'll put him on the phone, so you can explain where you're at. I didn't feel that it was my place. Would that be fine?"

Levi handed Van the phone, so he could hear the news from his mother. He thought that it be better to come from her then from him. Van might not have believed it coming from him, not knowing who he is.

"Mama, where are you, I've been waiting for you, for a long time."

He watched as Van would shake his head up and down, as if his mom was hearing him. He watched as tears came down the young boy's cheeks. Then he handed the phone back to Levi.

"My mom wants me to come see her. Will you take me there mister?"

"Yes of course, that is why I am here." Levi replied. "Are you ready?"

He looked at Van, just to see he was shaking his head up and down for his answer. Levi took the young boy's hand, to lead him to the car. Van pulled his hand away, as the two of them began to walk towards the car. Levi noticed that Van was not watching where he was going, his eyes were looking down; and he walked right onto a little tree that was out in their front yard.

"You better be careful where you're going young man, before you end up right next to your mom at the hospital. She just happens to have another bed, in her room. Now you wouldn't want that would you?"

After he asked that question, to his surprise the young boy came back with an answer yes.

Levi looked at him quite shocked, but once he thought about it, he could understand why he would feel that way. All he had was his mother, and after all she's in the hospital, so why wouldn't he rather be where she was at. It seemed right to him so he left it at that, without asking Van any questions of why he felt that way. It was a quiet ride to the hospital, the young boy sat in the front seat starring out the window the whole time. He would glance over at Van, and watch him as he would chew on his fingers. Levi was teasing him by telling him that he should be careful, before he ate some of his fingers off. Van didn't even look at Levi as he spoke to him. Then he told the young boy that they have arrived at the hospital.

The boy looked up and not noticing that the car hadn't yet come to a complete stop, had the door opened up and began to jet out.

Levi hit the brakes so fast, that his head jerked to where it hurt him, but nothing seemed to faze the young boy.

"Van hold on there boy, let me at least get the car parked, then I will take you into see your mom."

Van got back in the car, and waited for it to be parked. He was so excited to be able to see her that he was willing to get ran over by a slow-moving car, to get to her. Levi took the young boy's hand, and began to walk up the sidewalk. This time Van didn't pull away from him.

"Your mother will be very happy to see you, as you are to see her, I'm sure of it." spoke Levi. I know that you must really love her, the way you were willing to get yourself run over by me to get in here to see her."

The boy looked up at Levi with a smile, that reminded him of what he seen Yvonne give him just an hour before now "You have a smile like your mom's, has anyone ever told you that?"

"My grandma did."

As the two began to walk the long hallway to get to where she lay, Levi noticed the nurse that helped him out earlier.

"I see you found the missing link?" the nurse asks as she gave Levi a wink.

"Yes, I have, and he's in such a hurry to see his mama."

"I can see that, you better get him to her room."

They reached the end of the hallway, where just behind the door lay a mother waiting for her son to come see her. Levi opened the door quietly, so he wouldn't startle Yvonne in case she was sleeping. When Van seen his mother lying in bed, he let out a cry that woke her up.

Yvonne jumped as she woke up, opened up her eyes. "You're here!" she spoke as she held out her arms to embrace her son. "I was just dreaming of you and look here you are." She spoke with such love, as she held on to him before letting go, to thank Levi, for bringing him to her.

"Mama are you going to be alright?" he asked.

"Honey I am going to be just fine, you remember when I told you that Jesus see's everything we do, and everything that we go through?"

"Yes." he answered.

"Well son Jesus was with me today, when my life could have been taken. He made sure that I got out of my car in one piece. So, I don't want you to worry or be scared, just know that He loves us, and He is there for us."

"I know mama, I got scared when I came home from school and you weren't there. I didn't know where you were and I prayed and ask Jesus to help you be alright. And I knew that you would be after I prayed."

All the while Yvonne and her son were hugging, and talking, Levi tried not to listen in on them, but he heard the words that she spoke about Jesus being there for her, and for him when all this happened. He thought about how when he was in the ambulance ride to the hospital he was very angry at God, for allowing this to happen. And yet Yvonne lay in bed, thanking God for being there for her, and for him. They both came out safe, she might have a few bruises on her face and arms as she said but she's alive to tell about it.

"Levi, I thank you so very, very much for bringing him here."

Levi raised his eyebrows, "it was no problem. He was a bit frightened at first, but then he came around. Where will he stay for the night?"

"I'm not sure, I don't think that the hospital will allow my son to stay here with me."

"I see." Spoke Levi. "Would you like me to take him with me, I have a big home, I'm sure he would like?"

"I couldn't ask you to do that. I wouldn't want to be a bother for you and your family. I am very grateful for you going out of your way today, and picking up my son. I don't need to bother you any further,"

"First of all, it would not be any problem, for me to care for your son tonight." Levi spoke while rubbing the top of Vans head. And second of all, I have no family, at this time. I live almost alone, and I will have lots of stuff for young Van to enjoy himself at his stay." He spoke with a big smile.

Yvonne didn't answer him at first, she wondered what he meant by living almost alone. But she felt not to ask to many questions at this time, thinking maybe he was living with a girlfriend. She looked at Van and hung on to him again tighter then the first. "Are you sure, I don't want to put you out." she added looking up at him.

"You won't be putting anyone out. Now I don't want you to think about that, I know that if you could, you would get out of here right now to be with him. And since you have no one else you can turn to, I am offering you my help. I'll make sure that he gets to his school on time, or would you rather him come see you instead?"

She looked at Van, and asks him what he wanted to do.

"I want to stay with you mama." he spoke quietly then looked up at Levi, hoping that he didn't hear him.

"I fully understand that Van, I wouldn't want to go home with me either." Levi spoke while lighting up the room with a hearty laughter. "But I have no choice; I follow myself where ever I go." Levi was trying to get Van to feel more comfortable with him, for he knew that the hospital rules would never let the young boy stay there.

Yvonne wondered when Levi spoke those words of him following himself, if he ever thought about following God, instead of himself. But she quickly focused her attention to Van.

"Van I would like you to go home, with Mr. Ubani. I have a feeling that everything will be fine. I'm sure he will bring you back here tomorrow, as he said that he would."

"Do you remember when I say pray, and when you have the peace of God to confirm things? Son mom prayed when this first happened, and God has given me the peace that I need to have. You go with him, and after school tomorrow, I'm sure that he will bring you back to see me. And if everything goes right, when day light comes, I'll be able to come home tomorrow."

Levi stood close to her, listening to every word that she spoke. He wondered if God brought the two of them together, even in these difficult circumstances, to bring him back to knowing the things of God. It just seems to him that ever since the accident, he was hearing, everyone talk about God and His love. After all it could have been anyone that pulled out in front of him, but it wasn't, it was a Christian woman, Levi's mind began to wonder on all the why's that is in the world.

Why a Christian, why a woman that seemed to be so sweet and beautiful, that he was so attracted to. He knew that he was taken by the lovely Roxie, but the attraction he had for this woman that lay in bed right in front of him was leaving him to consider his feeling's for Roxie, why after all this time, right when he was considering asking her for her hand in marriage, now he meets Yvonne, and everything becomes confused with his thoughts and feelings for Roxie. He has seen many young beautiful women, and none have made him think differently. And then there was this young boy that reminded Levi of himself, alone without anyone but his mother, much like Levi when he was growing up. It's been years since going to church, but still when he heard of others talk about the things of God, it made him have the feeling that he was running from something.

"I'll take good care of him that is for sure. And right after school, I'll get him something to eat, and bring him right here to see you." said Levi.

"I don't know how to thank you, for what you're doing. It's like God waited for me to pull out on the road right in front of you. I know that sounds silly to say, and it's probably not really so. You could have been anyone; someone else could have been seriously hurt, or very wicked towards me after what I did. But you, well you are very kind and giving. I just thank you so very, very much."

Levi listened to Yvonne show her appreciation, as the tears rolled down her cheeks. He knew this was hard on both her and Van, to trust a total stranger.

He knew if the shoes were on his feet, he could never just hand his child over, to someone he knew nothing about.

"I want to thank you for trusting me, with your little guy here." Levi spoke as he placed his hand on Van's shoulder. "It will be alright young man, tomorrow after school you can come back here, and tell your mom all about the fun, that you had. But if your mother is ever going to get any sleep, we better get out of here so she can get better."

Van stood up, and then leaned over the bed for the last time, before they were to leave for the night. "Good night mama! I love you, and I'll see you tomorrow."

"Night my sweet boy, now don't you worry okay? Make sure you say your prayers before bed. Maybe Mr. Ubani can say them with you before bed, if he wouldn't mind." she spoke while giving Levi a wink.

"Sure! Buddy we can say them together if you'd like." *Yeah, he's going to be the one, to teach me how to pray.* Levi thought to himself.

"See honey, I know that it will be alright, this fine man will even pray with you. Now you go and let me get some rest okay?"

3

Levi and Van walked out the door, without any more words being spoken. It was a quiet ride back to Levi's home. He let Van sit quietly, the whole while he was trying to think. What could he do to make this young boy happy, and try to get his mind off of his mother? Then again, he let his mind think on thoughts that wasn't good for him to be thinking on. *What am I doing, I let a pretty young lady in the hospital get to me, now here I am taking her son home with me. What can I possibly do with a child? I have nothing in common with him.* Then he heard Van interrupt his thoughts.

"Where do you live Mister?"

"We are almost there, just around the corner up here, you'll be able to see the top of my home."

Van looked to where Levi was pointing at, and all he could see were tall trees. Then as he kept his eyes facing in that direction, until he seen something, that look much like a castle would look. Not saying a word, he felt a little scared the closer they got.

Once reaching his home, Levi stopped his car at the edge of the approach, to allow the gates to open up so he could continue to go up the long winding driveway.

"Wow! This is where you live, Is it a castle? I've never seen anything so big, in all my life." A voice with a great big thunder sounded. He was trying not to let fear get a hold of him, he remembered what his mom told him about putting his trust in the Lord.

Levi was pleased to see, excitement come from this boy that up until now seemed to have been very quiet. "Yes, this is where I live, and to answer your question, it's not a castle, I prefer to think of it, as my home. Although I have heard from time to time, a man's home is their castle." He spoke with a light laughter.

"Do you live all by yourself?"

"I do, unless you want to count my maid and my butler. I guess you would say that they live here, because they do live at the east end, of the home.

But I'm sure your stay here will be an enjoyable stay, I have lots of things that you can do."

After Levi parked the car in his twenty-four car garage, they walked inside, just to be greeted at the entrance, by and elderly lady named Mable, who is his maid. "Oh Levi, I'm glad that you made it home, safe and sound. I almost lost you earlier." the maid spoke with care in her voice. Then she looked down to see, that he was not alone. "And who's this young man you have with you?"

"Mable this here is Van McAlester. His mother was also part of the car accident that took place today." He was trying to let her know without putting blame on anyone.

"I see, and I trust the she is going to be alright." The elderly woman spoke while bending down talking to Van.

"She will be fine, she just needed to get some rest, so I brought the young man home for the night."

Then after school tomorrow, I'll be taking him back to the hospital to see his mother."

"Have the two of you eaten anything?" asked Mable.

"No, we have not had a bite, and I'm starved." Levi spoke with laughter, while rubbing his belly, and trying to get Van to warm up to him and Mable. "You'll eat won't you, young man?" he asked.

"Yes, otherwise I might get sick, like my mom." answered Van.

"Come on in and have a seat, dinner will be ready in just a few minutes." inquired Mable walking towards the kitchen.

Mable was an elderly woman that's been with Levi from the beginning of his wealth. Her and her husband Roman, were friends with Levi's mother for years before her untimely death three years ago. Knowing the couple all his life, Levi, offered them a place to live, as if it were there very own home. They had the whole east wing, all to themselves. Usually on their Friday nights they have friends come over and play some cards.

Levi never seem to mind them having that night for themselves. He was a very wealthy man, years before his mother's death. He had his home built, a year after his first million. He had asked his mother to move in with him. For a long time after she moved in with him, it was still hard for her to find her way around the seven thousand square foot home. Mable and Roman being such close friends to his mom, had lost their home to a fire. Levi had asked them if they would like to work for him, taking care of the place. The two had no problem agreeing to what he asked of them, after seeing the size, and the pay they would receive.

Levi had always treated them well, and let them pretty much run the home, as they see fit. The two have never taking advantage of his generosity. They have always respected anything that he might ask from them. They treated Levi like one of their own. In fact, a few years back, they thought that Levi would marry their daughter Teresa. The two dated for a while, but nothing more than friends ever become of their relationship. Although it made Roman and Mable sad, when things didn't turn out for the two of them. But they knew what a kind-hearted man Levi was, and they kept their friendship with him very close, he was like a son they never had, and treated him just like it.

"Van, would you like to take a look around, while we wait to be called to come eat?" Levi asked.

Doing the Unthinkable

"Yeah!" he replied with much excitement. "This place is so big, it'll probably take me a whole week before I can see everything." Van stated as his eyes were looking in every direction.

"You think so huh, well I'm not sure that it will take that long, why don't we start down this way." Levi pointed to a big open walkway that led him to a room with all kinds of game.

When he and Van entered the two thousand square foot game room, Van's eyes got so big, he let out a light scream. "Wow! You got to be kidding me. Really all this, wow this is so cool." He started to walk over to all the games. "You have pool table, hockey, air hockey, wow you even have your own two-lane bowling alley. You got pinball. How did you ever get all this stuff, you must be rich?"

Levi began to laugh, watching the excitement of Van. He knew by the way Yvonne and Van's home looked from the outside, that they never had much, so it pleased him a great deal, to see the young boy enjoying himself. He knew now that his mother was in the hospital, he needed some extra things to do, to help keep his mind distracted from thinking about his mother.

"I'd love to have a place like this, my mom's not rich, and so we don't have anything like this. After my mom gets out of the hospital, do you think that you will ever let me come over and play here?"

"I'd like that very much, but you haven't played anything yet. And Van there's a lot more to see."

"There's more than this?" Van asked, surprised that there could possibly be more to offer.

"Would you like to see, what else is here? Or do you want to play some games first?"

Just as he was about to answer, Mable called them on the intercom system, to come and eat.

"After we eat I'll show you around more okay, then if you want to come back here to play some pinball, or whatever you want, we will do it okay?" Levi felt sorry for Van and his mother, so he wanted to make sure that he had fun, while he was there. Not only did he feel an attraction for the mother of this young boy, but he felt like he needed to be there in the boy's life as well. He couldn't understand what kind of thoughts and feeling were being stirred up on the inside of him for the mother and son. But for now, he knew this was what he must do.

"Okay! Van answered with much excitement. I can hardly wait until we're done eating.

Levi took him by the hand, and led him to the kitchen. Van with wide eyes, looked at all the food that was prepared. He never saw so much food, in all his life. As he sat down on a chair that was pulled out for him, and all the while he tried not to stare at everything that was on the table.

"Does everything look satisfactory to you Van?" ask Mable.

"Oh yes ma'am, I never seen so much food before. We just usually have chicken and potatoes, maybe some corn with it. But you have a whole lot. What's this?" Van asked, pointing at a platter of food.

"That there is roast beef, in a gravy mix. It's one of my favorites, Mable makes it for me quite often, just about once a month." replied Levi. "I'm sure she did today, because I scared her when I hit into your mom's car earlier." He gave Mable a wink.

"It, sure smells good." Van waited for them to say their prayers before eating, but everyone just started to pass the dishes of food around, asking Van what he would like.

"My mom and I always say our prayers before we eat." Van spoke just above a whisper.

"Did you say something?" asked Levi.

Van now shaking his head up and down, spoke again, but this time a little louder. "My mom and I say our prayers before we eat."

"Of course, you do." said Mable then she bowed her head. "Would you like to say them?" she asked Van.

Van bowed his head, "Dear Lord, bless all this food to our body. Help it to make us whole in Jesus name, oh and God, help my mom get better so she can come home, amen."

"That was a very nice prayer, you said. Your mom must have taught you well." Spoke Mable.

"She taught me how to pray, when I was just a little boy."

Van spoke as if to say, he was all grown up now. Levi got a kick, out of listening to him talk. He could tell that he, was trying to sound all grown up, and that was okay with him. Levi never really committing himself to anyone or anything but his work found that he was truly enjoying his time with the young boy. He laughed more, today then he had in a long time. Well at least a real laugh, he would have some moments, where he and a buddy would talk, and a light laughter might come, but it was nothing to the laughter he has done today.

"Van you eat anything you want, trust me Mable is a very good cook. See how big I've gotten because of her cooking." spoke Levi with a big smile.

Van looked at Levi, wondering if that could be true. Levi was a man that stood to be around six foot in height. He had broad shoulders, and he had muscles which Van himself would want when he got older, and most considered him to be handsome.

"This is very good, this here meat stuff. I forgot what you said the name of it is." Van spoke while chewing on some food at the same time.

"It's called roast beef" spoke Roman.

Van looked up, like in shock to hear another voice, he had not yet heard. It was deeper then Levi's almost put a scare in him.

"Oh, don't mind him, his voice is a little rough, but he's as gentle as a lamb." Spoke Levi while watching the look on Van's face.

"He looks like my grandpa." Spoke Van.

"I do huh! Do you like your grandpa?" asked Roman.

"Yeah, but I don't get to see him very much. He doesn't live around here."

"Is that your mom's dad that you're talking about?" Levi asked.

"Yeah, they live in Florida. Me and my mom, was talking about moving over there. I mean my mom and I." He chuckled when correcting himself. "But now that she got hurt I don't know if we will still go."

"Do you want to move there?" asked Levi

"I don't know, I like my grandma and grandpa, but I will miss my friends. And I don't know if my mom will have a job, when we get there. My mom works here in town as a waitress. She might not get me everything that you have, but she tries to get me stuff for Christmas, and my birthday."

The room fell silent, for a couple of minutes. Then Mable thought it best for her to say something, or Van might think that he said something wrong.

"I'm sure that it will all work out for you and your mom young man." she spoke

"If you're done eating, I can take you and show you around. Or do you just want to go back in the game room to play some games?" asked Levi.

"I'll go and see what you have. Is that okay, then I can play some games you have in that big room?"

"Levi do you think that you should be doing any such activity, so soon after the accident?" asked Mable. "Maybe you shouldn't do too much, too fast, you think?"

"Thank you for your concern, but I feel fine. After it happened I was a little shaken up, but I'm fine now." Levi wasn't going to give in, to having a little bit of discomfort. After all he did feel fine, except whenever he got up to fast after sitting down, he would feel a little light headed.

He led Van out to the back yard, where he had a large pole barn. In side of the barn was a garden tractor, a snowmobile, a for-wheeler and several other kinds of things that would be fun to ride on. Van couldn't believe that any one person could have so much.

"How does one person, get so much?" asked Van. "I didn't think that one person can have all of this. I thought that you would need more people to have all of it, to be able to have any fun."

Levi laughed at the way Van would say certain things, he knew that he was surprised by everything that he was seeing for the first time. But he also knew that what he spoke about having more then just one to have fun, he was right. Levi had many things, but all the things he had never really seemed to make him happy.

He knew that there was really no sense in explaining where he got all his money from, the boy was just too young to understand work. While he was there, Levi wanted him to enjoy himself. Levi decided to take Van for-wheeling since he said that he had never been on one before. He noticed that Van's helmet seemed to be a little big on him, he kept pushing it over so he could see out the front of it, he would watch with a slight chuckle as it would turn on him. He could see that Van was having a great time that he didn't bother to ask if he had a smaller helmet. They rode, all over Levi's three acres of land. He had small hills that he would take Van up, then down. Each time he did this Van would start to laugh; he said that it tickled his stomach. Then Levi would take him to a wide-open stretch, and go super-fast, as Van called it.

After riding for an hour, Levi decided that it would be time to come in, he didn't want the darkness to fall on them as they rode.

"That was the most fun, I ever had. Can we do that again?" asked Van.

"We sure can, if your mom says it okay. I am sure glad that you came here with me today buddy, I haven't ridden any of my toys, in quite a while. I never realized how much I missed that kind of fun."

"You mean to tell me that you have all those big toys." Van now calling them what he heard Levi say. "And you don't go on them every day? I know you can't ride your snowmobile right now, but what about all the other stuff you have. If they were mine, I'd ride them every day. I think that I'd have to ride each one every day, or the other one might think that I don't like it as much, and it might not run very good for me. I play with most of my toys every day, because I don't want the others to be mad at me."

Once again, Van brought laughter to Levi. The young man didn't know why, when he spoke Levi would begin to laugh. He was just being himself, talking. But he felt that Levi was a good man, and he enjoyed his company a great deal. He felt as though he could talk open about anything that came to mind.

"I guess one of the reasons why I don't take them out very often, is because I work a lot of hours. Then I hang out with some of my friends, a lot of times." Levi stopped talking, in the middle of his sentence and changed the subject. He failed to mention the times he spent with Roxie. "I'm just very busy with work, but anytime you and your mom would like to come over, you are most welcome too. Maybe we can get your mom to ride along with us."

"Really! My mom ride one too? That would be great, I bet she never rode one before either. If she had, she never told me about it."

"Maybe you might want to ask her if she might want to come over some time to ride them with us?" He was going to use the boy to try to get his mother to come over. *"Am I doing this all wrong?"* he questioned himself. *"Should I use the boy to do something that I myself ought to just do myself?"* Van interrupted his thoughts.

"Don't your friends, come over and ride them?"

"Well not too much, you see my friends all have a family, and they work to. So, we don't seem to find the time, to play all too often. But I sure did enjoy myself today riding with you."

"Maybe my mom would like to come over, and go riding. She never gets to play like this."

"Anytime, the both of you are welcome." Levi spoke with a chuckle in his speech.

"Why don't you have any family, did your wife die, like my dad did?" Van asks as they were putting up their helmets.

"No, I was never married, I had a mother that lived with me, and then she passed away, three years ago."

"Were did she pass away at."

At first Levi just looked at Van, but when he noticed that Van was waiting for an answer, he then realized that the young man must not know what he meant by passed away.

"What I mean, is my mother died three years ago."

"Did you cry? If my mom died I would cry really hard."

"Yes, Van I cried, very hard. I loved my mother a great deal, she raised me all on her own, when my father left us when I was just a young boy, much like you."

"Who bought you this place? Did your mom, before she died?"

"No, I bought the property, eleven years ago. Then I had my home built on the land. After that I had my mom come live with me. She never did get used to the place, she always told me it was too large." Levi spoke while they walked up to the house, from the barn, all the while looking at the size of his home from the outside. Levi was a proud man, he was proud for what he had accomplished. He never had much all the while growing up, his mom worked hard to make ends meet, until she was able to start her own house cleaning business. She worked hard enough to put Levi through college. He was a good man, to those of less than he, often times he would give a great deal of money to the local charities. If he seen someone, on the street that was hungry, he would give them money to buy some food. Sometimes it was in the most inconvenience of times. He liked to show others that he had a lot of money, and he would flaunt his wealth.

"What game would you like to play, before going to bed for the night?" Levi asked Van.

Van looked around the room, to see which game looked appealing to him. "I'd like to play some pinball, if that's okay"

"Sure pinball is one of my personal favorites, I can get it way up into the hundred thousand. Let's see how far you can get it up to." enquired Levi.

"Okay!" Van was all excited, to play some pinball. He wanted to see if he could get anywhere close to what Levi's Score was. But to his surprise, on his first game it didn't even come close.

"Awe shoot! Man, I only got one thousand and two hundred points. I thought that I would at least, get close to your score. How did you get such a high score?"

"When I first started playing pinball, my score was much like yours. It took me along time of playing, before I could reach such a high score. If ever you want something bad enough, you have to work at it. When I first started my own business, I didn't know near what I know now I was just a beginner, and many times, I wanted to throw in the towel, and just give up. I never seemed to win any of my cases, then I started to watch lawyer's on tv, they always seemed to win their case's. So, I began to change how I did things." Levi began to think about how at times, he did things that was not so good, to get where he is at today. Some might even call it going against the law, doing things that were not legal. But that was for him to know, not anyone else especially this young boy. He continued on telling Van more. "I wanted more for myself, then I had when I was growing up. So, I worked long and hard, and the next thing I knew I was doing things in the court room that no other lawyers were doing, that were very helpful to many, many people. Big companies were willing to pay a great deal of money, to have me win cases for them. And that was the beginning of my success."

"I hope one day I can do that, so I can get a big house like this and lots of games, oh yeah and all the toys you ride on too." Van spoke while looking up into Levi's eyes.

Levi rubbed the top of Van's hair. "It wasn't so easy in the beginning. Many people just looked at the color of my skin, and the kept their distance from me. It took some people a while before coming around me, so I had to overcome quite a bit in the beginning."

"I didn't know that people look bad at the color of others. I have a best friend in school, that is black, and I really like him."

"That's very nice Van, I knew that I liked you from the very beginning." He chuckled. "Maybe one day, you will be a successful man when you grow up. Fine something that you like, and work hard, to see how you can make money doing what you like."

The two played games together for a while, and then they went to the kitchen, for a snack before bed. After eating, Van told Levi that he was tired. Levi took him up stairs, and showed him the room that he was to sleep in for the night.

"Wow! I get to sleep in this big bedroom all by myself. Man, that's a big bed; I've never seen a bed so big before. What size is that?" asked Van.

"That is what we call, a king size bed. I'm sure you won't be rolling out of the bed tonight, in case you roll at night."

"I never roll anyway, but I'm glad that I can sleep in this bed. I bet my mom would love to have a big bed, just like this." Changing the subject. "Levi can you say my prayers with me? My mom always prays, with me."

"You will have to let me know, how you and your mom pray together." It took Levi by surprise, when Van asked this of him. He had forgotten that back at the hospital, Yvonne did ask, if he would say bedtime prayers with Van.

Van looked at Levi then took him by the hand, as he knelt down next to the bed. Levi followed his lead, and knelt too.

"You can just repeat after me, if you would like to. Did your mom ever say your prayers with you?" asked Van.

"No, my dad's mom would take me to church with her, when I was a little boy. When my grandma passed away, my dad left my mom and myself. And I never went back to church again, and then I just forgot how to pray."

"Just say what I say then, okay."

"Okay." Levi allowed the young boy do the teaching now, he wanted to see how much this boy knew about praying.

Van began with, "Dear Lord Jesus, help me and my mom, and help my new friend Levi, Mable and Roman." He stopped there to say, "but you can say my friend Van instead." Levi chuckled under breath. None-the-less he said what Van had asked of him. After they were finished, Levi brought out a tee shirt of his for Van to wear to bed. He knew the boy never had any of his clothes with him. He told the young boy good night, and said that he would see him in the morning.

"Thank you, Levi, for taking care of me, for my mom. I'm going to tell my mom that you took good care of me, so then she will let me come over again." He had promised.

"You do that, it was great having you here this evening with me. Good night Van."

Levi left a night light on in the hallway, so the young boy wouldn't get scared in the dark, and would be able to find his way to the restroom if needed.

Levi was tired, and needed sleep, if the truth be told, his body has not felt the same since the car accident much earlier in the day. He held himself together quite well, never reveling to another that he felt some-what weak. He told Mable and Roman good night and he was off to bed.

4

He laid in bed thinking about all he and Van had talked about. He felt as if he knew the boy, for a long period of time. Although he was only eight years old, Levi knew by the way he talked, that he had gone through some tough times in his eight years here on earth. Van spoke a lot of his mother, And Levi felt like he was beginning to know her through her son, and that grew interest in Levi. Not only did she have great looks, but she was very nice. Not like the women that Levi was used to dating in the past before Roxie. He dated the rich and wealthy, much like himself which in his opinion, seemed to be stuck ups, and always thought that they were better than others. The type that liked to talk about other's behind their back's. Levi was never one of them kind of men to do that. He was really quite the opposite, always seeing the need in other's and helping when he could. It's no wonder why he never married, never finding one that matched him. But there was one lady he thought a lot of, she was not like all the others. Roxie Stratton, she had the looks, and the gentleness that Levi was always attracted to. But there was still something there that kept him from proposing to her. His friends had thought that the two of them, would get married one day. And until today, Levi had been thinking about asking her to marry him. But now everything has seemed to change, and he wasn't sure why all the mixed-up feelings he was having since the accident. When he seen Yvonne for the first time lying in the bed at the hospital, something inside him felt different. Levi fell to sleep trying to understand these feelings he had been having. He fell into a deep sleep, and began to dream of a wedding. He was standing at the front of the alter waiting for his bride. It seemed to him that he was waiting for a very long time, and yet he was not seeing his bride come down the aisle to meet him up front. He woke up as he was waiting for her. *"Now what kind of a dream is that?"* he asked himself. Putting the dream aside, and realizing that it was now morning, he knew he needed to get Van up.

"Good morning young man, it's time to get up, and have some breakfast, before school." He said waking Van up.

"Huh! Do I have to? I wanted to go see my mom today, instead of going to school. replied Van

"I told your mom, that I would make sure, that you went to school. And I'd pick you up after school, and take you to see her. Come on buddy, she just might be feeling well enough to get out today."

Van sat up, and put his head in his hands. "Okay, I'll go, but not because I want to, it's because I have to."

"I'll be waiting for you down stairs, when you're dressed alright?"

"Wait." Van shouted as Levi walked out of the room.

"Yes, Van what is it?" he asked coming back to see what he needed.

"I can't go to school."

"And why do you say that you can't?" Levi enquired.

"I never got to change my clothes, and my mom never lets me go to school in the same clothes."

Levi could see that he was doing whatever he could do, to get out of going to school. But none the less, he couldn't very well send a boy to school, wearing the same clothes as he did the day before.

"I believe you are right, young man. We wouldn't want others to think, these are all you have to wear." Levi agreed with him.

"No sir, we wouldn't." Van, spoke as he jumped out of bed, in a hurry to get up now.

"I'll see you down stairs. We'll eat then I'll take you to the store, to get you something new, and clean to wear, before going to see your mom. Would that be alright with you?"

"You mean you're going to buy me something?" Van asked with a surprised look.

"Yes! Would you like that?"

"Do you mean at a real store?" asked Van

Levi stood there speechless, for a moment. "What does that exactly mean? A real store."

"My mom never has enough money, to buy me new clothes, in a store. So, she takes me to a thrift store, and gets her and me clothes there."

"Oh, I see, well if you would rather me take you there, then I will."

"Are you kidding me, no way? I want to see, what the other stores have." Van spoke with such excitement, the very thought of him going, and getting something that was never worn by anyone else was so exciting to him.

"If we don't hurry along, all the stores will be closed, before we get there." Levi gave Van a wink, to let him know that he was only teasing.

"I'll be right down, where do you want me to put your shirt at, when I take it off?" Van asked.

"You can just leave it there, Mable will come and straighten things up here." With that note Levi was out of the room.

Van couldn't understand, why if he wasn't going to school, then why did it seem to him, that Levi was in such a hurry. He knew that he was only teasing about the stores closing before they would arrive there, so what's the big deal. Then he thought, maybe Levi has to go to work, but now that he was not going to school, he needed to figure something else out.

"I'm ready now." Van spoke as he found his way to the bottom of the stairs. "Levi can I ask you a question?"

"Sure!"

"Are you in a hurry, because you have to get to work?"

Levi chuckled. "No not at all, I would like to get up to the hospital, so we can see your mom. I'm not going into work today. I'll be spending time with you and your mom. Would you like that?"

Van took a hold of Levi's hand. "That would be fine with me." he replied.

"Good because, I sure like spending time with you."

"What about my mom, do you like spending time with her?"

"Well I don't know that buddy, the only time I got to spend with your mom, was at the hospital. And trust me that's not where I'd like to get to know a woman. If you know what I mean." Levi gave a smile to Van.

Van didn't answer Levi, he was too busy looking over at what they were being served for breakfast. "A man could get really used to eating like this." he spoke while getting some egg Benedict. Mable had to laugh, at the young boy's comment on eating. It was years for her since having a little one around.

"Sometimes you surprise, me Van." stated Levi, with a light laughter of his statement, about eating. "Not too many surprise me, but that was a good one." He, continued with a chuckle.

"I can see that you got used to it, I would love to have a maid cook for me." Van continued on.

"What do you call what your mom does for you, she does the cooking and cleaning don't she?" asked Mable.

"Yes, but that's my mom. She supposed to do that for me, isn't she?" he asked looking up at Levi.

"It's nice to have someone do those things for you, but you must always remember when someone does things for you, then it's nice to do for them also. You never want to take others for granted. "He spoke while giving Mable a wink. "Now I told you last night about how Mable and Roman are part of my family. That means, she's really a lot more to me, then just a maid, she's like a second mother to me, as well as Roman is the father that I never had."

"Yes, my mom told me almost the very same thing. She said that God said, do unto others as you would have them do to you."

"Your mother sounds like a very wise woman." spoke Mable. "And it sounds like you have learned a great deal of good from here."

"My mom is a good Christian, she's the best mom in the entire world, even though she can't buy me new clothes, in the store."

"Buying someone new clothes, does not make a good parent. But giving them all the love, and the right teaching, is what a good parent is all about. Spoke Mable.

"Do you go to church?" Van asked Mable.

Mable looked over at Levi, and then seeing he just shrugged his shoulders, she knew that she was all on her own with this one. "No Van I

34

don't go to church, but when your mom gets out, I'd sure like to go with the two of you sometime."

"Really! Van said all excited. "You promise, I know my mom, would really like that. Oh, I just remembered, we no longer have a car, my mom told me.

"I will come around to pick the two of you up for church then." She looked at Levi, to see if he was going to give any reaction.

"Really!" he asked

"Would you like that?" ask Mable.

"Yes, I would, and I think that you will like my church. We have a lot of nice people that goes there. I wish that Levi and Roman would come to." Van spoke while looking at Levi.

"You would like me to come with you, too huh?"

"Yes, and I know that my mom would like that to." Van spoke so sure of himself.

"Well, I think that we better get going, if we are ever going to get to see your mom today. No need to cause her any worry." He spoke rubbing the top of Vans head, trying to change the subject.

"Okay I'm done eating, we can go now if you want. Thank you, Mable for everything, that was very, very good.

"You are most welcome, it was all my pleasure. I hope that I get to see you again, and I'd love to meet your mom some day. I think that she is really lucky, to have a son like you." She said in a soft voice.

5

Levi took Van to the Birch Run mall, just like he said he would to do a little shopping. Van's eyes were fixed on everything that he passed.

"Would you like to go on the carousel ride?" asked Levi.

"What's that?"

"It's the horses over there. See how the people get on, just like the ones they have at the fair. You do go to the fair, don't you?" He asked the boy.

"Yes, when my grandpa and grandma came up to visit, the fair was going on. They stayed the week with us, while my mom was at work they took me to the fair."

"That's mighty nice of them, to come up and spend time with you and your mom. Is that the only time you get to see them?"

"No, they come up for Christmas too. They send me money in a card, for my birthday too. Can I ride the horses?"

"Yes of course. I did ask you, if you wanted to?" Levi said, as they walked over to the horses.

Van rode the carousel, as if he was riding a real horse. Levi watched him kick the horse, and say giddy up, faster, faster. He sat on the bench, enjoying the time he had with Van.

While watching Van on the horses, he noticed that he was getting some strange looks from some near by-standers. He tried to avoid the looks of others, and tried not to look their way to make himself appear to look guilty of a crime he has not committed doing. It was like he could read their mind, accusing him of wrongful doing. He began to think about Yvonne. He was remembering some things that Van had spoken about her. From the first time Levi laid eyes on her, he felt an attraction to her. He still wasn't sure of her race, not that it mattered to him any. He had friends of all race, he was never the kind to stereo type them. He knew that no matter the race, there were good in each one of them. Yvonne was very soft spoken, and that's one thing that attracted Levi to her. He could hardly wait to get to the hospital, just so he could get to know the person, he heard so much about. He spent so much of his time thinking about her that he hasn't thought much of Roxie at all.

"That was fun, Levi, I love horses." Van said with excitement in his voice.

"I'm glad that you like it, now let's get you some clothes, so we can get to the hospital to see your mom." All the while walking to a store in the mall, he could see the looks of others watch him walk away with a young boy that was not black. In some ways he could understand it, not having the mother there that had the same color as the boy.

"Okay, where do we go to get my clothes at?" asked Van.

"I thought that we could go to Younker's, they usually have a good selection."

"I've never been there before, is it here in the mall?"

"Yep, just down this way. I would like to get you a shirt and a pair of pants. Would you like that?"

"That would be great, thanks Levi. I've never had anyone buy me new clothes before, except for my grandpa and grandma, when they come up to visit. But they usually go where my mom goes to get clothes."

They reached Younker's, and began to look for young boys clothing. Levi went to where the eight through ten size was at, but Van had a different idea of clothing.

"Levi, can we get something that's a little big on me?"

"If you would like, is it because the style now days, everyone wears big and baggy clothes. Well except those that like their clothes to fit, like me. He spoke while tugging his sports coat."

"No that's that not why, I just hardly get anything new, and so I wanted it to last me awhile. I just might start to grow really fast, and I want them to still fit me."

"As long as we are friends, I won't let you go without clothes. I become quite fond of you."

"Really! I like you too." Van picked out the shirt that he liked, and the pants he felt fit him the way he liked them. He was very happy to have met Levi even under these circumstances. After Levi paid for the clothes, Van gave him a hug so tight, that even for Levi he could feel the squeeze. He in return gave Van a huge hug back. He was surprised by his own actions, on just how much he has taken to the young boy. He not only felt such and attraction, to the boy's mom after meeting her, he also felt a bond for the boy too.

Van spoke a lot, of what he thought that his mom would think, of his new clothes. The more he spoke about his clothes, the more Levi wished that he would have taken a little more time, on picking out another outfit. He was sure, that he would be able to buy for the young boy again. At least he had hoped that Van's mother, would have no objections, to him buying for the boy.

"We're here Van, would you like to change your clothes, and put the new clothes on, before going in to see your mom?"

"Yes please, I want to look nice for my mom, when she sees me." replied Van.

Van changed his clothes, all the while he was thinking how nice it will be to see his mother. I just know she will see me different, he thought. I hope she likes what I picked out, and I hope that she doesn't get mad at you, for not taking me to school."

"I hope not too buddy."

"I'm ready!" spoke Van coming out of the restroom. Do you think that I look nice in my new clothes?"

"I think you look very handsome, much like me." Levi said while tugging on his collar.

"Can we go to see my mom?"

"Lead the way, do you remember which way we go?" Levi asked.

Van looked down a couple of hallways, but was unsure which way was the right way. So, Levi led him to the door, where just behind it laid the woman that meant everything in the world to the young boy.

"Here we are, but she just might be sleeping so let's enter in quietly." Levi spoke with great concern, not to wake her if she was asleep.

When the two entered her room, they were surprised to see Yvonne was not in her bed, nor was she even in her room.

"Where's my mom, what happened to her. She's not here. Where is she at?"

Levi took Van by the hand; he could see fear in his eyes. He knelt down to the boy's size, and spoke to him with the same concern.

"I'm not sure where she is at, but I am sure that she is alright. Come with me and we will go ask a nurse, to the whereabouts of your mother."

Levi and Van walked down to the nurses' station, when not seeing the nurse that he had talked with before, he went to another.

"Can someone tell me where Yvonne McAlester is at? She is not in her room."

"Are you her husband?" asked a nurse.

"No, I'm a friend of hers, and this is her son." Levi spoke to the nurse, with authority.

The nurse walked over to the desk, and looked at some papers. Are you Levi Ubani?"

"Yes, that's me. Is she alright?" he asked.

"Could we talk alone for a minute; the young man can wait over there." The nurse pointed, to some chairs that were leaned against a wall.

Before Levi could answer her, his mind began to think on all the wrong thoughts. *Did she die, in the night? How could this have happened, she seemed fine, besides a few bumps and bruises.*

Before going any further, thinking negative. The nurse walked in and interrupted him.

"Mr. Ubani, could we talk for a moment?" "Yes ma'am, just let me sit him over here."

Levi told Van, that he must wait for just a few minutes, while he talks with the nurse. It will be alright, he tried to encourage the young boy as well as himself. He thought if he heard himself speak the words out loud, that it would make everything seem okay.

"What is it that you need to tell me, about Yvonne?" Levi asked coming right to the point. He knew if the news was really bad, that Van would need him at his side as fast as he could get there.

"I think her doctor, would like to talk to you. I'll page him now."

"Mr. Ubani, I'm Doctor Michael Palmer. I understand that besides her son, you are the only one here that I could talk to about what we have discovered about Yvonne."

"She has friends from church that she might want to call." said Levi. "But her son is here with me." He concluded.

"I had asked her, who I need to talk to about any matters of her. She had told me you sir. She did inform me that her folks lived in Florida."

"Yes, that is what she has told me. Can you please let me know, is she alright?"

"Last night when we tried to get her out of her bed, she was unable to move her legs."

Levi was in shock. "What are you saying? You mean to tell me that she's paralyzed?"

"We are doing more tests on her today, that's why she was not in her room, when you got here. We can't tell at this time yet, just how severe the loss of feeling in her legs are. We are checking her spinal cords, and we've taken x-rays. I cannot tell you, if she will ever get feeling back in her legs at this time."

"Wow I can't believe this, she is a single mother. How will she care for her son?" Levi was feeling so confused looking over to where Van was sitting. "Thanks Doc. Do you know when she will be back in her room?"

"She might be back there now, if not she will be anytime." The doctor informed him as he placed a hand on Levi with his last words he said. "Pray, all things are possible." Then he walked away. Levi stood there in shock, before returning to Van. He wasn't sure what to think, let alone what to tell the boy. How can I tell him, that his mother will not be walking him to the park anymore? How do I tell him, that she will be in a wheel chair? Levi walked towards Van, with all kinds of thoughts of how to tell him about his mother, everything that came to mind, sounded terrible. Van could see the look on Levi's face, and came running up to him.

"Where's my mom at, how come she's not here with you?"

"Van, I need for you to sit down, there is something that I need to tell you." Levi spoke while trying to get him to sit. Van was acting a very upset, not knowing where his mother was at. But Levi could fully understand, he knew if he were that age, and him not knowing what has become of his mother, he would be upset too, maybe even more then Van was showing. Levi didn't know how to tell the young boy, what happened to his mother. He decided to wait until he had talked with Yvonne first, she might want to be the one to tell him. After all he had just known them, for one day. He didn't really feel that it was his place to tell Van. He wasn't even family, why should he be the one to break bad news to him. Besides this could be something that just might be for only a day or two. He was sure hoping that would be the case. After all, he was having thoughts of the two of them, but how can anything develop between the two of them if she remained in a wheel chair. He wondered if his thoughts, were merely vain, wanting only someone that could walk.

"Van the doctor told me that your mom should be back in her room now so if you want, we can go back to her room, and see if she is there."

Van jumped to his feet so fast, ready to take off running towards her room, that Levi took a couple of steps back, before getting knock on his butt.

"Now hold on Van, we can't be acting like we're riding a horse in the hospital. We need to slow down, so we get to her room safe."

"Okay Levi, I just want to see my mom so bad." Van spoke with much sadness in his voice, and the look of a sad puppy dog written all over him.

"Let's go and see her, but let's try and stay calm, when we get in her room. We don't want to get her too excited, after all your mom's been through enough in the last two days."

6

The two arrived at her room again, and walked in quietly, so not to startle her. To John's surprise, she was sitting up in her bed.

"Mama!" Van cried as he ran to her bedside. "I missed you so much. Do you get to come home today?" He cried.

Yvonne sat there and starting hugging Van tightly. She looked at Levi, but was uncertain of what to say.

"I thought that you would be in school."

"Didn't you miss me mama?" Van cried out to her, you are acting like your mad at me for being here."

"Oh Van, I'm so sorry for acting that way. I didn't mean anything by that, I'm really sorry. And I am very happy to see you, I really am. You are my pride and my joy, now don't you know that by now?" She spoke to her son with all the kindness that she could, to reassure him that her love for him, was everything that he needed to hear from her at this time.

"Mama, do you get to come home today?"

"Sit up here son, I have to tell you something. It may be a little hard for you to understand, you being so young and all." Then she looked at Levi. "Did you have a talk with my doctor, about what they found out?"

"Yes." He spoke, but when he did he felt a lump go in his throat, that made his voice sound weak. "I did talk with him, and he told me what was going on, I did not tell Van. I thought that it should come from you."

Van turned around to look at Levi. "Then there was more to tell me, and you didn't." He spoke as if he was angry with Levi.

"I'm sorry Van, I just thought that it should come from your mom." Then Lev looked at Yvonne. "Would you like me to go outside the room, so you can have a talk with Van?"

"No! Please stay, I'd like you to hear what I have to say." She pulled Van closer to her, so when she spoke to him, she could wrap her arms around him, when needed to.

"Van after you and Levi left last night, the nurse's tried to get me to stand up, to walk to the bathroom." Yvonne tried to hold back her tears, as she spoke to her son and Levi.

"Are you okay mama?" asked Van

"I'm trying to tell you something, but it's not coming out very good." She spoke all the while tears, kept on fallen down her cheeks. Then she just came out, and said what was on her mind. "I can't walk Van, your mother can't walk."

Levi could hear the fear in her voice, he knew that she was scared at her condition. He was feeling so guilty, for not seeing that she was ready to pull out onto the road.

"What do you mean you can't walk, I don't know what you mean. You've always been able to walk. What happened?"

"They don't know for sure, they took different test on me, to see what they can find out. It may take a day or so, before the test come back."

All the while Yvonne sat there trying to make Van feel better, she wondered what would happen to Van and herself. "I don't know when I will be able to come home, and when I do come home, what we are going to do." She said as her words fell off her lips, and plundered to the floor.

"Yvonne, have you called your parents yet, to let them know what's going on?" Not that Levi thought they should come up here, and care for her. He just knew, that they should be told.

"No, I wanted to wait until my entire test comes back, so I know what to tell them. I don't want to worry them, anymore then I have to. My parents are getting up in age, and the very thought of my son and I, happen to move to Florida because of this." Her voice trailed off to a slow whisper, so slow that Levi never did hear the last words she spoke.

He looked down at Van, when his mother mentioned them moving to Florida. He knew that he didn't have any say so, to whatever they did with their lives. But the thought of him never seeing Van again, somehow cut right through him.

He hardly knew the boy, but for whatever reason, some that he couldn't even explain, he felt what he thought a father would feel for their son. It scared Levi to know he felt this way, for someone that he hardly knew. How could a man of his stature, even want a young child around? Now the woman that he felt so attracted to, from the first time he seen her is a crippled. As sad as it was for this unfortunate woman, to wind up in a wheel chair, and to have such a little boy that was pure joy to be around. There was just no way, he could give up his life, and be happy with a woman such as herself. Levi got all caught up in his own thoughts, that when Yvonne called to him, he didn't even hear her.

"Levi, earth to Levi." she continued to call.

Van began to pull on his sports coat. "Levi my mom's talking to you, do you hear her."

"Excuse me Yvonne, I am so sorry. My mind was thinking on how I can be of more help to you and young Van." "*What are you saying; do you even know what you just did? He asked himself?*"

"I thank you for the very generous offer, but this is none of your doing. I am the one that pulled out in front of you. I will call my folks, after my test results come back. I appreciate all that you have done for me and Van. I would however ask if it's no problem, can you care for Van again tonight. I was hoping to come home to care for my son, but I guess there's been a change in plans, rather I like it or not." Yvonne put her head down, on them last words. Levi knew that she was in no position, to care for Van at this time. He knew when he seen the two together, that they had a great bond. It looked to him as though this was killing her, to ask him, an almost perfect stranger to care for her son.

"Yvonne." Levi spoke as he reached down, and took her by the hand. "I don't want you to worry, about Van. I will take him home with me today, and after school, I will bring him back to see you. And maybe you will have found out more, about the test that was taken."

"You're not ready to leave yet, are you?"

"No, a matter of fact, I was going to ask if there is anyway, that you could go for a ride in that chair of yours outside, and get some fresh air. It's a beautiful sun shinny day. I think that getting you out of here for a little while, just might bring your spirits higher. I can take a ride up town, and pick us up some lunch." Levi felt a urge to do something spontaneous, at the moment. "Would you like that?" He asked.

"I don't know if they would allow me to do that." Yvonne said with a slight smile that brought hope to her. "Sunshine, I would love to go out and feel the warmth on my face."

"Let me go and see what I can do. I just may be able to take you outside for a lunch."

All the while Levi was gone, Van told his mother about his stay with Levi. "He lives in a mansion, it's so big I've never seen a place like that before. I was hoping that when you come home, that we can go there, so I can play games, while you guys visit."

"Van Mr. Ubani is a very nice man, but I don't think that he had plans for us coming over for a visit, when I get out of here."

"Yes, he does mom, he told me that we can come over anytime we wanted to." Van spoke with much enthusiasm when talking of Levi.

Yvonne sat there thinking, while Van was still talking. "*So, he is a man with great wealth, by the sounds of it. I wouldn't know that by the way he acts, he's so nice. I always thought, for someone with money, and a lot of it, that they were not so nice people. Of, course this is what I've heard.*" Yvonne in all of her twenty-eight years has never met someone with great wealth. She has heard from watching television, that the rich are stuck ups, and keep their nose high in the air. She had always thought this to be true. Could she be wrong what her beliefs have always been, or is this some kind of act. *But for what, it's not like he pulled out in front of me, where he thinks I just may sue him.* She was all caught up with wild thoughts of this man that she had just learned has a lot of money. But why does he seem to be so interested in me. I have nothing to offer such a man of his statues. Yvonne was interrupted by Levi coming back in the room.

"I have some great news." He spoke while getting the wheel chair, and brought it over to the bedside for Yvonne.

"Let me guess" said Yvonne. "He said that it would be okay for me to go outside for some fresh air.

"It's even better than that." He said that I can take you out to a restaurant. Would you and Van like to go out to a nice place to eat lunch?"

Yvonne thought for a minute, before agreeing to go out to eat. "I really have nothing to wear, but I would like to make it another day with you, if I may."

"Sure! That would be great, I'm sorry I wasn't thinking about you not having any clothes here."

"Levi I would like to thank you, for being so nice to Van and I, I see that you have bought him, some new clothes. When I get out of here, and get back on my feet, I'd like to repay you for all your kindness."

"Think nothing of it, I was glad to get him a little something. If you would give me your size, I would like to go pick you up something also."

"No that is quite alright; I thank you for the offer."

"Why not let him mama, he has lots of money. Don't you Levi?" Van spoke with hope that his mom would give in, so she herself would get new clothes to.

"Van you should not speak of someone's wealth, that is not what's important here. There are things that you just don't understand. I'm sorry for my son's boldness?" Yvonne apologized.

"That's alright." he spoke while putting his hand on Van. "He just wants his mother to have something new like him, there is nothing wrong with that."

Yvonne felt that for a man, she hardly knew, was offering just a little too much to folks he didn't know but for a day. In some ways, she thought that he was just being nice, but on the other hand, she was worried what his alternate motive really is. She had never known anyone that was willing to buy her, and her son things for no apparent reason. She prayed silently,

"Father God you know all things, and you see my need right now. I need your guidance today. Help me to know, what I need to do, for my son and I. I thank you, for watching over him and me amen."

"Well then if you won't let me do anything for you, then what can I do?" ask Levi, with a disappointed look on his face.

"Oh Mr. Ubani, you have already did so much for me. You took my son, when I had no one else to care for him. You bought him clothes that he so much loves. I want to thank you for that." Yvonne sat in her bed, looking as if she was lost for words.

"Mama, if you can't come home today, then who will watch me?"

"I will." spoke Levi before Yvonne could get a word out. "That is if you will allow me to, ma'am?"

Yvonne didn't answer at first, she sat there thinking on what she ought to do. She was waiting to see, if that same peace, she felt the night before, would come back. Then her mind was made up. "Yes, that is what I had asked at first, if you're sure that it's no bother. You can take him home with you for the night."

"No bother here, I enjoyed having a youngster around. My house is just too big, for me. Well there is." Levi stopped in the middle of his sentence. Van caught on to how he never finished. "Did you mean to say Mable and Roman?"

Levi looked at Yvonne, he didn't know what to say. He never wanted to seem, like he thought that he was above her with his wealth. He could tell that ever since Van told her that he had wealth, her actions towards him seem to have changed. Trying to cover, the fact that he had a maid and butler, he said they were friends of his mother, and he took them in.

"But they work for him mama." said Van.

At this time, Levi wished that Van would never have spoken of such things. He would have rather Yvonne getting to know the real him. For the first time in his life since becoming wealthy, he never wanted to sound as if he was bragging of his success.

"Mr. Ubani, it seems to me that you are trying to hide something from me." Yvonne said after she seen that he was trying to change the subject. "Is there something that I ought to know?"

"No, I'm not hiding anything. Your son is right, I do have a maid and a butler. It's just not something that I go around and talk about. I am aware, that there are a lot of folks that don't have a lot. And I would never want them to feel bad, because they don't have what I have."

"I see, the way I look at it is, the one that has the greatest of wealth, is the one that has the Lord Jesus Christ living, and dwelling inside of them. You see, man can have all that the riches of this world can offer. But if they don't have God, they don't have anything of worth." Levi stared at this woman that spoke about wealth meaning nothing to her. He could hardly, believe what he was hearing. He's worked hard all his life, to get what he's got, just to find that a woman that can't afford to buy her son something new said wealth didn't matter to her. "I'm not saying there's anything wrong, with having wealth. I'm just saying; I'd rather have Jesus over anything this world has to offer."

Levi stood next to her bedside, speechless. He had no words to say, to what her beliefs are. He could remember his grandma taking him to church, but what Yvonne spoke of having Jesus more than anything else, he never remembered hearing as a child.

Levi found words. "Are you saying that you would not want wealth?"

"No! I would love to have wealth. What I am saying is, the bible said, that God shall supply all my needs, according to His riches, in glory.

"Could you tell me just what that means; He shall supply all your needs?" Levi asks, not knowing what to make of the quote she just gave.

"Can I ask you a question Mr. Ubani?" asked Yvonne. "Sure, but will you please call me Levi."

"Do you know anything about the bible?"

"I know the verse that tells us that God so loved the world. I remember hearing that, when I was just a boy, in Sunday school."

"That would be John 3:16. I didn't realize you went to church when you were young. But why did you ever stop going?"

7

Just as Levi was ready to tell her about his grandma, her lunch was brought in to her. It was the nurse that he dealt with, when he first arrived yesterday. Levi loved how her hair was long, and flowing to the middle of her back. He had always felt that long hair was very attractive, on a woman.

"Well hello, Mr. Ubani. How are you doing?" The nurse asked while looking him up, and down with her eyes.

"I'm fine." Levi replied with half a smile, that when Yvonne seen it, she thought that he looked very handsome. "How are you?" He asked as if they were old friends.

"I'm very well thanks. I must say, you look better then you did yesterday?'

"Thanks, I am I think." Levi said, but was unsure just what she meant by that.

The nurse laughed, at what he said. "All I meant by that is, you looked as though you might fall yesterday. And today, well here you stand, all cleaned up looking very well?"

Huh, looking well. Was Levi reading this nurse, the way he thought the first time meeting her? Or was he putting too much, into it again. Maybe she says that to everyone, maybe it's her job. No, I know that's not her job, she's flirting with me. And right here in front of Yvonne, she's got a lot of nerve.

How does she know, if I'm not a married man? Levi was surprised at his thoughts. He wasn't usually the type to let his mind run wild, what is going on with me, he thought. Its like ever since I met Yvonne, something changed for me. His thoughts were interrupted, when the nurse was saying maybe I'll see you again, as she was walking out the door.

Levi didn't get to answer her, and she was gone out the door, and down the hallway. He then looked towards Yvonne, but he wasn't expecting what he heard next.

"If I didn't know any better I'd say that she was flirting with you. Did you know her before coming here to see me?" asked Yvonne.

"No, I met her yesterday for the first time." Levi answered her question, but at the same time he was wondering why she would seem to care if anyone was flirting with him.

"She's very pretty, and young." Yvonne continued.

"Oh, I didn't notice." He said without thinking, what he was going to say ahead of time.

"Look how Van fell to sleep next to you, now that's a picture." He spoke changing the subject.

"He must be tired to have fallen to sleep right now, did he stay up late last night?"

"I'm not sure what time you put him to bed, on a regular basis. But I had him in bed by ten o'clock. Was that too late?"

"When it's school night, I usually have him in bed by nine o'clock. But that's okay, I'm glad to have him here with me now."

"Do you know what you're going to do, about if you will be moving to Florida or not?"

"I've talked with Van about us moving there before, so I can be there for my parents. They are getting older now, and I wanted to take care of them.

But if, I'm not going to be able to walk, what good am I going to be for them, or anyone else." She was speaking from hurt and frustration.

"You remember when you told Van that God was there with you, through everything. Did you only believe that, when you thought that you could walk?"

Yvonne didn't answer his question, she started to cry.

"I'm sorry for what I said, I know that I had no right, to speak to you like that."

"You are right, how can I believe that God would only be there with me just because I can walk. I know He is there no matter where I'm at, and what I'm doing. I'm just all mixed up, not knowing what I am going to be able to do when I get out of here."

"Don't you think like that, you better eat something? You need to keep your strength up. You've been through a lot these last couple of days."

"I'm not really hungry. I just want to go home, to how it used to be. I don't know what I can do, to care for my son."

"I'm sure that something will come to mind." Levi spoke almost as he was uncaring.

Yvonne heard it in his voice, she felt bad enough the way things are going for her and Van. But now the way Levi spoke hurt her beyond words. I'm sorry to put this on you, I can see that I've put too much on you. I won't be a bother to you any longer."

"I'm sorry Yvonne, I know how that sounded, but I never meant it to sound like that. The truth is I was thinking that when you get out of here, I would be willing to let you and Van come stay with me, at my place." Levi wasn't sure what he was offering her, but one thing he did know is that she needed someone. This time he was offering help, for someone that had nowhere to turn.

Yvonne couldn't believe that Levi was inviting her, and Van to stay at his place.

She didn't have the words to say, to what he proposed.

"Do you think that is something that you are willing to do?" Levi asked.

"I don't know why, you would make an offer like that. You don't owe me anything, I don't know what to say. I know nothing about you." Yvonne was not sure of Levi's request, why he would care one way or another. She has never known anyone like that before.

"I know that my home is big enough, for the two of you to come and stay, and it's not too crowded. I can bring in a nurse, to help you. Maybe all you need is some physical therapy, and you can walk again."

"Could you please tell me something of yourself? I cannot go to a home, when I know nothing of that person."

"I can do better than that, when I come to visit you tomorrow. I'll bring all you need to know about me, with me."

"Bring with you" Yvonne was lost, she had no idea who she was even talking to really.

All she knew is what Van told her, and yet that wasn't much. To a child, anyone could have seemed to be rich, but then maybe he was, he did say he had a maid and a butler.

"Do you think that you should wake up Van, so he can get something to eat?" asked Levi noticing that lunch has well went by.

"Yes, I suppose that I should, he's been sleeping for a while now I haven't paid any attention, the nurse never came back to get my tray yet."

Yvonne woke Van up, but when it came time for him and Levi to go down to the cafeteria, Van didn't want to leave his moms side.

"Aren't you hungry yet?" asked Levi.

"Not really, I want my mom to come home with me. I don't want her to stay here, bad things happen to her."

Yvonne picked up Vans little face in her hands, and looked straight in his eyes. "I want you to listen, to what I have to say.

I put myself in here, by not watching what I was doing. It was I that pulled out in front of Mr." Yvonne caught herself ready to call him by Mr. Ubani, when Levi had asked her to call him by his name. "I pulled right out in front of Levi and that is why I'm here. So, honey I don't want you to be afraid, by me being here."

"Mama, why did you pull out in front of him? Didn't you see him?"

"No honey I did not I don't know what I was thinking about, when I did that."

"I never did ask you why, you were pulled over in the first place. Do you remember why you were pulled over?" Levi questioned.

"Yes, I was thinking about that last night, and then I remembered. I was getting sick, for some strange reason. I never get sick, but I began to hurt really bad in my stomach, so I pulled over. Please forgive me for pulling out in front of you. I just don't know why I didn't see you coming." Yvonne began crying, uncontrollable tears. Levi didn't know what to say to her at first. He believed that she would never have done that, after getting to know her, and he seen how much she loved her son. He watched as Van tried to bring comfort to her, and her cries brought pain to Levi, in a way that he never thought was possible. He went to her bedside, and found enough room for him to sit, and held her tight in his arms.

Yvonne could feel his strong arms embrace her, as she wept. But she was not going to even try, and pull away. It's been two years since having a man, hold her tight. She began to imagine, what it would be like to have such a man. A man of wealth is something that she never had before. She was never the type to desire the want for more, then she needed. She never went without, but she never could just go out and buy what she wanted either. Her sobs came to a quiet calm, her body now stopped shaking, as she began to feel peace surround her. As her head lay on Levi's shoulder, she felt him gently kiss her forehead.

Yvonne looked up at him, and gave a smile that lit the whole room up. Then she spoke words that Levi hung on to.

"That was very nice, I have not had a man kiss me since my husband. I know that you were doing it to be nice, and that's okay. But I just wanted you to know, that I appreciated it."

"That is quite alright." Levi spoke, all the while telling himself, that he was just trying to be nice, because he knew that she was hurting. But some how he felt as though he was lying, to himself. The kiss meant more to him, then just being nice. He could see himself wanting to kiss her lips and hold on to her and not let her go.

"Levi could you take Van, and get him something to eat." asked Yvonne, not wanting her son to go without eating.

"Sure, come on Van we'll come right back, to see your mom, when we are done eating."

"I don't want to leave, my mom. Mama come with us please, look mom!" Van pointed his finger, at her tray of food that has not been touched. "You never ate anything, mama."

Yvonne looked at Levi, and then she said. "You know he's right, I haven't eaten anything, and I'm getting a little hungry now."

"I believe that your lunch is all cold now, why don't you come down to the cafeteria with us, and get something hot to eat?" Levi asked Yvonne.

"I think that I will, I have felt sorry for myself long enough, now it's time to pull myself together. She could see, how much this was hurting Van. She was willing to do what it took, so he would not be hurt."

Van jumped out of the bed, and looked at his mother. "Can you walk now mama?"

"I don't know honey let's give it a try." Yvonne was hoping that whatever kept her from walking earlier was just some kind of weakness, but now has passed. "Do you think that you can help me try to walk?" She asked Levi.

Levi moved her legs over to the side of her bed, and took her by the hands. Okay try and push yourself up."

Yvonne tried, but she didn't have enough strength in her legs, to pull herself up.

Levi helped her up, and then asks her to move her legs.

"I moved it a little, did you see that?" she asked, all excited.

"It looked like it did a little to me too." Levi spoke with a smile on his face.

"Why don't we get a bite to eat, and when we come back here, I will let the doctor know. Is that okay?"

"That will be fine, let me help you in this chair."

The three went down to the cafeteria to get something to eat, over their meal Levi opened up the offer, he had already given to Yvonne earlier. "Would you consider, for Van and yourself moving in with me. At least until you are back to your old self. Or should I say moving in at my home. That might make it sound a little more appropriate."

"I have been thinking about it, ever since you asked me too. And I will accept if you are really sure, that is what you want. I just don't want to put you out, or inconvenience you in any way.

"That is one thing I can promise, you will not be putting me out. I have plenty of room for the two of you."

"He does mama, I slept in a really big bed last night. Levi told me that it was made for a king."

"Now that's not exactly what I said. What I said was, that it was a king size bed." Levi laughed at Van getting his words twisted.

"Wow you slept in a king size bed, all by yourself?" asked Yvonne.

"Yes, and I loved it, I know mama you will love it too. Levi can my mom sleep in that big bed?"

"I think that it might be better, if your mom was to have a bedroom down stairs. It might be a little hard for her, to get up the stairs, at this time."

"Oh yeah" Van said with a sigh. "I wasn't thinking of that. Do you have a bed down stairs, I don't remember seeing one?" he asked.

"As a matter of fact, I do. You know where the game room is at? It's just two doors down from that, and there is a big bed in there also. Your mom will have her own bathroom by staying in that bedroom."

Van was all excited, at the thought of him, and his mother coming to stay with Levi, for however long it may be. "I know that you'll love being there mama, its *soooo* nice."

"Thank you, Levi, for offering my son, and I a place to stay with you until I get my legs to work for me again." Yvonne spoke as if she already knew that she would walk again.

"I like the way you keep a positive attitude, in this. I don't, know if I could do the same." Levi spoke.

"I really believe with all my heart that I will walk again. I will not believe for one minute, that God would allow me to be a crippled, for the rest of my life. I do believe that I have a greater purpose in life, then what I have done so far."

Levi liked the way she held her head high, for the most part. He was glad that she had the faith, to believe she would walk again. He had no way of knowing if she would. But he wanted it for her, and Van almost as much as she wanted it for herself.

When the three of them came back to Yvonne's room, there were two people waiting for her return.

"Hello, my dear, how are you?" asked the reverend and his wife Patsy. "We have just received word, from hearing it on the radio that you have been in a car accident yesterday. So, we rushed right up here, to see how you're doing." stated Patsy.

"I was going to call, and let the church people know. But I was waiting to hear more news on what the doctor has found out earlier today."

"And what might that be?" asked the Reverend.

"I found out that after trying to get up out of the bed today, that I had no feelings in my legs."

"Okay, that is something that we will be standing in agreement in prayer about." The Reverend spoke while looking up at Levi.

"I'm so sorry, I wasn't excepting someone to be in here when I came back from lunch. This is my friend Levi, and you know Van."

"Hello, I'm glad to see that Yvonne has a friend, to be here for her right now she sure can use one, we love and care for her and Van a great deal. Have the two of you known each other for a long time?" asked the Reverend.

"No not quite, we just met yesterday." "Oh, I see."

"Reverend this is the man that I pulled out in front of on my way home from work."

"So that's what happened, we never did know what happened. We just knew that you were in some kind of car accident. But I must say I sure am glad that you are alright. And I trust the Lord that He will bring a complete healing to your body, in every way. Do you know how long that you will be staying here at the hospital?"

"No, I don't, I would like to get out today, but the doctor said that I will have to wait until more test are ran, and they can find out why I can't feel my legs anymore."

"Honey we're not going to stand in your way, of getting some rest. Let Patsy and I pray with you, before leaving. Dear Heavenly Father, we thank you for caring for Yvonne, and watching over her, as she now faces a change in her life. Whatever she must face now, we ask that you be with her, and Van through it all, bring healing to her legs as well as the rest of her, in Jesus mighty name amen."

"Thank you for coming, and for your prayers. I'll keep you posted, on what I find out."

"What will Van do while you're in here? I know that your folks are not from around these parts. Would you like the Mrs. And I to take him home with us?"

Yvonne looked at Van, then at Levi. She seen where Van's little hand reached out and took a hold of Levi's hand. "Thanks for the offer, but Levi was kind enough to offer, to let him stay with him."

"Oh, I see, well then. We better get going, and get out of your way. Levi it was a pleasure sir to have met you, I hope that when Yvonne gets out and comes back to church, we will see you there also."

"Thank you, and yes you will see me. It was nice meeting the both of you."

"Yvonne you call me at any time, you need me." said Patsy as she bent over and gave her a slight hug and kiss on her cheek.

"Thanks, I will goodbye."

She sat in the wheel chair until they exited the door, then she asked Levi if he could help her get back in her bed.

8

Levi talked with Yvonne, about what he meant by saying to the Reverend about coming to church with her when she gets well enough to go.

"Oh, that would be so nice, to have you come with Van and I. I am very glad to see that they stopped in to see me."

"Yes, it showed that they really cared, for you and Van."

"Mama, I didn't want to go home with them. I was hoping that you would say no."

"I could see that, when you reached out and took Levi's hand. I hope that was okay with you, that I told them he was going home with you."

"I wouldn't have it any other way. I had so much fun with him, out riding my toys, which is something that I just don't do that often anymore. And I haven't had a child at my home, in a very long time."

"Oh, did you used to have a girlfriend or family that had a child?" she asked.

"I'm the only child, and no I never dated anyone before that had any children. But my maid and butler have grandchildren that come up from time to time for a visit."

"You allow them to have their family come and stay at your house?"

"Yes, of course. They are my only family that I have. Although they are not blood, what's the difference, Roman is the only man I know for a father, and Mable she's just like a mother to me. I love the both of them a great deal."

"Levi, I think that is so very Kind of you, to let them come care for you, and your home. And they can live there as if it was their very own, I would really like to meet them one day hopefully."

"That would be nice, but first I need to let the doctor know you moved your leg before going to lunch."

Yvonne agreed to have the doctor come talk to her about her legs. She was opened to any suggestions that he could give her.

The doctor told her that there was more test that needed to be taken, to determine what steps he needed to do. She agreed to have the test ran before leaving the hospital.

After the doctor ran more tests on Yvonne, to determine why her legs could move a slight bit. He told her, that he could do surgery on her spine and that could possibly give her back, all the feelings in her legs again. Or it could do more damage, where she might never get to walk again. He told her that she needed to think long, and hard of what she wanted to do. He asked her to give it a few weeks, of therapy, to see if her movements of her legs came back. And if they never did, he would suggest her having the surgery.

The day came, for Levi to take Yvonne home, to stay at his place, for as long as she needed to. Since the time of the accident, Levi has only spoken to Roxie, once. She was out of the country, doing some traveling, when Levi called her with the news, about him hitting into another car on the freeway. He knew that she was due back, the following day after he would have Yvonne and Van at his home. He was unsure, of how to explain to her about the new in comers. It was his home after all, he thought. Why do I have to explain myself, she doesn't have a ring on her finger from me. Levi wondered why he really didn't seem to care, if she approved or not. He knew that Roxie was nice, and he even thought of marring her. But he must be truthful with himself, he cared more about how Yvonne would feel about him seeing Roxie, then Roxie feel about Yvonne.

"Are you ready to come back to my place, with me?" asked Levi.

"Yes, I am, but we will need to stop by my place so I can get some of Van, and my things if you don't mind."

"Not at all, your wish is my command." Levi spoke giving a bow towards Yvonne.

It was a talkative drive from the hospital, to Yvonne's home to Levi's home. Yvonne paid very close attention to how to get there. So, when she was able to drive again, she would know the way.

"Mama you will see when we get close to his house, that the roof is taller than the tree's."

Levi looked over at Yvonne, and gave a slight laugh. "Not really, it just looks that way, but it's not that tall, or else it really would be a castle. I live up on a hill, so it makes it look very tall from the outside of my driveway."

Yvonne just looked at him not knowing what she was getting herself into, how big is this place anyway she thought. I know Van said that it looked like a castle. No sooner did she think that when Levi said here we are.

Yvonne looked and to her surprise Van was right. "Van, you were not kidding me, when you said that he had a gate at the end of his driveway." Yvonne spoke looking up at the tall steel gate that held all intruders out, unless having the pass code to get on the inside.

"Levi this is a very beautiful place." she spoke while driving up the long drive. Yvonne was looking everywhere, to try to get to know Levi, through her eyes. She could see lilac trees, some dark purple, some white ones, and then there were the light purple flowers everywhere. She could see lots of tree's that held no flowers, but they held a beautiful shade that for when someone was hot, they could catch a nice breeze underneath of one. The only time, that she had ever seen this much beauty of such things, was on television, or in a magazine. This is a dream, she thought. "I see that you love your trees." Yvonne questioned.

"Yes, I do, and when in full bloom, I'll get some red blossoms on a couple of them. But I'm not sure of what they are even called. They were here before I built my home eleven years ago. It was a shame the amount of tree's that had to come down, so I could do everything that you see. If you would like, when you get all settled in, I can take you out in my golf cart, and give you a tour."

"Oh, I would love that, it seems to be very peaceful here surrounded by so many trees, where no one can bother you." After Yvonne spoke those words, she felt like she needed to correct herself. "I didn't mean it like it sounded. What I meant, was where I live, I have neighbors everywhere. There is no privacy anywhere. There are times that I'd just like Van to be able to go outside, and not have to worry, about someone kidnapping him. You see where I live, my yard is very small. The neighbors are always watching your every move. It will do me some good to take a break from there." Yvonne realized just how she was sounding, and she needed to quickly correct herself. She was always very giving, and thankful. But this was just not right. "I am so sorry for acting this way, this is not like me at all. Van what you just heard mama saying honey, I don't want you to pay any attention to okay?"

"Okay mama I won't."

Levi didn't reply to what he heard Yvonne say, it was not his place to give an opinion at this time. He pulled in the garage, as close as he could to the door, so it wouldn't take much, to get Yvonne in the house.

"Here we are I'm sure you will get to know the place, in no time at all. I called in ahead of time to Mable, so she could have your room all prepared for you. I made sure that the room I have picked out for you will be of one that has a bathroom in it."

"That is so very kind of you, going out of your way for me. I'll have to let Mable know how much I really appreciate her doing that for me."

"Think nothing of it, I am very happy to have you and Van come stay with me here. It will be nice to have company. And Mable, she loves to help people, you'll see when you meet her."

Mable met them at the door. "Hi, you must be Yvonne, I've heard so much about you. It is very nice to have you, and young Van come out to stay with us. I hope that you will let me know, if you need me for anything."

"Thank you, I will. And it's nice meeting you too. Levi told me that you prepared a room for me, thank you so very much." Yvonne, replied.

"You are very welcome my dear, and please let me know if there is anything that I can do for you."

"Okay I will, but you also let me know, if there is anything I can help you with. I may be in this chair for now, but I can still help some okay." Yvonne stated.

"Okay, thank you."

"Mable could you show Yvonne her room, while I go get their things, out of the car?"

"Sure, I can, let me help you with that chair.

Yvonne was looking at everything, in the home. She never has seen so many nice things, in all her life. She knew just by looking at Levi's things, she could see, that he had great taste. When she entered her bedroom, it was so much more, then she could have ever hoped for. The light from outside, come shining through the soft cream-colored curtains that hung from the windows. There was the prettiest queen size brass bed that she has ever laid eyes on. The cream-colored bedspread with a mixture of flowers that matched the wallpaper, made her feel all warm inside. She felt like the queen of England, it was like everything she ever dreamed of, was coming to pass, all in a day's time. "Oh Mable, this is a beautiful room, thank you so much, for your kindness."

"You are very welcome, I'll leave you for now you can call me on this intercom, anytime you need me."

"Thank you." Yvonne spoke, as she rubbed her hand over the bedspread, to feel the material. "Thank you, God, for sending me such wonderful help, and a beautiful place to stay." she prayed.

Levi and Van came walking through the bedroom door, with arms full of Yvonne's things. "Where would you like me to put your things at?" Levi asked.

She wasn't sure how to answer him, the room was much bigger then what she was used to back at her home. She could see that there were three doors in her bedroom, and she wasn't sure of what they were. She sat there looking around. "I guess you can put my bags on the bed, so it will be easier for me to put thing away. Levi this room is so much more then I would have ever expected. Thank you so very much."

"I like pretty things." He said as he gave her a wink.

Levi put her suitcase on the bed as she had asked. "Now Yvonne, I don't want you to worry about doing that. I can have Mable do that for you, she won't mind at all."

"That's okay Levi, I can manage. I'm not used to having people do things for me. I do appreciate the offer, but I know she must be busy doing house work, or something."

"We will be having supper soon can I do something for you before we eat?" He asked, knowing that her mind was already made up, about not letting Mable help her.

"You can show me what door is the closet, so I can hang up my church clothes?" she asked with a smile.

"Well let me see, it's been a number of years since I've been in here, myself." Levi opened a door, but it led to the bathroom. "Well I know where your bathroom is." he said, then slightly chuckled.

Then he tried another door. "Here you go, but the pole might be too tall for you to reach, sitting in the chair. Why don't you let me help you?" He asked.

She looked at the pole, and stretched her arms up, to see if it was possible to hang her own clothes up.

"I see that you're a woman, of a strong mind. You like to do things your way, and I can respect that." With those words Levi walked out of the room, leaving Yvonne to tend to her own clothes. He felt that he was putting too much pressure, on her. He didn't want to push too hard, he was afraid that it just might scare her away, before getting settled in. He knew that if anything, she would ask Van for help, if she needed it.

Levi walked into the kitchen, with a lost look on his face, and it troubled Mable.

"Levi, what's that troubled look on your face?" She asked putting her arm, around his waist.

Levi leaned his elbow on the counter, and put his face in his hands. "I'm just thinking, trying to decide what I can do to make Yvonne feel more at home."

"Is she not happy here?" asked Mable.

"Give her some time boy." Spoke Roman. "If you push too hard, you're more than likely going to frighten the girl." Spoke Roman. "You know that I have always thought of you like one of my own. So, I'm going to talk to you now, as if you are my own."

Levi looked over at Roman unsure if he wanted a lecture right now. "Okay." He agreed to one anyway.

"I'm telling you right now that you need to give her some room. Don't crowd her, or push too much. This girl, for what I understand, has lost her husband two years ago. Am I right?"

"Yes, that's right." Spoke Levi.

"Until five days ago, this woman had a job, which she went to everyday. She had her own home, for however small or great it was it was hers. She walked, or drove to where ever she wanted to. She had her own circle of friends; you get my point don't you. She needs to find her own way here, at her own pace. And if you let her alone, she will find it. She just needs to adjust. Give it some time."

"Okay, I won't push. But I need to let her know that Roxie is coming home tomorrow. I'm sure she will want to come over, and hang out."

"Her again, did you tell Yvonne about her yet?" Mable asked all disappointed.

"No! Every time I've tried, I just couldn't get the words out. I don't know what's wrong with me, it's just silly. Why is it every time Roxie comes out this way, you run and hide yourself away. If I didn't know any better, I'd say that you don't care about her at all. Am I right?"

"I don't mean you any disrespect Levi, but coming from a woman's point of view. That girl is after one thing and one thing only"

"And what would that be?" "Your money, what else."

"I don't know how you can say that, she has her own money."

"That very well can be, but if you were just a nobody. Like one with no money really to speak of, would she still be hanging around? I know that you are a very handsome man, but that is not what keeps a girl like that. Trust me I know, I've seen it all my life. She is after your money, not your charm."

"Hum I never really thought about that. Maybe deep inside that is why I never married her after two years."

"I wouldn't doubt it, at all. You need a woman like Yvonne, now she's not after your money. She would like you if you only had two cents to rub together."

"Son why do you think that you are having such a hard time, telling her of Roxie?" said Roman.

"Because I don't want her to feel she's getting in the way of anything."

"No, my boy, that's love. When two people are in love, things can seem a little confusing at times." Roman implied.

"Love! Are you telling me, that you think I'm in love with Yvonne? I hardly know the woman, I only met her five days ago."

"Then let me ask you, why it would be so hard for you, to tell her about Roxie? And why did you make sure that her and her son, came here to stay? You could have found another place, if that's what you would have wanted. Or had an in-home nurse, come stay with her at her home."

"I don't know." In love, Levi whisper to himself. Standing next to the counter in a daze *I can't be in love, what kind of life would that be for me. I would have to give up everything, to be here with her in a wheel chair.* His mind was running wild again. He couldn't believe just how selfish, he could think. Then he told himself, that he was just helping a friend and nothing more. Roman didn't know what he was talking about, with all that love stuff. In fact, I can hardly wait to see Roxie, he told himself. I think that I will move forward, with our relationship when she returns.

Levi was sitting on the couch in deep thought, about purposing to Roxie, when he was interrupted by hearing Yvonne calling out to him. He jumped to his feet, and run back to her room. She was sitting in the chair, with her church clothes on her lap. It looked as though she had tears in her eyes.

"I'm sorry to have yelled for you, but you are right. I can't reach the pole, in the closet, and Van I think is in the game room playing."

"I'll help you in any way that I can." Levi told her as he reached down to grab a handful of hangers.

"I'm sorry, for earlier. I know that you were just trying to help. You see, it's hard for me to except help from another. I've been alone, all the time since Mark my husband passed away. I learned to do everything for myself, and now to have to ask for help." There was a long silence. Then she finished with. "It will take some getting used to, I hope that you understand."

Roman was right, she just needed time. "I do understand, and I'm sorry if I seem to be too pushy. I just don't want you to be afraid to ask for help."

"There all the clothes are hung up, would you like to come out into the living room?" He asked her.

"I think that I'd like to see where Van is first, if you don't mind."

"Not at all, I'll take you right to him."

Yvonne was right, Van was playing some pinball and when he seen Levi. He got so happy to show him his score. "Look, I got up to six thousand now."

Levi looked at Yvonne, then he told her how Van, has been trying to reach his score, of over a hundred thousand. She smiled, and told Van it will take time.

"If you would like, we can go to the living room now or you may take me for that stroll, you were telling me about. I wouldn't mind seeing more of your home, if you don't mind."

"Not at all, I'd love to show you around." Levi began taking her to all the rooms.

"This is a very nice room here, do you call it a sun porch?

I love sitting in the light, to read, or to have a cup of coffee and meditate on the things of God."

"Yes, it is the sun porch and very bright. I think its kind of a pain for Mable, to clean all these windows. But I do like to sit out here and have coffee thinking."

"Does Roman ever help Mable with the house work?"

"I'm sure he does, I've seen him watering the plants on the inside, as well as those outside. He helps her cook, also. But to say how much, I can't really say. Up until Van started to come out here a few days ago, I wasn't here that much."

"I don't want you to feel, just because Van and I are here, that you have to stay home all the time, when you have your own life to live."

Levi never commented on what he heard her say, He just began to push her chair, into another direction. "You said that you love to read, well here is the library. If you ever want to come here, to read any books, I'm sure that I have just about every kind you would like."

She knew by looking at the room, that it would become one of her favorite rooms. "Levi this is awesome, I sure would like to come in this room. That is if you really wouldn't mind."

"I would be disappointed, if you like to read as you say, and never used this room. Back when I built the house eleven years ago, I liked to read to. I guess I can say that I kind of got out of all the reading that I used to do."

"Why would you do that? Whenever I had the time between work and Van, I would read something that would speak to me."

"I guess it was all the extra work that I did all the time. Then I met, well I met friends, and allowed a lot of time to hang with them. Now this room is never really used, unless Roman or Mable comes in here."

"Not for long, Van will be going to school, and you to work. I think this room will find me coming into it."

"Very good, it's nice when the winter is here and the fireplace is all hot. You can get all snuggled and cozy sitting by it. Why don't I take you to show you more of the house, so you can begin to get used to everything here."

9

M able called for everyone to come and eat, she wanted the first night for Yvonne, to be something very special. She brought out the best dishes to be used, only for special occasions. She lit some candles, that made the room smell of lavender. When Levi and Yvonne enter the dining room, they could see that the table was set just for two people.

"What's going on, where is everyone else at?" asked Yvonne surprised to see only two place settings.

Levi stood there shocked to see the same as she did. "Huh your guess is as good as mine. I wonder where Vans at?"

"I was just thinking the same thing, do you think that they are doing this on purpose? But why would they?"

"Let me help you into a chair, and then I will go and take a look around, and find out what's going on."

As Levi was helping Yvonne in her chair, Van walked in with a platter of crab legs. Roman followed by coming in, with a platter of fried scallops. Mable walked in carrying, a platter of fish. Before they knew it, there was a five-course meal of all seafood, waiting for Levi and his guest to begin to eat.

"Everything looks very good Mable, but I need to ask you what the three of you are up to? I have never had you eat in another room, we have always eaten together. So, would you mind telling me what this is all about?"

"Van ask me if we can make the first night, of his mother being here a special night. He told me that she liked seafood, so the three of us worked to put this together for you. We have our food in the kitchen, we just thought a quiet evening eating for you would be nice. I hope that I haven't offended, any of you."

Yvonne was lost for words, she sat there looking at everyone. Then she spoke to Van." So, you wanted my first night to be special, huh. Thank you for thinking about me honey and my night is going great thanks to all of you. And Mable I can tell you worked very hard putting this together and Roman thank you for helping in everything to." She reached out and took Vans hand and gave it a light squeeze, thank you honey."

The three of them exited the room leaving Levi, and Yvonne sitting at the table lost for words. The two sat in quietness, for a few moments. Than Levi decide to break the ice.

"I was just as surprised, as you were. We might as well enjoy, this time alone. I really don't know what they were thinking, but we might as well eat."

Levi and Yvonne agreed that they believed they were being set up, by the rest of the household. They laughed together over their meal, and talked about what it must be like for Van being in the middle of what was going on.

"Some how he must think, that the two of us, are planning on getting together. I don't know why he would feel this way. I've never given him any reason to think, that the two of us would be together. Do you know why he felt like we should be having a meal for just the two of us?" asked Yvonne.

"No not at all, I tried to think, if we could have said something, to make him think this way, but I can't." Levi looked at Yvonne when talking to her, and noticed her head look down, as though she felt bad. "Yvonne you are a very lovely woman and you seem to me to be very exciting. I will be honest with you, I am very attracted to you. But I have to tell you something, when I asked you and Van to come stay here, it wasn't because I wanted a relationship with you. It's because, I wanted to help you."

"I know that, I never thought once that it was because you wanted anything more. I don't know why you would think that I thought more."

Yvonne spoke her peace, and then went on to eat, then after a few more bites, she said something else that came to mind. "I will make sure that I talk to Van, about what is really going on. I want to say that I am truly sorry, if you were put on the spot tonight."

"Why don't we just go on like it was before this happened, can we do that?"

"Yes, please let's." Yvonne replied, in agreement.

After supper, Levi and Yvonne sat in the den, talking about everything that would come to mind. Yvonne found that Levi had a lot of ways that was pleasing to the Lord. She felt like the two of them, had known each other for years. Levi was so easy, to talk to. All the while the two talked, he had in back of his mind that he needed to tell her about Roxie. He didn't understand why it was so hard for him, to just come out and tell her that he has been seeing someone for two years. It felt almost like he would be telling her that he was unfaithful, but yet he knew that was just silly thinking that way. They both had established that, tonight at dinner.

"What time did you want Van to go to bed?" Levi asked. "What time is it?"

"It is about nine o'clock, and Van has been playing in the game room ever since we ate."

"He has school tomorrow, I'd like to say his prayers with him, so he could get some sleep." Yvonne said. "And yes, have our little talk, so he could get the illusion of the two of us out of his mind."

Levi didn't say anything after that statement, but went on to act as if he never even heard her last comment. "The bus will arrive, at about six thirty in the morning. Do you think that he will be alright, on a different bus?"

"It might take him a couple days, to get used to it, but he will be fine. I know he sure liked staying here with you, when I was at the hospital. Now that I'm here, and he knows that I will be here, when he comes home from school. I don't think that it will bother him to ride the bus. Levi I just want to say, how much I really appreciate, you taking him to school, and bringing him up to the hospital to see me, after school every day." Yvonne began to have tears of appreciation, when thinking just how close she came to death, and not knowing what to do with her son why she was in the hospital.

Levi took her by the hand, and gave it a light squeeze. "You are welcome. I am very glad, that we have met. I know that might sound wrong to say, because how we met. I just can't help but think there was a reason for it. Maybe that sounds silly to you, I'm just saying what came to my mind."

"Can we talk about this, after I put Van to bed?" Yvonne asked.

"Oh, sure we can, I'll go get him for you."

Yvonne thought about what Levi said, she never felt that it was entirely silly. She herself had thoughts, that there had to be a greater reason, for them to have met. But until now, that's all it was, just a thought.

"It's bedtime already?" Van asked in a disappointed voice.

"I'm afraid that it is. You have been playing, in the game room, ever since six o'clock. And now it's past nine. Let's say your prayers, then off to bed for you, young man."

"Okay mama."

Levi listened as the two of them, were saying their prayers. He liked to hear them pray, it reminded him of when his grandma was alive, and would pray with him. He could tell that Yvonne was a good mother. Just the way she would talk, and pray with Van. Then he heard her begin to tell him about the two of them.

"Van, we need to talk about something, that happened tonight."

"What mama, are you mad at me, did I do something wrong? You act like you're mad."

"No honey I'm not mad at you, I just have to talk to you about Levi, and myself. I think that you got the impression that he and I are going to be together, is that right?"

"Uh huh, aren't you mama?"

"That is not why we came here honey, so that he and I can be together. Van right now, I need some kind of help, I can't work to make ends meet. Levi was so kind, to take you and I in to help us at this time. I am so thankful for that, but Van that all it is. He is just a man that I believe for whatever reason, God has brought into our lives. You can't be trying to get the two of us together, I know that Levi really likes you, because he has told me that he does, but I don't think he thinks of me in the same way, as you wanted him to okay."

"Okay mama I'm sorry, are you mad? Is Levi mad at me?"

"No buddy neither one of us are mad, we just didn't want you to get your hopes up okay."

Levi walked in from the other room, hearing the last of their conversation getting over.

"Good night mama, night Levi." Van said as he gave his mother, a good night kiss. "I love you, mama."

Van began to walk away to go to bed, when he heard Levi tell him that the bus, would be here to get him at six thirty in the morning.

"I have to ride a bus, but I don't want to ride a bus mama."

"Van we already talked about that earlier, you knew that you would begin to ride the bus, when I moved in here." Yvonne stated.

"I just thought that you might change your mind, and Levi could take me."

"No Van, I had asked Levi to let the bus pick you up from here on out. We can't be expecting him to do that every day. Besides Levi will have to go back to work soon, so I need you to work with me, on this and be good okay?"

"Okay mama, I'll ride the bus. Good night." Van said as he went up the stairs to his bedroom.

"You seem to of handled that quite well." Spoke Levi.

"I don't want him to start thinking, that it's your job to ride him to school every day. I think that for the past few days, with you taking him, he was just hoping it would continue, I know that you haven't been going into work much at all, a couple of hours here and there. But when I first met you, you told me that you worked all the time. I just don't want Van, and I to inconvenience you more then we already have." She spoke then gave him a nice smile.

"I will have to go into work at times, but I don't have to go for long hours, like I used to, unless that's what I want to do." Levi spoke then with a chuckle. "I'm the boss, I don't see me getting fired."

"Yes, that would make it easier, not showing up for work when you're the boss." Spoke Yvonne. "I made a few things clear, with Van about the two of us. I think that he understands what I said. So, there shouldn't be any more silliness coming from him."

Levi and Yvonne stayed up for half the night, laughing and talking. They went into the kitchen long after Mable was in bed, and got out the ice cream, and pop. Yvonne made an ice cream float, and she and Levi shared it.

She felt so at home with him, and Levi did with her. Yvonne knew that if she was ever going to get up with Van in the morning that she would need some sleep.

"Levi you made my first night here, so special. Thank you for that. I have to tell you, that before coming here I was a bit afraid. Not knowing what to expect, but you made everything just right."

"I had a lot of fun too, I really liked the part where we shared a float." Levi told her raising up one eye brow, and giving her a wink.

Yvonne went to her bedroom, feeling happier then she has felt in two years. She couldn't understand where all this happiness was coming from. After all she should feel unhappy, not being able to walk. Yvonne knew that in most cases, someone losing their ability to walk. They would be very unhappy, sulking in self-pity. But she knew that she had something to live for, there was a call on her life. Not knowing what that call was yet, she trusted the Lord to reveal it to her on His timing.

Levi went to bed, feeling that same kind of happiness that Yvonne did.

He was not sure where it was all coming from, but one thing he did know. His life was had been wrapped around work, friends and Roxie. None of them bringing fulfillment, to him until he met Yvonne, and Van. There was a new excitement, something fresh. The hours that he slept, seemed to give him the same newness that he had before bed.

Yvonne had a dream that she was walking again. It was her wedding, Van was the ring bear. As she walked down the aisle, to be with her husband to be, she could not see his face. She felt like maybe she should turn around and run, but something kept drawing her forward. The closer she got to the front, the stronger she felt the pull. She tried to resist, and run. Just when she reached the front, she woke up.

Oh my, what was that, or better yet who was that man that I was ready to marry. Why didn't I see his face? She asked herself. Then she remembers something about that man which stood there waiting for her. He was wearing, a black tuxedo with diamond cufflinks.

Why this kind of dream now, she had never had a dream of her getting married before. She fell asleep again, and then the next thing she remembers was waking, feeling anxious to see Levi. She knew that it would be a challenge for her to shower, at the hospital she had a nurse to help her, now she was on her own. There was no way she would call Levi in to help her.

She knew that Mable would be willing, to help. But she didn't want to appear, to look helpless. There were just some things, she would have to do for herself, and this was one of them. Yvonne picked out, a bright blue V-neck, tank top. She got out a pair of white shorts, to go with it. She managed to shower, and wash her hair on her own. At first, she felt like she couldn't do it by herself, then she asked God for strength. Upon getting her self all dressed and going out into the living room, Levi was patiently a waiting her arrival.

"Have you been up for long?" Yvonne asked Levi with a smile, he was becoming quite fond of.

"No not for that long. I see you managed to dress yourself. I could have helped you there, you know." Levi spoke with a slight grin.

"Thanks, but no thanks. I managed quite nicely, to shower, and dress by myself. Besides I don't believe that two people should see each other, unless they were married. Or if it was a job, such like being a doctor or nurse. That you are not, are you?"

"I was just teasing you, I know that you are not that kind of woman. If you were then I would not. Levi stopped right in the middle of his sentence.

Yvonne looked at him, wondering why he never finished what he was saying. "Why did you stop, please continue." asked Yvonne.

"I better go upstairs, and get Van up. His bus will be here in forty-five minutes, if I don't wake him now, he will miss the bus." Levi said, as he went up the stairs, to wake Van.

Yvonne wondered just what Levi was going to say, but never finished.

Van stomped coming down the stairs, all dressed and ready for breakfast.

"Good morning honey, you look very nice for school today. Yvonne said. "Are you ready to eat? And why you making so much noise coming down stairs?"

"I wanted Levi to take me to school. I didn't want to take the bus. Will you and Levi be eating with me?"

Yvonne looked at Levi, for the answer that Van was waiting for.

"Sure, we're going to eat with you; Mable has everything ready for us." He spoke, as he led Yvonne into the kitchen, with her chair.

"Something smells really good." spoke Yvonne. "What do I smell?"

"Mable likes to make southern gravy and biscuits, you might be smelling that. Let's sit down and she will bring the food in for us."

"You are right, it is biscuits and gravy. I have always liked them very much." stated Yvonne.

Levi passed the food to Yvonne, and she dished up Van and her food, and then handed it back to Levi. After saying the prayers, she tasted the food, when she looked at Levi. "Wow this has got to be by far the best, I have ever had. I don't know what makes her's taste so much better, then the others, but this is awesome."

"THANK YOU." A voice from the other room made itself known.

"Van you better finish up, so you can catch the bus."

"I'm almost done mama."

"I'll go with you to the end of the driveway buddy, I want to make sure that the bus stops here for you."

Levi and Yvonne watched as Van got on the bus, for the first time since the move. It was hard for Yvonne to see her son, going to school from a place that was not theirs. She knew that it was bound to happen, but to watch him, was altogether different. She didn't quite understand it herself, maybe just because it was different not being at home, since he started school it was from her home. Levi noticed that she had tears that rolled down her cheeks, onto her shorts. At first, he didn't react to this, not really knowing what to do. He continued to push her chair, up the long drive. Then he came to a stop, and knelt down in front of her.

"I watched you cry when he got on the bus, I thought that is what you wanted. Did you change your mind?" He asked sounding a little, worried that she was unhappy with him taking the bus.

"No, I never changed my mind, it's just, silly really." she said holding back her words.

"If it made you cry, then it can't be that silly." He replied, hoping that she would let him know why she was crying.

"It's just ever since Van started kindergarten, he rode the same bus, now this is scary for him, to be on a different bus. I just don't want him to be afraid, to do something different. Does that make any sense to you?"

"Perfectly" He replied, then without another word, he walked to the back of her chair, and began to push her all the way to the house.

Yvonne looked at all the beauty that surrounds her and Levi as they walked. She began to think, *what if I would have met Levi under different circumstances. Would he even have noticed me, or Van. Would he ever have invited either of us, out to this beautiful place he has made for himself? Not likely,* came to mind, it saddened her to think, that she was only here, for one reason and that reason was, to get better. And better she will get, she will not stay at a man's home out of guilt, or whatever reason he had underneath that he wasn't going to share with her. *No one can be this nice, for no reason. Maybe it wasn't my fault, the accident happened after all. Maybe it was his, and that's why he's being so nice to both Van and I. Maybe it's because if I really could remember what happened, he might think that I would sue him for everything, he has. And he wouldn't want that to happen, after all he did say that this has been his whole life for the past eleven years.* Yvonne knew that she was allowing her mind, to work over time. That is not a place that she would prefer to go. She knew just by those thoughts coming to mind, that she has not been reading her bible much lately.

When reaching the front door, of the home. Levi asked Yvonne, if she would like to go out back, for a ride in his golf cart.

"Not at this time, I haven't been reading my bible like I should. If you wouldn't mind, I'd like to go to my room for a while, and then if you're not busy, after lunch, we can go."

"Sure, that's no problem at all. Why not study in the library, you might find that to be much more suitable for you. It's up to you, I just know yesterday, that you made a comment on how that would become your favorite room, in the home."

"You remember that, wow that's impressive." You are right, it would be much nicer of a place then the bedroom. There's only one problem with it."

"What, just say the word, and I will try to fix it for you." Levi replied.

Yvonne started to laugh, "I don't know how to get back there." Yvonne couldn't help but laugh, the way he had offered to fix it for her.

"Oh good, I thought that I might have to tear down a wall, or something a little harder, but finding your way there that's easy." Levi walked away, leaving Yvonne sitting in the living room. A minute later he came back with colored paper.

"What are you going to do with that?" Yvonne asked.

"It's simple. I'm going to make you arrows that will point you anywhere, you want to go. I'll just put them here on the wall." He spoke as he cut out his first arrow, and then taped it to the wall. "There, I have the name on it, pointing you in the right direction. Now I'll go to the end over here, to show you where this one will take you."

Yvonne couldn't believe this man, going the second mile for her. She felt guilty, at what she had thought of this kind man, when coming up the driveway. "This is so kind of you, I've never had anyone do anything like this for me before. Putting all these arrows everywhere, so I know where to go. Aren't you a bit afraid that it will mess with your decor that you have?"

"No not really, if it will help you to get from one place to another, that's all that counts. Beside you have never met me, before. I want to make you happy. You said no one has ever done anything like this for you before." He spoke giving her a big smile. "I just want you to feel free, to go where ever you want to go, without feeling you're asking too much from one of us here. I don't think that any of us, would mind helping you around. I think I got to know you a little last night, when we talked about each other's ways. You like to do things for yourself, without feeling you need help from another, am I right?"

"You paid close attention that is just how I feel. Even when Mark was alive, I did a lot for myself. It used to drive him crazy, when we first married. He always wanted to do more for me then I would let him do."

"Like what?"

"Like change a tire, or fix a broken lamp. Anything little like that."

"You call changing a tire little, you are a very small framed woman, how did you ever managed to change a tire?"

"I may be small, but my dad taught me, the greater things in life when I was young, and I never forgot them."

"Speaking of your dad, when did you say that your parents are due to come in? They are still coming, aren't they?"

"Yes, they called last night, and told me that they will be at my home, Friday afternoon, around one."

"They are more than welcome to stay here with us, if you would like."

"My dad told me that they would rather stay at my home, no disrespect. But my parents are a little old fashion and they feel it's wrong for Van and I to be here to."

Levi didn't say a word, just shook his head.

"I know I tried to tell them, that my bedroom is down stairs and yours is up.

But they said it don't look respectable, for a mother and her son, staying at a man's home. They mean well, I don't think that they fully understand, what's really going on with Van and I right now."

"This must be hard on you, trying to get them to understand your situation. Do they even realize that you are in a wheel chair right now?" Levi asked, trying not to sound upset.

"They know that I am, but I think they don't really understand that at this time I really can't walk. I think they think of me, as I just hurt my legs. And it's easier to sit in this chair, and then try to walk. Does that make any sense?" Yvonne asked confusing herself.

"Yeah I think so. The bottom line is they need to see you to understand, where you're coming from, and why you are staying, here with me."

"That's it." she laughed. "Okay I'm going to follow these arrows, and I trust that I will find my way around." She smiled at Levi, as she began to move her wheel chair, to go the direction of the arrows.

"Yvonne!" Levi called out, as she was headed down the hallway.

"Yes!" She answered, as she stopped her chair, from going any further.

"I'm headed to my office, for a while. I thought that would give you some time to read, and pray. But if you need anything, you can call my cell phone, or ask Mable? Is that alright?"

"Sure, I'm not here to stop you, from doing whatever it is you do. I'll be fine."

"I'll be back for lunch, I plan on the two of us, going for that ride that you promised me."

"It's a deal, after lunch. We'll take that ride." With those last words, she was on her way back down the hallway.

10

On his way to the office, Levi got a phone call from Roxie. She was letting him know that she was coming home, and wanted to spend some time with him. Levi not wanting to get into any long conversation with her didn't mention to her that he had a couple staying at his home with him. Now he needed to figure a way to tell Yvonne about Roxie. *Why is it so hard to tell her, I'm just going to have to come right out with it? It shouldn't matter to her one way or another. She so much as told me last night, that there will never be anything more to us then friends anyway. Why do I feel like I'm doing something wrong behind her back by not telling her about Roxie?*

Yvonne enjoyed her time with reading God's word, and praying. Often times, she would hear God speak to her heart, and give her direction for her life. Now she prayed that when her parents arrived it would be of one that would be of joy, not sorrow. She knew what her parent's beliefs were, and she too believed the same, that a man and woman should not live together, without being married. But she also knew that her, and Levi did not fall under that category. She would just have to show them, that their relationship was not at all the same. "Lord Jesus, help my parents to understand, what I am doing is not because I have walked away from you in anyway, it's because I need help at this time. In Jesus wonderful name I pray."

Levi was true to his word, he was back for lunch, with a dozen of roses. "These are for you, to brighten up your day." He spoke while handing them to Yvonne.

"White roses are my favorite, color of roses. Thank you so much, but how did you know?"

"Know what?" Levi asked.

"That the white ones are my favorite?"

"I didn't." He said with a big smile. It's just when I look at you, to me you are pure and clean. So, I wanted to buy white, their clean, and fresh looking to me."

"I never thought of that before, they do look clean. No wonder I always liked them, better than the other colored ones." Yvonne said with a light chuckle. "I love the vase, you put them in. If I may say, you have very good taste. I have never seen a vase that looked as though it was made of pearl. This is very pretty, thank you." Yvonne was amazed, at what steps Levi would do to make her happy. She was in shock, that someone would do so much, for someone they barely knew. Yvonne began to see him in a whole new way, where she found herself looking at him in a fondness she had not had before.

"You are most welcome, shall we go get a bite to eat. I'd like to enjoy the outside with you, if you." Levi stopped again, like he did the day before, in the middle of a sentence.

"There is something that you have been trying, to tell me, so will you please just come out with it. It seems you get so close to telling me, and then all of a sudden you just stop." Yvonne sat very stern looking up at him. Levi, if we are ever to truly be friends, then we must be honest with each other, even if it makes us a little uncomfortable."

"You are right, I do have something to tell you. It's not that I tried to withhold it from you, it's just every time, I tried to tell you, I could just never get it to come out."

"Please just tell me, you got me wondering what's going on now I am very understanding."

"Okay I'll tell you. I have a friend, of mine that will be stopping over tonight." Levi spoke keeping his head turned, away from her.

"Now why would that matter to me, I have friends too. And someday, they may want to come out to see me, I'd hope you wouldn't mind."

"No, I wouldn't, but my friend is a lady, that I have known for a couple of years." Levi was still having a hard time, coming out, with who this person really was.

"Are you trying to tell me, that you have a lady friend, that's not just a friend?"

"Yeah sort of you see, I wasn't sure how you would feel about it. Her name is Roxie, she and I have been seeing each other for two years."

Yvonne never spoke a word for a moment, getting caught off guard so-to-speak. Then she found the courage to go on. "Levi it's okay, I know that you have a life outside of Van and I. You could have told me before. If you would like, Van and I will stay in the game room, or in my bedroom, while she's here."

"Not at all, now that would be just plain silly, to hide you away, as if your very presence should be hidden. I will not hear of it. This is your home for however long, only time will tell. You and your son will not hide yourselves away for anyone.

"I can't believe that you thought you needed to keep your girlfriend hidden from me. If I had a boyfriend, I wouldn't want to keep him from you." Yvonne stated wondering why this was the first time of hearing about Roxie, and trying not to sound bothered by the news.

"I met her through some friends of mine, a couple years ago. She is a very nice lady, she's been traveling for a couple of weeks, and she came home last night. She called to ask, if she could come out this way for a visit." Levi went on explaining how she and he have met, as if he needed her approval who he can have come out to his home.

"Levi this is your home, I am only a guest. You do not need my approval, of who comes out to see you. I will be happy to meet your girlfriend tonight."

Levi heard the words that Yvonne spoke, but he couldn't help but feel a little sorry, that she hadn't shown she cared, to whom he would have over. Some how he had hoped that she felt, like he felt towards her. Levi thought about how many times, he wanted to tell her about Roxie, but he couldn't bring himself into doing it. And now that he had, she didn't care cither way. He should have already known that she wouldn't care, after their talk. He wondered if Roman could have been right after all, did he indeed love this woman, that didn't seem to love him back.

"Are you ready to go in and eat?" he asked Yvonne with disappointment written all over him.

"Yes, I can use a little something to eat. I don't know why, because I know that I ate a lot for breakfast, but my stomach has been just a growling."

The two went into the house to see what Mable had fixed for their lunch. After they ate Yvonne excused herself from the table and went to her bedroom.

Levy sat at the table feeling troubled, and it was written all over his face.

"Okay, I can see that you are troubled. Tell me what it is that has got you looking like you lost your best friend?" Asked Roman

"I told Yvonne about Roxie, I figured that I better get it out before she was to show up here." Levi said looking at Roman, and Mable.

Mable looked towards Yvonne's bedroom, and made a statement, that surprised even her. "I wish that she would never have come back from her vacation." Surprised by what she just said looked over at Levi, to see if he was going to bawl her out, or at least have something to say back to her.

"Well don't hold back your feelings, there Mable." said Levi.

"I'm sorry Levi that was not my place to say anything like that. Please forgive me, for speaking of Roxie like that."

"You don't need to be forgiven, for speaking how you feel. I'm aware that you two have never really seen eye to eye. Even though I really don't know why, it must be something that I'm really blind to."

"Or it could be, that you might have seen it, but never really wanted to address it, or face it." spoke Roman.

Levi looks at Roman. "Do you feel the same way? I was beginning to just think that it was a woman thing. That we men aren't even aware of."

"No son, I have to say. Every time I see Roxie, I get very uncomfortable. That's why I always make an exit." He quickly changing the subject. "You never said why you been sitting here looking so sad."

"And here I just always thought that it was to give her and me some time alone. What am I, blind to something, that the two of you see, and I don't. And to answer your question, the sadness that the two of you are seeing is because I am so confused in my feelings for Yvonne."

Yvonne came back out to join them at the table while they were all talking. Everyone kept right on a talking, she was absorbing what was being said. Yvonne sat there not knowing what to say, she would look at whoever was doing all the talking. Then she mentioned something that made everyone else stop talking. "Why don't we just wait for tonight, for me to meet her? I've had people say to me many times before that I am a great judge of character. If you wouldn't mind, Levi I'd like to be given the chance to see for myself." She looked at everyone sitting there. "Please, I'm sorry if it sounds like that the two of you are not just as good as I am by judging characters. I surly never meant for it to sound that way."

"Sure, why not, everyone else seems to think that they know more than I do. I would like to know what you really think. I know Mable has always felt that Roxie is after my money, when she has her own. And I'm not sure what Roman's reason for not liking her is." he spoke looking at Roman.

"Let Yvonne meet her, and I bet she will think the same as I do. Not the right one for you." Roman added.

"And I suppose the two of you, think that you know who's right for me."

"We know it's not Roxie." Mable said looking at Yvonne, as if to imply that she was the one for Levi.

Yvonne trying to change the subject said. "Mable, you have outdone yourself, again with the meal. If ever you would like some help, please just ask. I have been known to whip up a pretty good meal, from time to time. Of, course it's not as good as your cooking. I just don't want you to make a fuss over Van and I. I want you to know, that I'm free to help, if you ever need me please don't hesitate to ask." Yvonne didn't want Mable to feel as if she wasn't a good cook. She liked someone cooking for her, she never had that since living at home many years ago.

Levi listened carefully to Yvonne, as she talked with Mable. He could see why the attraction to her, was so great. She chose her words so careful, as to not hurt another. How could he ever see Roxie, the same as he did Yvonne? Although Roxie seemed to be nicer then the wives, of his friends, he never remembered her, ever caring, what others thought of her. Maybe that is why Roman and Mable didn't care for her. She was very out spoken and never did he ever remember her telling Mable thanks for anything before. Let alone to offer to help her with cooking or anything else. Wow

I can't believe I never seen that before, how could I have been so foolish and blind, to have not noticed. What am I am going to do now? He questioned himself.

He needed to stop thinking about Roxy and focus on better things, yes better things such as Yvonne. A woman of character, a woman that has great love like I've not seen since my mother. A woman that others see as of great value. He stood a way's off watching Yvonne from another room, thinking about the time they had spent together. And how in just a few short days, it had meant more to him, then in the last two years he had spent with Roxie.

Approaching her slowly. "Do you like to play board games?"

"Yes, I do, do you?" she replied.

"I like all kinds of game, just not head games," he said then started to laugh. "I'm sorry, I just had to say that."

"I don't like head games either." she said giving him a big smile.

"Van will be home soon, would you like to go outside and wait for him?"

"I would like to meet him at the end of the driveway, if you don't mind. I want him, to see me, when getting off the bus."

"Okay, we'll start to head out there." He told her, he also wanted to meet Van too, when he came off the bus.

Levi carried her out to his golf cart, then drove down to the end of the drive, so he could give Van, a ride back, to the house. He wanted to hear all about his new bus, and the ride back to the house.

"Here they come now, I hope that he had a good day today." Yvonne said all excited to find out how his first day went on a different bus.

"I hope he had a great ride, it might take him a few days, to get used to it, but I'm sure he'll be fine." Levi gave his opinion on what he thought.

The bus came by as though to stop, but yet it went right on by leaving Levi, and Yvonne just sitting there.

"What just happened, did they just drive by not seeing us. Or did they not realize that my son is on that bus." Yvonne looked at Levi, horrified. "Now what do we do, there not coming back. Oh Levi, Van must be scared out of his mind. He's only eight years old. That's not right, that they just drove by and never stopped. What did they think, we were doing out here?" Yvonne was getting all upset, not knowing why they didn't drop her son off.

"Let's get up to the house, and call the school. I don't understand why they didn't stop, when we were waiting right there. Didn't they remember, picking him up, this morning?"

Levi called the school, to find out where Van was. The school hadn't heard anything about the bus driver not dropping him off. They placed Levi on hold, so they could contact the driver of the bus. After doing some checking as to his whereabouts, they found out that Van had taken his old bus, and was dropped off at his old address.

"Why would he get on his old bus?" asked Levi.

"I'm sure that he just got confused, can we go get him. He must be worried, sitting there all by himself."

"Yes, we better hurry, I don't want him thinking that something went wrong again. Last time he was there by himself, he found out about the car accident."

Levi and Yvonne drove as fast as they could, without breaking the law, to get across town to where Van was at. When pulling up to the driveway, they could see him sitting on the front porch, much like the first time Levi met him.

Van came running to the car. "I got mixed up, on what bus to take. I'm sorry, are you mad?" he asked.

"Van, I'm not mad, I thank God that you are alright. We didn't know what happened to you, we were waiting for you at the end of the driveway, but the bus drove right past us, I got worried. You need to remember what bus, you ride on from here on out, okay buddy?" Yvonne scolded, while giving him hugs, to let him know, she was glad to see that he was okay.

"I'm glad that you're okay too buddy, I was starting to get worried. I tried to be strong, for your mom. I think I had a little anxiety, going on for a while there. Tomorrow I'll give you, a piece of paper that you can carry in your pants pocket, with the bus number on it. That way this kind of thing doesn't have to happen anymore, okay."

"Yes, I wish I would have had that today, I was starting to get worried if my mom was alright or if she wasn't." Van spoke reaching up from the back seat, and touched his mother's shoulder.

Yvonne knew that he would be getting worried, if they didn't get to him quickly. She patted Van's hand when he touched her. "I am glad that Levi was home at the time the bus came by, otherwise I don't know what I would have done." It was her turn, to give Levi a wink.

Changing the subject, Levi thought that he better let Van know about Roxie coming over. "We have company, coming for supper tonight."

"Is it grandma, and grandpa?" asked Van.

"No honey it's not them yet. They will be here this weekend. Levi has a friend coming over, so I want you to remember your manners okay?"

"Yes ma'am" A soft voice spoke.

"She's a good friend, I've known for a while now, I'm sure that you will like her." spoke Levi.

"Levi, you and my mom are boyfriend and girlfriend aren't you?"

"Van, what ever made you say a thing like that? You know that Levi and I are just friends." Scolded Yvonne, and then looking over at Levi apologizing. "We just had this talk, I told you we would not be thinking these thoughts, do you remember?"

"Yes ma'am."

"That's alright, maybe in his mind, that's the way he see's things. Or maybe, it could be what he wants it to be like." Levi spoke to Yvonne in a low tone, so Van couldn't hear him.

Yvonne never commented on what Levi said, but she did sit there pondering, on what he said. The rest of the ride home was a quiet ride. She sat there thinking, about what it's going to be like to meet, Levi's lady friend.

"We're home, and it looks like Roxie is already here." Levi looked at his watch. "She's early, I wonder what time she arrived?"

Van sat up, to look out the front window. Yvonne began to feel, a bit uncomfortable. Her mind began to race, what if this Roxie woman gets upset with Levi, for letting Van, and I stay here. What if she convinces him, into having us leave?

Levi pulled his car into the garage, and without saying anything, he walked around to Yvonne's door, and helped her out, and into her chair.

"I'm feeling a little nervous, now that I'm going to meet her. Do I look okay?" Yvonne asked.

"You look fine, and there's nothing to be nervous about. I'm sure that you and Roxie will get along just fine."

When they walked in the house, Yvonne was not expecting what she saw. Before Levi could introduce Yvonne, and Van to Roxie, she grabbed a hold of Levi, and planted a big kiss on his lips. Levi got embarrassed of what just happened, he wiped his lips, and pulled back from her. "Roxie, I'd like you to meet my friend Yvonne, and her son Van."

Roxie looked past Levi, and then looked down to see who he was talking about. Without saying anything to Yvonne, or Van she just looked back at Levi. "I didn't realize that you had company. I thought that it would be just us, after I've been out of town for a while. And since when do you wipe off my kisses?" Roxie spoke in such a way, that Levi felt like he didn't even know this person that stood in front of him.

"Excuse me Levi, Van and I will go in the game room, and leave the two of you alone. I'm sorry to be intruding on the two of you." Yvonne spoke, as she attempted to wheel her chair down the hallway.

"You will do no such thing." He looked at Roxie with such disappointment in his face.

"It's okay really, we don't care to be out here right now."

"Oh Levi, don't tell me that you have this woman, and her son staying here with you. I see all these arrows, posted on your walls everywhere. When I ask Mable what they were here for, she just said ask you."

"Who are you?" Spoke Levi, in a very sarcastic way. "I don't even know you, you go away out of the country, for God only knows how long. Then you come to my home, and treat my guest, like they have the plague. What is this all about Roxie?"

She stood there, looking into Levi's eyes. She could tell that he was very upset, with the way she had acted, towards Yvonne and Van. "I'm sorry, I just wasn't thinking, seeing some woman here in a wheel chair, and her little boy. If you want me to, I will go tell them that I'm sorry"

"Roxie, I think that it might be best, if you just go. I don't believe that we have any more to say to each other." He told her as he reached down to grab her purse, and walked over to the door, and opened it up for her.

"You've changed Levi, what's got into you all of a sudden. Since when do you have the poor come and stay with you. It's one thing, that you are always giving your money away, on the streets to them, but now your bringing them home with you."

"Roxy!" Levi shouted. "Not that it's any of your business, but those two wonderful people, are not off the street. Yvonne is the woman I hit with my car, and came close to killing her, I crippled her, when I hit her."

"Why didn't you tell me that, right away? I would never have acted the way that I did."

"You never gave me a chance, and what different does it make anyway. People are people, in my book. If anyone should know that, you should. Now just go, if she will have me, I'm going to ask her to marry me. I'll invite you to the wedding." Levi had a big smile come across his face, as he enjoyed telling her that.

Still not leaving, Roxie stood there hearing the words, marry, coming from Levi. She had always thought that one day, he would ask her to marry him, but what is this I hear him saying about marrying a crippled. she thought. "You just can't be serious, marry, what are you saying?"

"What I am saying is I believe she is the woman for me. So, you might as well, put your eyes back in your head, and go gossip about me to your friends, because I know that's what you're going to do anyway." With those words, he closed the door, behind her. He was shocked, from the words he heard himself speak to Roxie, marry wow where did that come from? She just makes me so mad, he was telling himself. But marry Yvonne, hum I don't think she sees me that way, and I'm not sure I do her. I never pictured me marring anyone, in a wheel chair before. Maybe one day, she will walk. He stood in the living room, in deep thought. He heard Yvonne coming down the hallway.

"Levi, Van and I have been talking. We think that it might be for the best, if we don't inconvenience you any longer, and go home. I will work out something when my folks get up here, tomorrow."

"You don't have to do any such thing, I can promise you, that Roxie will not be coming here any longer. And I'd like to apologize, for her actions. I can't believe that I have never noticed how vain she really is. I must have been out of my mind, to have wasted two years of my life on her."

"Levi, I don't want to be the one, to keep your friends, from coming to your home."

"If all my friends acted like she did, I wouldn't want them to stop over either. Tell me that you will stay."

Mable overheard part of their conversation, and thought that she would give her opinion on the subject. "Yvonne, honey I wouldn't let the likes of Roxie chase you and your son away from here, if my life depended on it."

"I just don't want to be a bother, to others." Yvonne said as she held Van's hand.

"Why didn't she like my mom and I?" asked Van.

Levi didn't know how to answer Van, he didn't want to say the wrong thing, like telling them that she thought the two of them were homeless. He knew that wouldn't be the best way to go about it. "Some people just don't see anything, but themselves. She has changed, since the last time I seen her. I never remember her being so closed minded before. Or maybe it's I who's changed, and I don't care to hang with people that don't care for others."

Van looked at his mother. "Please can we stay mama, I love it out here. And I won't miss the bus anymore, I promise." He begged.

"If you're really sure, that we won't be a bother, we'll stay."

"I'm really sure you're no bother, now it's settled. The both of you will stay, for as long as you like." spoke Levi in a deep voice.

It's funny how Yvonne, never took notice, of how deep Levi's voice is until now. She wondered why that was, she has talked with the man, many times, but now it seemed to had gotten deeper then it was before, now it sounds as though his voice has changed. She shrugged the thought of that aside, to think about how Mable and Levi wanted both her, and Van to stay. She was willing to put her feelings aside, to do what was right, for her and Van.

"Okay now that, that's all settled. I'll be more careful, of whom my friends are." Levi spoke giving Van a rub on top of his head. "I don't know about you folks, but I'm getting hungry. Are you hungry there young man?" He asked Van.

"Yeah, are you mama?"

"I think I can eat a bite." answered Yvonne.

"I sure hope you can eat more, then a bite." spoke Levi. "Mable has made my favorite meal, you know what that one is don't you Van?"

"I sure do its roast beef."

"You remembered I knew after you tasted the way Mable makes her roast beef, you would never forget it. Come on let's go eat." Levi spoke rubbing his hands together.

"It, sure smell good, I can hardly wait to try it" Yvonne said, as she began to wheel her chair, towards the kitchen. "Everything smells great Mable." She then tried a bite, "Yummy," she commented on Mable's cooking. "I believe this just might become one of my favorite meals also. I just want to say thank you, so much, for asking my son and I to stay. It's really hard for me, to depend on others, so thank you for not minding, the extra."

"Now you never mind about the extra, it's good to have more around here. I seem to cook, for more than three all the time, and the food then goes to waste. It's been a long time since Levi was at home, for this amount of time. He was always at work, now he seems to be enjoying life a bit. I want to thank you and Van for that. I worried about him, working so much, and not doing anything else."

Yvonne gave the woman a smile, "He told me that he worked a lot, I'm glad that he is doing something else too. I know that Van, and I have been enjoying ourselves here hanging with you all."

"I quite agree. Levi has spent much, too much time with his work that he forgot about life. My wife and I have been with him since his mama passed, and we have never seen him this happy, as he has been, for this past week." Roman added in.

Yvonne looked up at Roman, surprised to hear him speak. Then with a slight grin she said. "I was beginning to think, that you didn't talk, you're so quiet." She laughed lightly.

"You will hear from him, whenever he feels the need, to let you. Otherwise, he keeps pretty much to himself." Mable implied.

"I see why this is your favorite meal, it is absolutely fabulous. I have never been one to cook, a very good roast beef. Although I'd love for you to teach me, some time. That is if you wouldn't mind. I'm sure Van would love, for me to cook this meal for us, when we return back home."

Mable looked at Levi, when Yvonne mentioned going back home. She knew how much he needed Yvonne here with him right now, even though he would never admit it. Before she and Van came here, Mable could see that he was not looking so well, she and Roman worried over him all the time. They had thought that he might have been sick, but when he went to the doctor, all his test came out negative. But since Yvonne, and Van came his life has changed. "I hope that the two of you will be staying, for some time longer, before returning to your home. I hate to see Levi forget, what life is all about." Mable spoke giving Yvonne a wink.

"You two, make it sound like I hadn't lived, at all before. I did manage, to go to the clubs, from time to time." He said looking at Yvonne. "I will have to admit, it's been great having the two, of you here."

"The clubs, now what kind of life is that. That's not life. Mable stated.

"I know that's not really a good place to hand out, if you want to meet a good woman that's for sure. I'm glad you decided to stay here." he said looking at Yvonne and Van.

"Well I thank you, for all your nice words you have spoken about Van and I. I am sure that we will be here, for a while longer. I have to figure out, how to make a living, before heading back home."

"I have called a nurse for you, and she will be coming tomorrow, to start your physical therapy." Levi told Yvonne.

"That's awesome, I can hardly wait. I want to walk again, as soon as possible."

"Did your doctor, tell you, that you would walk again?" Mable asked, while everyone sat waiting for her answer.

"No, he didn't, but he didn't have to. I know that I will walk again. I just need a little help right now, it may take some time, but it will happen, I don't believe that God would have me stay in this chair, for the rest of my life. In fact, I had a dream last night." She stopped, and chose her words carefully. "I had a dream that I was walking again. I believe that God gave me that dream, so I wouldn't lose hope."

Levi wondered why she stopped, right in the middle of her sentence, then continued to finish. Was she leaving something out, that she didn't want the rest of us to hear.

Levi and Yvonne played games that evening, until they were tired. They laughed, and tossed popcorn at each other like they were kids again. Mable and Roman could hear them clear, from the other room. They could hear laughter of all kind's comings from the front room. They came to see what was going on, with the two of them. When they came close, to the dining room, they stopped. Looking around the corner as they hid from them, they watched the two enjoying, each other's company. They could see, how much Yvonne being there, was helping Levi to feel alive again, even though he was too proud, to admit it. They stood there watching, then came the part that sent them on their way. Levi reached over, and gave Yvonne a kiss. They knew it was time for them to go.

Shocked, Yvonne sat there looking at Levi, she was unsure, of what she should say, or what really just happened. What was this for, was it just a nice friendly little kiss, or was there more to it, she wondered.

Levi surprised by his own actions, apologized to Yvonne. "I'm sorry, I should have asked you first. Please forgive me." He asked, feeling as if she might not have liked him giving her a kiss.

"That's alright, it took me by surprise a little, but I didn't mind." She gave him that smile that let him know she liked it. "Can I ask you something?"

"Sure, ask away"

"Why did you kiss me like that, was it because of how Roxie treated me. And you felt sorry for me?"

"Is that what you really think? Yvonne, from the moment I laid eyes on you at the Hospital, I was attracted to you. I would, or could never kiss someone, just because I felt sorry for them. I can't say that I didn't feel things for her at first. What I can say, is that I thought, that I knew who she was, but boy was I ever wrong. I felt like I let you, and Van down, after telling you, she was a nice person."

"I'm glad, that you never felt sorry, for me. I wouldn't want a kiss from a man, just because he felt sorry for me." she spoke with a light laughter.

It's good to see, that my kiss can make you laugh. I guess it's better than making you cry." he said laughing.

I must confess, from the first time, I saw you. I thought that you were a very handsome, man."

"Oh, I see, you thought that I was." He spoke with redness coming to his face. "So, have you changed your mind now that you have got to know me better?"

"No, it's not like that. You're being silly. I still think that you're handsome, it's just not something, that a person goes around saying." Yvonne was laughing at this time. Now it was her turn, to have a red face.

"There's something that I have wanted to ask you, but just never did. What nationality are you?"

"I have Part Indian, French, English, German, and some Scotch, Why?"

"I have been trying to figure out, where you got your dark brown eyes, and the darker skin, I wasn't sure, if you had Mexican, or what it was."

"Does race matter to you?"

"No not at all, look at me, I'm black as they come." He laughed again. "I think you're a very beautiful woman Yvonne, from the inside out. And I don't care what you have in you. I'd like to get to know you more, I mean in a way, that's more than just friends."

"You surprise me Levi."

Levi wasn't sure if that was good or not, the way she said that. But he sure was going to find out.

"Oh, how's that." he asked." I hope it's a good thing, not bad."

"All this time, I thought that you were just being nice to me, because you hit into me, on the highway. But now you're asking me, if we could be more, then friends, am I right?"

He was the one surprised now, he somehow would have thought, that she would have jumped, at the thought of becoming, more than just friends. But what he was hearing, didn't sound like she was jumping, at being anything to him. "Its fine if you just want to be friends." He spoke, with embarrassment written all over him, for even suggesting, that they be more, then friends.

"Levi, I didn't say no, I was just trying, to understand, if that is what you were asking me. I like you very much, and I think you are a wonderful man. You took Van, and I in, after the accident, and you didn't have to do anything like that. It was my fault, what happened to me, but yet you have forgiven me for pulling right out, in front of you. I could have taken your life, as well as my own, you never judged me, or accused me, for the wrong that I did. You have been there for Van, and I more than anyone has. If I were to see anyone, I would hope *that* it would be you. You not only have been very kind to my son and I, but I see the kindness that you have shown to Mable and Roman too. I don't know what ever, compelled, you to care, for my son, and I like you have. But I'm sure glad that you did."

"If that be the case, then why do I hear in your voice, that you're not so sure about us giving it a try?"

"I'm not really saying no, what I am going to ask, is if you will give me time, to think and pray. The bible tells us as Christians to be not with an unbeliever. God said that we should be with a believer. I need to just have some time to pray, about what God is wanting from me, in my life. Does that make any sense to you?"

"I do believe, just because I don't go to church, doesn't make me an unbeliever."

"One thing that God, does ask from us, is that we fellowship with one another in the same body. Meaning Christians, God ask us to go to church, and worship. I just don't want anything, or anyone that will ever discourage me, from the things of God."

"I would never do that, in fact last night, when I went to bed, I thought long, and hard about a lot, of things, and one of them is getting back into church. I would really like this Sunday, if I could go with you, and Van."

"Really, I would love that, and I know Van would to. Why don't we see, how things, go after church on Sunday? I would never want you, to come to church, just to please me. Come because you want to come."

"I do want to go, I want to see what I've been missing, all these years. Not to change the subject, but have you talked, with anyone from your church lately?

"Yes, I got a phone call last night, from one of the ladies. She was asking me, if there was anything, that anyone, from the church, could do. I told her everything was fine, and I'd see them all at church."

"I'm glad that you told her, everything was fine. Now I know that Mable, and I are taking pretty good care of you." He said and gave her a wink.

11

Yvonne took the next day, getting to know Levi more. She would watch him from a distance when he didn't know that she was watching him. She knew that if she would take him in consideration, to being her new bow. Then she would have to watch and pray. Levi went into work, while the nurse came to help Yvonne with her therapy. She wanted to walk so badly, she thought if I ever am to date Levi, it would be nice to walk again. A couple hours past and Levi was home. When Yvonne heard him, she came out of her room.

"Levi, how was your day at work?"

"It was busy for the couple hours that I was there, but I knew I should be here, so I left early and came home."

"My folks, will be at my house anytime, do you think we can go and see them?" Yvonne asked with excitement, in her voice, as she came out of the bedroom, and down the hallway.

"I must say, do you ever look nice. She looks very nice, don't she Van?" he asked as Van stood there, saying nothing.

"Yes, mama, you do look nice. I can't wait to see grandma, and grandpa. Are you guys ready now?"

"Yes, let's get going." Levi, opened up the garage door, to let Van, go first. Then he carefully led Yvonne, out to the car. The whole way to her home, she fidgeted, with her fingers. "Are you nervous, about seeing your parents?" asked Levi.

"Yeah, I guess, I am a little. I haven't seen them, in quite a while. I don't think that they really realize that I'm in the wheel chair for now, to get around. And that worries me."

"How is that?" He asked.

"When they really see, that I'm in the chair, to get around, I wonder what kind of effect, it will do to them, being older people. My mother usually, will take things to extremes."

"It might take some time, for them to adjust, but I'm sure they will, in time." he spoke.

"I'm hoping that I will be walking in no time, I did rather well today with my exercises I had to do."

"Mama, when will you walk again?" asked Van.

"I'm not sure when, but with the nurse helping me I'm sure it will come soon." Yvonne replied, to her curious son.

"But when will that be, I want you to walk now, what does the nurse do, that I can't do?"

Yvonne chuckled at Van, and his comments. "She helps me, with my therapy, in ways you would not be able to. She went to school, for this kind of thing. I know you want me to walk, as well as I want to walk. It will come, I know that it will, but we must be patient."

"Sorry for not asking you how things went today, I meant too, just was caught off guard when I came in the home." Levi spoke, then continued on. "When I was at work today, did everything go good with the nurse?"

"Yes, she is a very nice person. I did a lot of leg pulling, I'm not sure what all she will have me do later. But she said that we'll work on more come Monday, when she comes by."

"They're here! They're here Van screamed looking at his grand parent's van in the driveway.

"Here it goes." said Yvonne looking at Levi. "I don't see them outside anywhere, they must have gone inside already."

"I'll get your chair out." said Levi. "I must admit, I'm a bit nervous, to meet them."

"I just don't want them, being upset, seeing me in the wheel chair. I don't know, what they will think."

Van jumped out of the car, and began to run up, to the house. "Where here! Where here."

Levi was pushing Yvonne, towards the house in her chair, when her parents came out on the porch.

"There's my big boy." Spoke Marilyn, Yvonne's mother looking towards Yvonne as she was pushed up the sidewalk. She put her hands, over her mouth. "Oh, my honey just look, at our girl." She, spoke to Jack, Yvonne's dad.

"Let me help you get her up, these steps." Jack said as he took a hold of the bottom, of the wheel chair. "Thank God, that you are alive, I never thought that I would see the day, where my daughter would be in one of these." He bent down and gave her a kiss.

"Hi mom hi dad, I'm so glad, that you made it up, here. This here is my friend Levi. Van and I have been staying at his home, while I'm in this here chair."

"You can't walk at all? Have you tried?" Ask Marilyn.

"Mom, it's good to see you too. Do you really think if I could walk, that I'd be in this thing?" Yvonne responded with sarcasm.

"I'm sorry dear, I didn't mean to say you like that chair or anything, I just wasn't thinking."

"No! I'm sorry mom, I didn't mean to speak to you like this. I wish that I wasn't in this thing. I hate not being able to walk, and then to have others do for me. What I should be able to do for myself."

"I thank God that you're alive, and breathing." Levi interacted, trying to break the ice between Yvonne, and her mother.

Yvonne, looked up at Levi, "I'm sorry, I know this is no way to greet, my parents." Focusing her attention on her mother she stated. "I'm sorry mom I don't mean to worry you, and dad. I wondered, how the two of you, were going to handle this whole thing."

"Us, you don't need to worry, about the two of us." Spoke Jack. "You just get yourself well, as soon as you can, you hear me? Levi, I want to thank you, for taking care of my baby girl." he spoke as he shook hands with Levi.

"It is my pleasure sir. I've become quite fond, of the two, of them. And while you and the Mrs. are up in the states you are more than welcome, to come stay at my house, if you would like."

Jack looked over at his wife, to see if that's what she would like. "No thank you, I know, you mean well but we will take care of Yvonne and her son while we are here." Spoke Marilyn, in a stern voice.

"Mom, I don't know why, you're giving Levi a hard time. He has done everything, to help Van and I."

Marilyn stood outside on the porch, with her arms crossed. Not saying a word to what Yvonne, had asked her.

"Can we go inside, I don't want the neighbors staring at us." Yvonne asked, looking at some of the neighbors gathering close.

Levi took her inside, and then knelt down, to talk to her, where others couldn't hear. "Would you, like me to go, while you spend some time, with your folks? It's your call, I'll do whatever you want."

"You don't have to do that, she will just have to get over it." Spoke Yvonne.

"Then would you mind, if I left for a couple of hours. I think that you need to spend some time with them, without me."

"Okay, maybe it is for the best. Just call my cell, when you're ready to come back okay?"

"You got it." Levi replied giving her a tap on the shoulder. "Van, I'm going to go for a while, so you, and your mom, can spend some time with your grandparents."

Van came running up to Levi, giving him a big hug. Looking up at him, "you're coming back, aren't you?"

"Yes, little buddy, I am."

Levi left on that note.

"Mom why did you treat him with such little respect? You were very rude to him, I want to know why?" Yvonne tried not to be upset, but what her mother, had done was just wrong, in her eyes.

"He could have killed you." And here you are, staying with him, at his house. And he is black, what will people think?"

"Mom!" Yvonne snapped, at her mother. "How can you say that? It was not his fault, it was mine. I could have killed him. And black? Really, since when does the color of another make a difference?"

"How can you say that, he hit you? And then he has the nerve to invite you, and Van to stay, at his home, to ease his continuous."

"That's not fair. Mom, I wish that you would just listen, dad will you talk to her please?"

"I tried, she got it set in her mind, that he almost killed you. Now rather that's true or not, it's what she sees."

"Then she sees wrong, Levi is a wonderful man. And I really like him, I wish that you, would give him a chance, and not be so hard, on him. I know once you got, to know him, that you would really like him too."

"So, are you going to stay there, with him, or here with us?" asked Marilyn changing the subject.

"The bus comes, and picks Van up there, and all our clothes are there. Levi will bring me here, to see you, and dad. Another thing, he's hired a nurse, to come do therapy on me every day, to help my legs get stronger. So, I need to be there."

"Honey, I'm sorry that you had a car accident, and now you are in this chair. I'm so glad, that you are alright. And this young man has helped you out it sounds to me, like you found a really great man."

Thanks dad, I needed to hear that. Levi has asked me, if I would like to see him more than just a friend, I told him that I needed to pray, and think things through. One of the things that I prayed was I had asked God, to let you see Levi as part of my life."

"I believe he is the one, for you, I can tell the way he looks at you, that he would make you, a great husband, and Van a great dad. Now that doesn't mean that I'm right, that means that's what I saw. You continue to pray, before making a choice."

"I do believe that Van, would agree with you. He loves Levi, and I know Levi does him to."

"I'm glad that you're alright too honey, I don't know what your dad, and I would have ever done, if we would have lost you. I'm sorry for hurting you, the way I talked to Levi, and about him. I don't know what ever came over me. When he returns, I will ask him, to forgive me."

Yvonne reached out her hand, for her mother. "I forgive you mom, and I want you to know, that everything is going to be okay, for Van, and I."

"Does he go to church?"

"He did when he was young, but hasn't gone in years. He said that he wants to start going back, this Sunday with us. That's a start, of something good I believe." She looked at both her parents. "How long are you and dad going to be here for?"

"As long as you need us for I'm just not sure, that you need us at all. It looks to me, like you have everything that you need."

"It's funny to hear you say that, you know I've been alone without a man, for three years. I never thought that, I would meet one from a hospital bed. I am praying, and asking God to show me, if he is the man, for Van, and I. And mom, to say that I don't need the two of you, that's just silly. I always need, the both of you."

"He seems to be, a very good man, and I would want nothing less for my daughter." Spoke Jack.

"How does he make you feel, when you're around him?" asked Marilyn.

Yvonne looked at her mom, to answer her question. "When he walks in a room, I get butterflies, in my stomach. I feel so good around him, like someone, very special."

"I like him too, he has a lot of stuff, at his big house, for me to do." Spoke Van.

"What kind of home, does Levi have?"

"He has a real, real, real big house and a really big game room. It has everything in it to play. Don't it mama?"

"That's right honey, he does have a very nice home. And he does indeed, have a big, game room, that you love to hang out in." added Yvonne.

"Is this man, a wealthy man?" asked Jack.

"I don't know if we should talk, of what he has, and don't have. Why don't the two of you, come out there, for supper tonight. I could call Mable up, and let her know, that we will be having company."

"Mable! Who is she?" Marilyn asked as though, it could be Levi's wife.

"Mom calm down, don't get so excited. Mable is his maid."

"His maid, well I'd say he must be wealthy, to have a maid. Isn't it the wealthy, that has maids." replied Marilyn.

"Mother, you act as if it's a sin, to be wealthy. Yes, if you must know, he is very wealthy, just how much I don't know. It's none of my business."

"None of your business, well it should be every bit of your business."

"Marilyn! Now you have said some thing's since being here today, that I thought was just wrong. But now I am telling you that will be enough of drilling our girl. We should be thanking God, for saving her life, and be happy, to be here with her. Not questioning her, every move. Now I will hear no more, what this man has, or does not have is none of our business. I would like to apologize, for your mama, and myself honey."

"It's okay dad, I know you guys are just concerned. But we are okay. Levi is a really nice man, and until God tells me to leave, or get away from him. I will stay, and except his help."

"We accept your invitation, we will come out tonight, and get to know him better. And we will see, what big game room, he has that my little grandson loves to play in." Marilyn said as she pulled Van close to her.

"Thanks mom, I know that you will find him, to be a very kind man. I'm going to give Mable a call, she is very kind, and also, a very good cook. She and her husband Roman have come to live with Levi, when they had a house fire, some years ago. Now they work for him, and have become part of his family."

"That was very nice of Levi, to open up his home to them." stated Jack.

"They were friends of his mother. They knew him since when he was a young boy." Yvonne filled in everything that she was told by Levi, and Mable. After she made her phone call to Mable, she let her parents know that supper plans had been made.

Levi called Yvonne up, to let her know, that he was on his way back. He asked her, if the coast was clear, for him to come back, he let out a chuckle when asking her.

"Yes, the coast is clear." she whispered low enough so the others could not hear.

"Levi, I'd like to say how sorry that I am for acting, the way that I did towards you. Pay me no mind, whenever I get to acting up. My husband tells me that I'm just a bag of hot air." she laughed slightly to ease the tension between the two of them.

"That's okay I understand. I probably would have acted the same way if she were my daughter."

"Levi, I called Mable, to let her know that we will be having my parents out for supper tonight. I hope that was okay to do."

"That's nice, I'm sure she will like the extra company. Mable and her husband Roman are like family to me. She loves having people stop by for a visit."

"Thanks for having us." said Marilyn.

"Is everyone ready to head on over to the house then, if we get there before supper, we could show your folks around?" Levi asked with caution, not wanting to make them feel like he was rushing them.

"Yep we are already, just let me lock up the place."

12

"I hope that your parents will enjoy their visit tonight."

"I hope so too, I don't like it when my mom begins to act up." She smiled after saying that."

Did Mable say what we were having, for supper?" Levi asked, on their way home.

"No, she never mentioned it. But to answer your question, I know they will love your home, and I'm sure they will love Mable's cooking. Van and I told them, all about your beautiful place, when you left earlier."

He left his garage door opened, so Jack, and Marilyn could park their van in next to his car.

"You have a very nice place here." spoke Jack.

"Thank you, sir, let's go in through this door over here." Levi spoke while pointing to the door that led them into the living room. "That door there, will take you to the basement." He spoke about the one that Jack was headed for.

Mable greeted the guest at the door. "Welcome, you must be Yvonne's parents. It's very nice to have you here."

"Thank you, it's nice to be here." said Marilyn, as she looked around the room. "You have a very lovely home, Levi."

"You will notice, as you look on the walls, I have arrows pointing in different directions. I put them up, so it would be easier for Yvonne, and Van to get to know the place better, and to find the rooms they want to go to."

"I see, has it helped you Yvonne?" asked Marilyn.

"Yes, a great deal, I still don't have everything memorized yet. But I'm getting there. Let me show you around. You don't mind, do you Levi?"

"Of course not, I'm going to go into the kitchen, to see what Mable is cooking up for supper tonight. Excuse me folks." He said as he walked away, in the opposite direction.

"Mom, dad first I want to show you, my room, it's a very nice bedroom."

Yvonne started down the hallway, and then Van wanted them to see the game room.

"Look, this is what I was telling you, back at home. See how big it is? Grandpa you want to play a game of pinball, with me?"

"Not at this time honey, your mama wants to show me, and you're Grandma around first, Then I'll play one with you. Is that alright?" Jack spoke, as he was checking out the game room. "This is one big room, wow! I've never seen a room that was so big. Maybe you and I can play a game of bowling. What you think Sport?"

"I'd like that grandpa."

Yvonne opened, up the door, to her bedroom. "This here is my room, Oh, mom I really love it here. I've never had anything so nice before."

"It sure is pretty." she spoke looking at all of Yvonne's things. "What's this here?" Picking up leg braces.

"These are braces, that the nurse puts on me, to help sturdy my legs, as she has me stand. She has to hold, onto me, but this helps keep them straight. Come, let me show you, my bathroom, how big it is."

"Does Mable do all the cleaning, in this big house?"

"She and her husband Roman, do it. But they don't have to clean, every room every day. There are days that no one goes in some of the rooms. I pick up, what I can, to help out. I wouldn't feel right, if I didn't do something to help. They are all very good to me, I couldn't ask for more. I can't go upstairs, and pick up after Van, or fix his bed. But I do manage, to clean, my own room.

I thought that after supper, we can all go out back. He has a beautiful pond, back there. A man has come here to build a bridge, and gazebo, over it. He has bird houses, all over back there. I can go on and on about this place. I've never seen, a place so nice, in all my life, except those on TV, or in magazines."

"I'm really happy, for both you, and Van. I just want to see you, walk again. It hurts me, to see you getting around, by that chair."

"I know dad!" She stopped talking, and looked at Van standing there, listening to every word, that was being spoken. "Van will you go into another room while I talk to your grandparents please."

With a sigh, he turned and walked out.

"Dad, every morning I wake up, and the first thing, on my mind, is will I walk today. But when I try, I can't move much of anything."

"Do you get some kind of movement, in your legs?" asked Jack.

"Before I got out of the hospital, I moved a very little. Now when the nurse, was here to help me, I pushed my legs forward, just a little. But it's coming, I know it is." She spoke, with conviction, in her voice.

"We'll keep the faith that it will take, to get you back, on your feet." Jack said.

"I'm standing in agreement, for you too honey." Marilyn said.

"Thank you both, I knew that you would be praying, for me."

They turned, when hearing a knock, on the door. "Can I come in?" asked Levi.

"Come on in."

"Everything is ready for supper, if you would like to eat." enquired Levi.

Yvonne looked at her parents, "Are you ready?"

"We sure are, honey. Whatever she made, sure smells good." Jack said, patting his stomach, with a smile.

Over the meal, Yvonne's parents questioned Levi about how he came, into money. She had heard, the same story, told to her, just two nights before. It was nice to hear, some of the same things, she already knew. She could tell, by the look on her father's face, that he liked Levi. As for her mother, she could see a slight glimmer, come on her face that she just might like him to. It was important to her, that her folks, like the man, that she, was beginning to fall in love, with. The more she heard him talk, the more she knew that she was falling head over hills in love with him.

"Yvonne, you never did tell us, what the doctor told you about, moving your legs a little. Did he give you any hope of getting better?" asked Marilyn.

Yvonne, wasn't ready, to get into talking about her legs, at this time. But by the looks of everyone, in the room, she could see that was indeed, becoming the topic of conversation.

"He told me, that after looking over my x-rays, he could see where my spine was hurt. That is what caused, my legs to become paralyzed. He also told me, that he believes that surgery, could fix the problem." As she said that, Levi's mouth fell opened.

"Why haven't you mentioned, that to me before?" he questioned, in shock of hearing the news, for the first time.

"I wanted to but I also wanted to wait, and see if I could walk after the nurse working with me. The doctor, told me to give it a couple of weeks, working with the nurse. He said then if I'm still not walking by then call him, about possibly having surgery."

Levi sat there staring at her, wiping his mouth, with a napkin. "Why possibly, having the surgery, might I ask?"

"He told me that, there is always a chance at every surgery, that something could go wrong. I guess right now, I have a great chance, of getting my feelings, back in my legs. But there's always that chance, that I won't, and surgery may, or may not help me be able to walk again."

"I believe that you will walk again, honey." Jack said, as he reached over, and gave her arm a squeeze.

"I do too. In fact, God gave me a dream, and showed me, that I was walking again."

"Oh, how wonderful, that is great news. Praise God for that honey." spoke Marilyn.

"Levi, I told my parents, that after supper, we could go out back, and show them your beautiful land, would that be alright with you?" asked Yvonne, as she tried to change to subject.

"Sure, I'll get the golf cart, and come back and pick everyone up when we are done eating." He focused his attention towards Jack now. "You care to walk with me back there in a bit?"

"Sure!"

"This food is wonderful Mable." Spoke Marylin.

"Thank you, I've glad that you are enjoying it."

After they ate, the two men walked, back to the pole barn together. All the while Jack was looking at Levi, he could tell that the man had something going on in his mind. He wasn't sure how to ask him what it was, after just meeting today for the first time. After thinking how to asked, he decided the best way to ask, was just ask.

"It looks to me, that you have a question, for me. Is this true?"

"You can read me, pretty well there, Jack. Yes, I do, I'm just trying, to figure out, about dreams. How do you know when dreams are from God?" He asked.

"When you live for Jesus, as my wife and I have for many years. We brought Yvonne up to know, and trust God also.

When you spend time reading His word and praying. What happens is that you develop a relationship, with Him. You begin to know, Him, and what He does for His children. The bible talks, about getting to know the Lord. He shows some people, visions, some dreams. He has His way of confirming His word to us.

Yvonne has had many dreams that God has given her before that came to pass. This is one of her gifts that she has. She also can sing beautiful, did you know that, have you heard her yet?"

"No, I haven't, but would love to, one day."

Jack turned his attention to elsewhere. "You sure do have a nice place here, going for you. Might I ask you a question?"

"Sure!" Levi said with hesitation.

"What are your intentions, for my daughter?"

"Well sir, that is a fare question, and one I'll try to answer, the best that I can."

"That's all I can ask." spoke Jack.

Levi walked, trying to choose his words, carefully. "When Yvonne and I first got in that car accident, it turned my whole life, upside down at first. I didn't know, what happened, why would someone pull out, in front of someone else, unless it was to kill their self, or because they were drinking. I was in complete shock, never having been in a car accident, before. I thought I had my whole life, planned out for me, just when it seemed that everything was going as planned. My life took a complete u-turn. When I hit into Yvonne's little car, I was not harmed, just maybe a little shaken up. When I saw her, the first-time she was bleeding, and she was knocked unconscious. I hurt for her in a way, I didn't know that I could hurt. I wanted to know all about her, from that time on, I went to the hospital, to see her hoping, and praying that she was alive. When I heard that she was alive, I wanted to meet her with every fiber of my body, I was drawn to her. I can't explain it, but that's how I felt. Then after meeting her, and Van, well I really care for the both of them a great deal. The two of them has brought a whole new meaning, of life to me."

"I think that it's clear to say, that you're in love with my daughter."

Levi never said a word, he just thought about the words that he heard Roman say, just a few days earlier. "I believe you are right, I tried fighting, my feelings. But the thought of losing her, and Van, is more than I can bear. I love to know they're both safe, here with me. I don't want to lose either of them."

"Have you told her how you feel?"

"I did in some ways, I mean I ask her if we can take our relationship to the next level. She told me, that she needed to think and pray, about it."

"Does that bother you?"

"No not really, just what if she feels God, is telling her no, then her and Van leave."

"Trust me dear boy." Jack put a hand on Levi's shoulder. "I don't believe God will tell her that, but if He did, you wouldn't want her anyway, because God would have someone different for the both of you. He doesn't want us to marry, someone that's not for us, that is why there are so many divorces, like there is. People marry the wrong, person, all the time."

"What makes you say, that you don't believe, that God will tell her that, I'm not the one?"

"Dear boy, there are just something's, a parent knows. Now you will have to talk, with her, about the rest. If we don't get back to the house, they will think that we got in some kind of scuffle." Jack spoke given a chuckle.

"I suppose that your right." Levi laughed at Jack, noticing where Yvonne gets her sense of humor.

The two, got into the golf cart, and rode up to the house to pick the two women, and Van up.

"Sorry it took us men awhile, we were busy gabbing." said Levi. Yvonne I'll help you in the front. Jack you and Marilyn can ride couch. And Van you might want to hop in the back, where you will be able to see everything from behind."

Levi took them all around his three acres, not wanting to miss anything. There were things that Yvonne was seeing for the first time. With Levi not doing what he should have, he had forgotten certain things that he had done many years ago. He was also seeing things for the first time himself.

He stopped the cart, and pointed to something new they were all seeing for the first time. "Look right over there, I have never seen that before. It must be something that Roman and the other helpers did, when I was too busy to care."

For the first time he was looking at the prettiest water fountain, in his pond, but on the other side of his property. He had seen where his property came to an end, and where the neighbor's property began. He knew that they could get a nice view of the water fountain. What he couldn't understand is why he would have a water fountain so big and nice way out back, for the neighbors to see and not them. He knew that this was one thing that he would be asking Roman about at another time.

"That sure is a pretty water fountain, and you mean to tell me that you have never seen it before?" Marilyn asked Levi, surprised that a man can have such a big beautiful object, and yet not know that he does.

"You are right about me not knowing, like I said before, I was so busy hardly ever home, before Yvonne and Van came here. I have giving Roman and Mable the right to run this place as they see fit. As long as nothing was getting torn up, or ruined, it didn't really matter to me. I'm just wondering why way out here, and not close to the house where we could see it when we go out to the pond."

"That's nice of you to trust them like that. You must be very close to them." Marilyn mentioned, in a sarcastic voice.

"Mother, why are you acting like Levi is doing something wrong, by trusting the two people that have been here with him, for three years, not to mention was his mother's best friends. There is nothing wrong with trusting someone. Maybe you should stop thinking, that there is so much bad in everyone."

"I'm sorry Levi, I had no right. Yvonne is right, I have had a hard, time trusting others, and I'm not even sure why. Besides, it's none of my business what you do."

"That's quite alright, I had a hard time trusting some people in my life before too. I guess it's just one of those things, where you have to really know someone to have complete trust."

Levi started to head back towards the house, not much being said, the rest of the ride. Then a loud voice came from the very back.

"Grandpa, will you play a game of pin ball with me now I want to see if you can get as much as Levi does."

"Sure son, I'll play a game. But I hate to tell you, I have only played pin ball a couple times in my life."

"That's okay, we will still have fun playing it together." spoke Van, all excited that his grandfather would be playing with him.

13

It was a long night, for Yvonne's parents. They decided, after the time spent getting to know Levi, they too would spend the night at his home.

Yvonne was so excited, that the night went well, with her parents. She wondered for a while, if her mother, would ever warm up to Levi. After jokes, and some serious talk, much laughter came to all of them. She knew without any doubt, in her mind, that Levi was the one for her.

"I think the night, went very well. I like your folks, very much. Your dad and I have a lot in common." He spoke.

"Oh really, how is that?" she asked with a big smile.

"We both love, and care for you, and Van a great deal. And we love beautiful women."

Did I hear him right, *love, and care?* Was I just imagining, things? "Did you just say that you love me?" she asked.

Levi picked up Yvonne's hand, in his. "Yvonne, I know it sounds like a line, some school boy talking. But from the first time, I saw you, something inside me, was forever changed. Ever since that first day, I have wanted to know, everything, about you. When I'm not with you, all I do is think of you, when I lay down at night, all I do is dream of you. I know that we have only known each other, for a little over a week. But if you would have me, I want to spend, the rest of my life, getting to know you more." Levi got down on his knees, and tucked inside of his shirt, he pulled out a little black box, wrapped in a gold ribbon. "Yvonne, will you do me the honor, of becoming my bride."

Yvonne, had tears that were streaming down, her cheeks. "I wondered if I was going to get another chance. Yes, yes, yes, I'll marry you Levi Ubani." She wrapped, her arms around, his neck, pulling him in closer to her. "I love you to, and want to get to know you, the rest of my life."

"Aren't you going to open, the box?"

"Oh yes! Or course." she began to untie the bow.

"Oh, Levi this is the prettiest ring, I have ever seen." She spoke while he, took the ring out of the box, and put it on her finger.

Then the excitement wore off her face, as she lowered her head.

"What, what's the matter, is there something wrong? Please tell me, what just happened, to make you frown?"

"I was just thinking, I want to walk, down the aisle, when I marry. I don't want to be in the wheel chair, I'm just being silly, I never even asked you, when you wanted us to get married."

"First of all, I fell in love with you. It doesn't matter to me, if you're in this chair, or not. I love you, and if you would rather, wait, and see if you start to walk, with the nurse helping you. Well then we will wait, how long did the doctor say, have the nurse work with you?"

"He said a two, or three weeks, and if that didn't help, then I could have surgery, to see if that would help."

"The nurse, worked with you, for one day now Has it seemed to help, in anyway?"

"Yes, it has. When I put my leg braces on, and she has me try, to walk. I am able to slide my feet. When she first started yesterday with me, I could barely move at all. But before she left, I could feel the difference."

"Why didn't you ever tell me any of this? Did you not think that I would care?"

"That's not it, I wanted to surprise you. I wanted to work with her, for a few weeks, and then come out of my bedroom walking. Now this has given me, a whole new reason, to practice my walking more, then I have been doing. I really want to walk, when I get married."

"Then the two of us, will work together, to get your legs to work again. You learn, the routine, and then we will work together aside what your nurse does."

"I'd like that, for the two of us, to work together, that will be great. But right now, I'm a little tired, and I know morning comes early. I will, have to get Van up, for school. So, I will say good night sweet heart, I love you, and I'm so glad that God has brought you, in my life."

"Yvonne, did you forget, that tomorrow is Sunday. I know it's been a long day. So, you go ahead, and get some sleep. I'm going to go down to the library, and read some of the bible, and spend some time, getting to know God."

"Levi, I'm so happy, for you. That is so important, in a person's life. I will see you in the morning." She started to turn, her chair, when Levi reached out and held on to it.

"Aren't you even going to give your fiancé, a kiss?"

Yvonne looked at him, with tears forming her eyes. "I would have never believed that I would have met, such a wonderful man, the way that I did. Please be patient with me Levi, I just haven't kissed a man since Mark." She reached her hands out for his, and then with determination, she began to pull, herself up, to stand next to him. Levi held her tight, to help her keep her balance. With a passionate kiss, the two embraced each other, like they never had with another.

"Wow! So, this is what I got to look forward to huh, then why can't we marry next week." He said with a smile that stretched across his face.

"Levi, your being silly now." She said with light laughter. "I don't know, what came over me. I just stood up, and I could feel the floor, underneath me. Before, I could move my legs, and not feel the floor, but this time I felt a hard surface underneath me. I was beginning, to wonder, when this would happen."

"That's great, this shows me your dream is going to come true, you will walk again. I have no doubt, in my mind anymore at all."

"You know when I told you, about the dream I had, about me walking. That wasn't all, that I seen in my dream." she looked up at him, sitting back, in her chair.

"What did you leave out?"

"I not only was walking, but I was walking down the aisle, of my wedding. I saw our wedding, Levi. And it was beautiful."

"Why didn't you tell me, that before? And when I ask you, to be my girl, you said that you would have to pray, and think about it. Why would you, do all that, if you already knew that we would marry?"

Yvonne thought, that he was sounding, a little upset with her. "Levi don't be upset with me, when I had that dream. What I told you was true, the only thing different, was that I never seen the man's face, I didn't know until now, that you are that man. His back was all I could see in the dream. There was one thing that stood out to me, in the dream. I saw diamond cufflinks that he was wearing, well that you were wearing."

"I'm not mad, I was just trying to figure out why, you never told me. But now I see why. And I do have a pair of diamond cufflinks. Honey you look so tried, you better get some sleep. We have church in the morning. I love you, and will see you in the morning, good night."

"Night." she was headed down the hallway, with so much joy inside, that she wanted to shout it out to the whole world, all about it. As she lay in bed, she tossed, and turned picturing, what her wedding would be like.

Levi lay in bed, thinking about Yvonne's dream. *Wow I can't believe that she actually had a dream of our wedding. I guess Jack was right, I wonder if I would have believed her, if she would never have mentioned the diamond cufflinks. It doesn't really matter.* He told himself, all that matters is she said she will marry me, and be my wife. Levi fell to sleep, thinking about a wedding.

"Good morning! Sun shine, how was your sleep?" Levi asked Yvonne when waking up to the sun shining bright through the windows.

"It was very good, and how was yours? Did you have any nice dreams?" she asked, giving him a slight grin.

"I am not one that dreams, a whole lot. I can probably count, on one hand, how many times I've had a dream. It sounds to me, as if you're the one that dreams. I talked with your dad, and he told me, that you have had a few dreams, that came to pass. Is that correct?"

"Yes, that's true, one of my dreams, was about a big flood. I could see it flowing, and destroying, many places. Right after that, it was all over the news, that floods were washing away places, and people were drowning. Many times, God gives me dreams, that show good things are about to take place. Like our wedding for one, then there are times, that it's dreams of warning that something bad can happen. Whenever I get a bad dream, I begin to pray hard. But when I get a good dream, it makes me feel, very happy. I know something good is about to happen. I remember praying, after I found out, that I couldn't walk. I asked God to show me, when something good will happen That's when He began, to give me hope that I would walk again. Oh, look at me, carrying on not giving you, any room to talk."

"That's okay, I love to hear you talk. I want to know all about your hopes, and your dreams. Whenever you feel, the need to talk to me, about something, then I want you to feel comfortable, enough with me to do that."

"Thank you, I am very comfortable around you. I feel like, I can talk to you, about anything. I want you, to feel the same with me, I want us to always feel, this way with each other."

"No matter what the case may be, rather you walk again or not I want you to be my wife.

"I will walk, for our wedding, my legs, keep getting stronger, all the time." She then changed the subject. "Do you know if my folks are still sleeping?"

"I think that they are, I haven't seen them come down stairs yet."

"We need to wake them so they have time to get ready for church. And Van needs to get himself ready too."

"Do you want to go to the kitchen and see what Mable has got made for breakfast?"

"Sure, I'll go and see. But can you please go and wake them all up? Do, you think that they might be lost up there?" she asked, being silly. "My parents aren't used, to being in a place so big. I haven't got to see, your up stairs yet, so I have no way of knowing."

"Trust me when I say, they're not lost. It's not that big, but I am going to check in on them and to wake Van. Honey, this week I am going to have someone come out here to have an elevator installed so you can come up and down, anytime that you want to."

"That would be great, but there is no need to go through all the trouble for me. Would you mind, terribly to go check on them? I want to make sure, everything is alright."

"Not a problem, I shall return." he said with a smile, and a raise, to his eye brows.

Yvonne could feel every day, that she was becoming more in love with Levi. She couldn't hardly wait, until the day, she would become, Mrs. Levi Ubani. She pictured the dream, she had about, their wedding. What a beautiful, dream that was, she thought. Now I get to take him to church today, and show him off to all my friends there.

"They are sound to sleep, I knocked lightly to wake them, but when I heard nothing, I carefully, opened, the door, to check on them. I'm so glad, that they were covered up. That would have been, very embarrassing, if they would have woken up, when I opened the door, and them not being dressed."

"Yes, I could imagine. But don't you think that we should get them up, so they have time to eat before church?"

"Yes, I guess you're right, I'll go back up there and try to wake them up."

"Thank you so much for all you are doing for me."

"Not a problem, I thought that if you, and your folks, wanted to, we could have a bar-be-cue, out on the veranda, after church. I haven't had one this whole, year so far. It's a beautiful, day out. It's already, seventy degrees out, and it's only going on eight o'clock. But let me get them up first before we plan that."

"That sounds wonderful, to me. Let's hope, my parents, have nothing else planned, for the day. I don't think, that they do, they never mentioned it last night."

"I'll go see, what Mable is making for breakfast, why you wake up my parents, and Van.

Mable asked Yvonne, "What do you think that her parents would like to eat."

"I can't say for sure now, but I know my mom, used to make ego waffles for my dad and herself. I don't get to see them much, whenever they came up here to visit, I was always at work, it seemed. They would take care of Van, for me, and take him to the fair. I was usually gone, before they got up, in the mornings. Anything you want to cook, would be fine, for them, Van and I."

"I know that I can make some waffles, if you would like. Do you want one?"

"Sure, do you make them by box, or homemade?"

"I don't believe I know how to cook, from box. Everything I make is homemade. Trust me, I seen how you eat, and you will only be able to eat, one of my waffles. They are rather big, then the toppings that you can chose from, with homemade whipping cream, yummy. There the best, if I say so."

"You're making me hungry, I would love to try, one of your waffles."

"Okay I'll start them now." said Mable.

"I know my parents, will eat some too."

"That's fine, I've never been one to make small batches of anything. That's one reason I like you, and Van being here. It helps me use up some of my food that I cook." she spoke with a grin, to let Yvonne know she was only teasing.

Levi came down stairs, and whispered in Yvonne's ear. "Later on, I'd like to talk to you, about something. That concerns you."

"Do we have to wait, until later? Can we talk now, while we wait, for our waffles? Now would be a good time, there's no one else, to hear us talk." She was excited to hear what he had to say, she knew it would be good by the look on his face.

"I've been thinking, about having that elevator installed, to take you up stairs, when you want to go up there. And after we're married, I think that you would rather, have the bedroom, that I have. It would fit both, our needs much better, than the room you have now."

"How can you do that, where would you put one in at?"

"In the hallway, that leads us down to the library. It's wider than the others, it would give us plenty of room, to have a small one put in."

"I thank you, for wanting to do that, for me. But I really believe that I will be walking soon. Then I can go up, and down the stairs."

"This would still make it quicker, for all of us. Then there is Mable, she's getting a little older, and she's up and down those stairs, every day." He said giving her, a puppy dog face.

"This is your home, if you feel the need for an elevator then by all means, if you can afford it then do it."

"First of all, this is going to be our home, when we marry. And yes, we can afford it, Yvonne honey, I have plenty of money, for whatever it is we want or need. I know that we, have never really talked about, money. But I do have plenty, of it."

"Would you think terrible of me if I was to ask, how much you have. But first know that it doesn't matter to me, if you had none."

"No, not at all, you have the right to know all of my business before we get married. It is hard to say, my accountant would know, more than me at this time. I have money coming in all the time, and I have stocks and bonds also. I do know that I have a million or more. Yes, I believe it to be more, by now. I made my first million, when I was twenty-three years old."

"You are a millionaire? I knew that you had money, I just didn't dream, it to be that much." Yvonne said covering her mouth, with her hand.

"For some reason, I thought that I had shared all this with you before. Maybe I was just thinking, about when I would."

"I don't remember you telling me anything, about it before. I think I would have remembered something like this."

"Well good morning." said Jack. "You two, look as though you were in a deep conversation. Am I interrupting you?"

"No dad, it's alright. How did you sleep? I hope mother and you slept well."

"I did indeed, that has got to be one of the nicest beds that I have ever slept in."

"I'm glad that your sleep was a pleasant one for you, as well as I hope for your wife." said Levi.

"I'm sure it was for her, she's still not down here." Jack said chuckling.

"Oh, here she comes now with Van." Mable commented.

"That is a very comfortable bed you have there Levi. I didn't want to get out of it today."

"Is everyone ready to eat? Mable is making her wonderful waffles for us today." Levi looked around the room, to see if they were all hungry, and everyone agreed they could eat something, before leaving for church.

14

"At the breakfast table, Levi decided to make an announcement, he wanted everyone to hear, what he had to say. "Everyone, can I have your attention, just for a moment?" Mable, and Marilyn stopped talking, to hear what he, had to say. "Last night, I had asked Yvonne, to marry me, and she kindly accepted."

"Congratulations, to the both of you. So, when's the big day?" asked Roman.

"We haven't set the day yet. I want to walk, down the aisle." said Yvonne.

"Are you sure, this is what you want to do? You have only known each other, for a short time?" Marilyn said.

"We know this mom that is why it won't be, for a while. We want to get to know each other, more over the next few months."

"I think, that would be wise, I do believe the two of you, will be very happy together." stated Jack.

"Mom, you and Levi, are going to get married? Does this mean he will be my dad now?" asked Van.

"Van, I will never be your real dad son, but what I will be is a father to you, and I will love, and teach you everything, that I know to help you, learn to be a good man."

"And you will teach me, how to become rich, like you."

"Van! What have I told you about that?" Yvonne scolded.

"I'm sorry, mom. I thought you, only said that it's not nice, to talk about how much money, someone has, when it's somebody else. I didn't know that you, were talking, about Levi because he's going to be my dad. I just didn't think that it counted."

Yvonne didn't righty know what to say, she believed, that he thought, that it was okay, to talk, about his soon to be dad's money.

"Van, what I think that your mom is trying to say. That its not polite, to talk about another man's wealth, because not always does that man, want others to know what he has. Do you understand what I mean?" asked Levi.

"Yes, I do." Van said with a sigh, while holding his head down. "I'm sorry, I just want to make money like you, when I get big too. Are you mad at me?"

"No, I'm not mad at all. I think every little boy, dreams of being rich, when they get older."

"They sure do Sport, I know that I did, when I was a kid. I just never got there, but I did find happiness, without being rich." Jack said.

"Well I want to be rich, just like." He stopped, and looked at his mom. "I just want to be rich, that's all."

Everyone started to laugh, at Van. They all knew, who he was thinking, about.

"Levi has decided to help me, with walking. The way we see it, the more, I move my legs, the faster, I should be able to walk. The nurse comes in for three days a week, and each time it's for an hour and a half each time. With the extra help, it should be good for me."

"You want to make sure, that you know, what you're doing." said Marilyn.

"I don't think, by us doing the same thing, that the nurse, has done, can hurt me any, if anything it should help."

"I hope that you're right, I wouldn't want anything to keep you from getting better." stated Marilyn.

"How long, are the two of you, going to be here in Michigan?" asked Levi.

"We thought that we might stick around, for a while. We won't be a bother, for you here. If Yvonne, don't mind, we would like to stay at her home, all the while we're here."

"Of course, I don't mind, you know that dad. You and mama are always welcome, for as long as you like."

"We just kind of want to stick around, for a while to see, how things go for you."

Levi looked at the two of them, then at Yvonne. Not saying anything after Jacks comment, but giving Yvonne, a strange look, as to say they don't trust him, enough to care, for their daughter. Then he thought about if she was his daughter, he would feel the same.

Yvonne seen the way, he looked at her, even if her parents didn't. It bothered her, just knowing, that it did him. She had hoped, after last night that her parents, would have gotten to know Levi a little better, and see what she sees in him. She couldn't understand, why they couldn't see, how happy she really was.

"I wasn't going to say anything, but I have to. Dad you said that you, and mom, want to stick around to make sure everything is okay with me. What do you mean, by that? Do you not think that Levi, can care for Van, and I?" she asked sounding all upset.

"Oh no honey, you're missing the whole point. I wasn't thinking, of that at all. I was talking, about you walking again. Your mom and I weren't here, when you got hurt. And that has hurt, the both of us, very much. We would like to be here, when you walk again, that's all."

Yvonne started to cry, she felt a shame, for acting the way that she did, towards her parents. "I'm sorry, mom and dad. I thought that you thought, that Levi wasn't caring well enough for Van, and I. And it hurt me, because he is a great guy, he really is the best."

"That I can see he is honey, I do not worry how he will care for the two of you. You both, will be very happy together, I just know that you will."

Mable started to clean, up the dishes, as Roman was putting them, in the dishwasher. Is there anything special, that anyone of you would like for lunch?" she asked.

"We will be having a bar-be-cue, today out on the veranda. You, and Roman are welcome, I insist you join us." Levi requested.

"We wouldn't want to impose, on your company. Mable said.

"Now you know that you are family, so come join us today. You can have a rest from cooking. Yvonne, and I have this one, say you two will join us."

Roman looked over at Mable. "Yes, we will join you."

"Who's all going to church? We better get ourselves together, it's going to be starting in an hour." Yvonne said to everyone as she looked up see who was going.

"We can all drive in the van together, if you like." Jack mentioned.

Levi looked at Yvonne, and Yvonne looked at Mable. "Sure, I don't mind, I'll ride with you."

"Us to." said Levi. "It looks to me like all of us are going, except Roman. Come on Roman, if I can do this, then I know you can. I've been missing out for way to long. Why don't you come with us today, hey you never know, you just might find that you have been missing out on a lot too."

"Why not, I got nothing else to do. My Sundays are usually pretty boring, maybe this will give me something to do on my Sundays."

"Glad to hear it. Let's everyone get dressed, and we'll meet in the living room, in a half hour." Levi told everyone.

Everyone went to go get dressed in their Sunday's best, after a short while, they were all in the living room.

"Well, don't everyone look nice. I think that we are going to be the best-looking bunch there today." Jack said bringing a smile to everyone's face.

"Yeah, I think so to grandpa. We all look good."

"Let's everyone load up, I hate to be late. I think that we just might surprise, Reverend Thomas." said Yvonne.

Everyone started to get into the van, when Jack mentioned about how nice it will be to see the Reverend and his wife Patsy.

"I met them only the one time, it was at the hospital. They seem to be very nice folks. I told them that I would be coming with Yvonne. I just wondered if they believed me." said Levi.

"Unless you gave them a reason not to, then I'm sure they did. That's the kind of folks they are. Very sweet, I've known them for many years. It's always good to come back for a visit, and see them when we are up." Jack told them with much excitement, to get to see his old friends again.

"You'll find a lot of people that will want to shake your hand, it's just what they do here. I think just about everyone that goes here, are very nice people." Yvonne thought to warn them, ahead of time about the shaking of hands, so not to scare them. She didn't know how much they knew about such things.

Yvonne was right, there were many that approached all of them, even down to little Van, that was shaking their hands. Levi didn't seem to mind, to the most part. He just would return a handsome smile, and say it's nice to be here. Roman and Mable would give a smile.

"Good morning folks." The Reverend spoke from the front of the church. "I like to take this time to welcome back, are dear sister Yvonne and her son Van. Most of us have heard about two weeks ago, she was in a car accident that could have taken her life. But God and His goodness reached down and kept her from leaving us at this time. I want to say welcome, to her friends, Levi Ubani, Roman and Mable Smith. I'd also like to give a warm welcome to my long-time friend, Jack and his wife Marilyn, Yvonne's parents. It's so nice to have them join us once again. Welcome everyone, I'm sure we will be seeing more of you. Now for our singers, come."

Yvonne watched Levi, Roman and Mable, as praise and worship songs were being song. She could see them try to sing along with everyone else. She knew that they didn't know the songs, but she so badly wanted the songs to touch their heart.

"Now I'd like everyone to turn in their bibles, to Jonah 1. I'm going to be talking about, a man that tries to run from God. This man Jonah was called by God to reach people that didn't want God. But Jonah said that he didn't want to go speak to them, he said why they wouldn't listen to him anyway. The Reverend was talking about how Jonah ran from God and wound up in the belly of a great fish. How after three days and nights being in the fish's belly, Jonah cried out to God. He said then, he would go speak to the people that God told him to.

Yvonne could see by the look on Levi's face, that it was touching him. Possibly he was thinking about his own life, how for years he himself has ran from God. At least this is what she was hoping that he would be thinking. Maybe a great fish never swallowed him up, but sin did. All the years he spent on going to the bars, and drinking and fooling around. He was running, from God. She sat there silently praying, Dear Lord Jesus, please touch Levi's heart. Help him to come to you today, with all that he has and all that he is. In Jesus mighty name, amen.

The Reverend had an alter call, when he was done preaching. Yvonne not saying anything, to anyone watched to see if anyone of the three new comers would answer the call. The next thing she seen was all three walking towards the front, she began to cry. Her prayer was being answered. This was a new beginning for all of them. She could hardly wait to hear what Levi had to say, about the service.

After church, Yvonne introduced Levi to some of her friends there. She noticed how some of her friends had known who he was, and what he did for a living. On their way home Levi went on and on, about how when the Reverend started to talk about Jonah running from God. It hit him right in his belly, he said how he could hear God say to him, that it was he that's been running for all these years. And it was time to run no more. He put his arm around Yvonne, and made a statement that everyone in the van could hear him say.

"Yvonne, I know that I've told you before, how sorry I am that I ran into your car, that this has happened to you. Don't take this wrong, please. But if I wouldn't have hit into you, I wouldn't have come to church today, and accepted Jesus Christ as my Lord and Savior. I'm not happy you're in this chair, but I'm sure glad that we have met, I only wish it could have been from a better circumstance."

"I know you don't mean anything by that, I'm not glad that I pulled out in front of you either. But I'm sure glad that we met too. And I will walk again, every day that goes by, I keep having more feeling in the bottom of my feet. I can feel it tingle, many, many times."

"I can hardly wait, until the day that I call you my wife. Mrs. Levi Ubani, that has a very nice sound to it don't it?"

"It sure does, I to can hardly wait." She replied.

After getting home, everyone changed out of their Sunday clothing, and into summer clothes. Levi started up the grill, where Yvonne began to make up a salad.

The day was filled with fun, and excitement. Levi took Yvonne and her parents out to the pool in the back, where they could choose from swimming, or going into the hot tub.

"Can I go swimming mama?" ask Van.

"I don't care, as long as you put on a life jacket. I know the pool goes over your head."

"I know mama, you tell me that every time I go swimming. Grandpa will you come swimming with me?"

"I would love to, but I didn't bring my shorts with me. I wasn't aware that there was a pool, I would have brought my swimwear."

"Jack, over in the swim house, I have every kind of swimwear there is. Help yourself and enjoy the pool. Does anyone else care to go?" He asked looking at Marilyn.

"I don't care to, but I will sit in the sun and watch." spoke Marilyn.

"I'll join you mother, although I'd love to get in the pool. It looks so refreshing right now."

"Why don't you get in then?" asked Levi.

Yvonne looked at him surprised, by what he said. It made her sad to think that he wasn't aware of what he was expecting from her. "Levi, I can't move my legs well enough to swim."

"You won't have to, I don't know why I haven't shown you this before." Levi got up and walked over to a gray little building, that was near the pool, and the swim house. "In here is all kinds of floats, there is some that you can just sit in and do nothing. The water movement will push you around. But if you're going to get in, I'll get in and push you around." he spoke lifting up his eye brows. You won't even have to change in swimwear unless you don't want to get a little splash getting on your clothes. The pool is large enough that if we stayed at one side, your dad and Van would splash all they wanted to, and not get us wet."

"Oh. that's sounds wonderful. It's been a long time since I went swimming. I would like to just stay in the clothes that I have on if that's alright. Is that alright with you mom if I visit with you in a little while?"

"Yes, of course, get in and enjoy yourself honey."

125

"If you don't mind, I think that I will put a pair of swim shorts on before I get in. Let me show you what we have for floats." Levi pushed Yvonne over to the float house, to see what she would like to use in the water.

"That yellow one looks nice I don't think that I'm too big for it."

"You have a tiny enough frame, you could just about use anyone of these floats, and it would be fine." he spoke with laughter.

"Oh, come on, you make it sound like, I'm built like a little child."

"Oh no, not at all, trust me when I say, there is no child that can have what you have."

"Levi! You surprise me." She looked around hoping no one else heard what he said. She didn't want to give them the wrong thought of him.

"Well I'm sorry, but you know what I mean. You may have a tiny frame, but that's just your frame. You weigh one hundred and five pounds soaking wet. And your five foot two inches. Now you look at me, I'm six foot three inches, and I weight one hundred and eight five pounds."

"You look very good at your height and weight. I get your point, I don't weigh a lot and most of these floats will hold me up. But I still like that yellow one, it looks very comfortable."

"Okay the lady said yellow, so that's what the lady gets, is yellow." Levi was trying to be funny, playing around in a joking manner. "I'm going to go in the swim house and change my clothes, and then I'll help you get in this."

"I'm not going anywhere." she said smiling at him.

Levi came out wearing a tan color swim shorts that showed off his dark legs. Yvonne never had seen him in anything that went above his knees before. Now she was seeing all the muscles in his legs.

His chest was all buffed, showing off his six pack, underneath all the hair. She sat there looking at him when moving the float, from one place to another. To get it just right for her to get in it, his muscles would flex, and show off just how big they were. She found that it was very attractive, and she could hardly wait till the two of them to be married.

"Are you ready my dear, It, took me a while to get this tied up so it doesn't move, when I put you in it."

"Okay" She answered, as she looked over at her mom sitting in a lounge chair getting some sun, as she watched Jack and Van swim at the shallow end of the pool. "Mom, are you sure you don't want to come in the pool?"

"No honey, I'm fine. I think that will be just a little too much for me. Your father is the one that has always liked to swim. I've never cared much for it."

"Okay I just wanted to make sure, before getting in."

"You enjoy yourself. Get some sun, it feels beautiful just sitting here in it."

"It's all tied now, let me pick you up and put you in. Are you ready?"

"Now you aren't going to drop me, are you?" she asked laughing at him, carrying her.

Levi pretended to trip a little. "Just a bout did, do you really think that I am not capable of carrying you, without dropping you?" He said with laughter.

"I know that you are I was only teasing you." she said as Levi was putting her in the float. "This feels very nice." Yvonne spoke, putting her hands in the water tossing some on her legs, to see if her legs could feel the cool water.

"Would you like me to push, you around?"

"You don't have to, you might as well enjoy the water, and swim."

"I'd like to push you around, and I'll float next to you." "Okay."

"I hope the meat will not burn on the grill." She mentioned.

"No, it won't, I have it turned way down so we can swim awhile."

Yvonne and Levi swam for about an hour, before getting out of the pool.

It was time for the meet to come off the grill and the rest of the lunch to come outside and onto the table, so everyone can eat. There was laughter and joy, that afternoon. Everyone talked as if they had known each other for a life time. Then the sun was coming down as the evening was approaching. When going in the house, Yvonne noticed how Van wanted his grandparents, to go play in the game room. And they followed behind him to go play games.

"This is a shocker, "Yvonne spoke seeing her mother playing a game of pinball, while Van and her dad where bowling. "I never thought that I would see the day, where you would be playing pinball."

"I never thought that I would either. Van talked me into it, he wanted to see if I could beat him at the game."

"So how are you doing on it, have you beaten him yet?"

"No, I'm not even sure what I'm doing. I watched him play a game, and it looked easy. But now that I'm playing it, I'm not getting a very high score. This is my third game, and he's beaten me so far. Let me finish this game, and then I'll come out and visit you."

"You don't have to stop, on my account. Levi and I are coming, in here anyway. We like to sit over at that table by the bay window, and watch Van play games. Or Levi and Van will play some games, and I watch."

"Do you play any games with them?"

"Oh yeah, at times I do. But I mostly bring my bible in here with me, and study."

"I'm glad that you have been reading, the bible. I'm glad honey that you're happy." Marilyn told Yvonne as she was sitting down, at the table. "I'll watch the guys with you."

"Okay, we can talk about my wedding plans, if you like."

"Your dad and I wanted to help you in any way that we can to help you pay, for a nice wedding."

"Mom thank you, but you know that there is no need. Levi will take care of everything."

"I thought that to be so, but I still wanted to offer." "Thanks mom."

"Yvonne honey," Levi said as he came into the game room. "I want to talk with Roman for a while, do you mind?"

"Of course not."

"I'll be back in a minute. Is there anything that you need before I leave, for a few minutes?"

"No thank you, I'm fine."

"Roman, can we talk for a minute?" Levi asked when coming into the front room.

"Sure, what's on your mind, is something wrong?"

"No nothing wrong that I know of. It came to my attention yesterday, as I took Yvonne and her folks out for a ride in the golf cart. That there was something on the other side of the pond, I never have seen before or even knew about."

"And what is that, you seem to be a little upset with me Levi."

"No, I'm not upset, I'm just a little surprised that there is such a big beautiful water fountain, in the pond where none of us could see it. But the neighbors, right across the property can see it. When did that even get put in? Have I really been so busy, being gone that I'm unaware of things being put in my pond that I haven't noticed."

"That was a request of your mothers." Roman answered.

Levi stood there looking at Roman with such a surprised looked. "My mothers, how could that even be?"

"Not long before your mother suddenly died, she had asked me and the other men, if we could have someone put that in the pond for her. I can't believe that you didn't know this."

"No, I never, but why would she want that put in way back there?"

Roman looked at Levi in shock. "You mean to tell me that you didn't know that your mother was planning on having a little home built for her back there."

"WHAT! You have got to be kidding me. This is the first that I have even heard of such talk. Why am I just now finding this out?"

"I just assumed you have always known. If I would have known that you never knew about this, I would have brought it to your attention a long time ago."

"Why did my mother, want a house built for her way back there?"

"I guess because she thought that this house was just too big, for her to get used to."

"You know you're probably right, I do know that she would tell me that it was just too big." He spoke hanging his head low, like to feel bad that he never paid too much attention to her, whenever she would tell him how she felt. Now with the quilt that was resting on him, was more than he could bare, after hearing a message at church that showed him that not only was he running from, the things of God. But he was also into himself so much, that he never really took the time, to care how his own mother felt living in such a big home.

"Now son don't you be blaming yourself, for not being aware about your mother's plans. If she thought that you needed to know, then I'm sure that she would have told you."

"She tried to tell me all the time that this place was just too big. I should have cared more. But I was so wrapped up, in all the things that

I wanted. That I just never gave her time, to tell me what it was that she wanted. Now it's too late, she's gone and I can't even ask her to forgive me." Levi sat down, sulking in self-pity.

"Now I want you to pull yourself together, son. You can't be any good to anyone by blaming yourself. Right now, you are thinking of yourself again. I hate to be so blunt with you, but right now, you have a very special lady, that can't wait to become Mrs. Levi Ubani. She needs you to focus on her and Van, not something that happened over three years ago. If you think that I'm talking out of line, then I'm sorry. I just know that your mother would never have wanted you to torment yourself like this. Now that's all I have to say about the whole thing." Roman walked away, wondering if Levi was upset with him for being so blunt.

But he knew now was not the time to find out nor stick around, to find out. He thought it best to just leave it at that, and to give him time to think about what he said.

I know he's right, my mother would never want me to feel bad for what has happened. But how do I just get passed, what I did. It was like Levi heard a voice say to him. Don't feel sorry for yourself but think of others. *That's just what I'm going to do, first of all I'm going to stop feeling sorry for myself, then I'm going to go see my bride to be, and plan a wedding.*

Levi walked in the room where Yvonne was sitting talking to her mom. "Can I interrupt you, I'd like to talk with my lovely bride to be." He walked in the room with a whole new attitude.

"Sure, what do you want to talk about?" asked Yvonne. "OUR WEDDING!" He busted out loud with excitement.

"My mom and I were doing just that."

"Do you know where you want to have it?"

"No, we haven't got that far, beside that's something that you and I should plan together. As well as how big of a wedding do you want?"

"Honey if it was just us, that's all I care about. I don't need a big one. But I want what you want, if you want a big one then let us have a great big one and invite everyone."

Yvonne, could tell whatever his talked with Roman was about, has given him a new excitement. Although she had no idea what the talk was about, she liked seeing him happy.

"We will have lots of time for that, why don't we all play a board game together." asked Yvonne. "How about that board game that you told me about."

"Are you talking about dreamopoly?"

"Yes, that's the one. Does everyone want to play?"

"Sure, I will play, your father and I play with some friends of ours in Florida." Marilyn said.

"I'll play, that is a fun game." Jack said.

"Okay, it sounds like the four of us, are all in agreement. I'll go get the game." said Levi, knowing what he really wanted to do was plan a wedding. But he knew that Yvonne was right about waiting for it to be him and her alone to talk more about it.

As the four of them were playing the game, they had a guest that they didn't expect stop over. Mable heard the door bell, and she went to see who could be there at this time of hour.

"Hello Mable, I want to talk to Levi, if you wouldn't mind getting him for me." Roxie demanded.

"I don't believe that he was expecting you. He has company, and I'm sure he can't be disturbed." Mable spoke sharply.

"This cannot wait." Roxie spoke pushing her way, past Mable.

"Levi! Levi!" she began yelling throughout the house. "Levi, I want to talk to you, right now."

"Is that someone yelling?" asked Yvonne, trying to make out the voice.

"Levi, I must see you right now." Mable asked in an excited voice.

"Mable! What seems to be the matter?" asked Levi, as he began to pull his chair out from under the table.

Mable stood at the door of the game room, so Roxie would not come through.

"Yes, Mable what could be the problem? Is everything alright with Roman?"

"So, there you are how can you do this to me?" shouted Roxie.

"How did you get in here? I thought that I had seen the last of you, the other night. The way you embarrassed me in front my Yvonne, I see I'm going to have to reset my code, at the gate."

"Your Yvonne? You, have got to be kidding me, throw me away for a cripple? What has gotten into you lately? I go out of town for a couple of weeks, and come back to a man that I don't even recognize." She looked at him with her hands on her hip. "So it's like that, Yvonne now huh? It has been the two of us for two years, now you change after hitting her car. What's up with that? People get in car accidents every day, they just don't break up over it."

Yvonne and her parents, sat at the table hearing everything that was being spoken. Levi tried to get her to leave the room, but to his dismay, unless he was to pick her up, and handle her in an improper manner, she was not leaving on her own.

"Roxie, it is over, the way you acted in front of my guest. You showed me what other's have seen in you all along, and I was just to blind to see. I really didn't know you at all. I've always spoke very kindly of you, I guess your true colors were never exposed to me before. And the thought that I even considered marring you. What was I thinking?"

"Levi may I say something to Roxie?"

"Sure honey, go ahead."

"Honey what the heck?" Roxie said all upset. "So, its honey, how can you decide just like that, we're done? And now you have a new girlfriend."

"It's the way you acted, when you came here that made me decide, that I can't even be friends with you. Will you leave like a lady, or do I need to remove you, like a man?"

"Wait! Can I say something here please?" Yvonne asked, while the rest of the family stood there watching and listening.

"You have nothing I want to hear, I don't know what you want but this man here." She was pointing at Levi, shaking her finger. "He is not the man I knew just over a month ago, what did you do to him? Did you threaten to take everything he owns? I know you did something, to get him to let you and your son stay here. This is pathetic."

Yvonne turned her chair around, with tears in her eyes, and pushed herself down the hallway, towards her bedroom. She had never been so abused, with such careless words before. She didn't even want to be there no more, all she ever wanted since the death of Mark was to find a man, to love her and Van. But this was not what she had expected. She just wanted to pack her things, and go back home. *Why did I ever have to pull out in front of him, now look at me in this stupid wheel chair. What am I going to do, I just can't stay here, with people thinking I'm here for the money. She was allowing Roxie's cruel words get to her.*

Levi could see that Yvonne was very upset, and that upset him. He took Roxie by the arm, and followed her to the door. "How can you treat my fiancé, like that? Not to mention, my, soon to be in laws."

"WHAT! You have got to be kidding me; you mean to tell me, that you are really going to marry a crippled?"

Levi opened up the door. "Get out! I do not ever want to hear from you again. In fact, I'm going to go change the code, at the gate right now that way I know you won't be showing up here, anymore." With that he began walking down the driveway, to change the code.

"Levi please don't do this, I'm sorry, I'm sorry." She yelled at him, as he ignored her and kept walking. Roxie stood there watching as he walked away, she didn't know what else she could do, to make her wrong right. *I can't believe he dumped me for her, what makes her so special. What does she have that I don't have, when she can't even walk? Sure, she might be pretty, but what else can there be.* She stood there thinking, when Levi came walking back up the driveway.

"Why are you still here? There is nothing here for you anymore." He opened the door, and closed it behind him, leaving her standing there alone.

Levi hurried down the hallway, to Yvonne's room. After her not answering the door when he knocked, He got worried and walked in. "I'm sorry for just walking in, but you wouldn't answer." He was so busy talking, that he never noticed that she was packing clothes, in her suitcase.

"I'm sorry Levi, for everything. I think that Van and I should be going back, to my home now."

"What are you saying? Leaving! Why?"

"I can't be having people think that I'm here to take your money, or hold something over your head. I just can't, I love you but maybe I don't belong here."

"Please let's talk, everything that Roxie said, is just because she's jealous. She is right about me changing. I did, and it was for the best. You and Van have changed me for the better, don't let anything that woman has to say, come between you and I. Van will be so hurt to leave, he loves it here."

"Your right." she said as she looked up at him. "I'm just being silly, acting like a child, aren't I?"

"I wouldn't really say a child, maybe a bit silly." He said laughing.

"I am being silly, will you ever forgive me, for acting like this?"

"I already have. I wish you would marry me right now I don't want to wait, I want to hold you, like a husband holds his wife." Levi spoke as he knelt down in front of her.

Putting her head down, with tears running down her cheeks, "I'm sorry, really I am. I really want to walk. Please try to understand."

"I do, why don't we go down to the game room, and let everyone know that you're okay. I'm sure that your folks might be wondering."

"Okay, let me put these clothes away, and then we can if that's alright?"

"Let me help you, put the clothes back in your dresser." He took a hand full of them and carried them to her dresser. "Yvonne, I want you to promise me that you never will listen to Roxie, or any other person that tries to come between us ever again."

"I'm sorry, and I will never let anyone come between us again. Shall we go in the other room, and put everyone's mind at ease."

"I want to take a look in the monitor, just to make sure that she did leave. After Levi closed the door to his gate he went into the game room.

"I want to apologize, to everyone for what just happened a little while ago. That lady was someone I used to know. I don't think that any of us will have to worry about her anymore." he spoke looking at Yvonne.

"I sure hope not, she was, just awful, acting like a spoiled child."

"Mom she was a girl that Levi used to like at one time, now it's hard for her to let him go. She'll find someone in time, and leave Levi and I alone." Yvonne spoke like to reassure herself, of this.

"Honey I think that your dad and I are going to pass on the game at this time, and go back to your place. It's been a long day, and I'm starting to get tired. I see your dad, sitting here just a yawning. Do you mind?"

"No not at all, you go and I'll probably see you tomorrow."

"Are you sure that you don't want to spend another night?"

"Thank you, Levi, but we have most are clothes back there. And I think that you two need some time alone, to talk."

"Okay, I'll open the gate for you, from up here. Then I'll close it."

"I thank you honey for everything." Marilyn said giving Yvonne a hug good night. And thank you Levi for everything, please tell Mable I said thank you."

"Will do, you two must come by soon okay?"

"We will, and I want to have the two of you to come over to Yvonne's sometime this week for supper."

"That's sounds great. Just let us know when."

Levi and Yvonne watched as her parents walked out the door. Yvonne looking up at Levi made the statement. "I think that their warming up to liking you." she said with a big smile.

"Oh, you really think so, me and all my charm? You mean to say I have them won over.

"Honey Van went up to bed about an hour ago, would you mind us taking a rain check on playing dreamopoly, I'm getting tired myself, and could use some sleep."

"It has been a long day today, by all means you go get some sleep, and I'll see you in the morning." Levi spoke bending down to give her a kiss goodnight.

15

Weeks have past, and Yvonne was doing very well at her walking. She and Levi would take walks in the day, and in the evenings. Many times, Van was next to her too, now that school was out for the summer.

It's been a month since my parents, have gone back to Florida. I am doing so much better, than I did when they were here. Thank you for working with me every day, I think that I surprised the nurse, by telling her that I wouldn't need her help any longer."

"That's a good thing, it just shows that two people in love can accomplish anything together, as long as there is a will there's a way."

"I think that if we keep taking our walks, like we been doing every day. I will be as good as new in about three months."

"You think that it will take you that long? It seems to me, that you've been walking really well I thought that we could get married real soon. It feels like I've been waiting for ever, to marry you."

"It's been three months, since we met. But I agree it seems like we have talked about marriage forever. What kind of wedding do you want?"

"It could be just us and Van, and I'd be happy. But it's not just about what I want, it's about what we want. What do you want for a wedding?"

"I would like the groom." she said laughing. "Do you think you will make It?" still chuckling.

"Wild horses, can't keep me away. I'll be there, with bells on my feet, just as soon as you say it's time."

Yvonne looked at Levi, and took his hand. "If you really don't care about having a big wedding, then I say let's get married."

"Do you mean it? Did you really say that we can get married?"

"There are a few things that have to be done before we can get married."

Okay, and what are those things?" he asked.

"First of all, we need a marriage license, and then we need to talk to our Pastor. He already knew that we have been talking about getting married, so this will not come as to much of a surprise to him now. Then we need to figure out where we want to get married at?"

"I think since you, and I both love the outside. Maybe we should get married, in the back yard. Do you think that would be alright?"

"I think that is a great idea, I'd love to marry you at our home."

"Do you know that is the first time, that you have called this place your home. It sounds very nice to hear you call it your home and not just mine."

"You know I did, didn't I. That makes me feel good to." She said with an ear to ear smile that lit up on the inside of Levi.

"After are walk, we can go up to the court house, to get our marriage license. Then call Pastor. Maybe we should figure out a date, before calling him up. Don't you think that would be for the best?"

"Yes, I do. So, when do you want, to get married?"

"If you wouldn't mind, I've gotten to be pretty close, to Mable since coming here. I'd like to talk with her about our wedding plans. We've talked of it before, and she said that it would be nice if we had a big wedding. Maybe we should have a few guest come, you think?"

"Honey I know that you have friends from the church, and I guess since I've been going now for a while, they have become some of my greatest friends too. I think if we didn't invite them, we would have a lot of people very sore at us."

"I agree, why don't I talk to Mable, and then we can get this all figured out. Then once we do, I can call my parents up, and have them come back for our wedding."

Yvonne talked with Mable, and the two decided that it wouldn't have to be a big wedding, but it should be one that was with friends, and a dinner that would follow. They would have all the food catered so Mable would not have to do a thing for the wedding, except be there. Yvonne couldn't wait to tell Levi, that they would be getting married in about a month. She knew that she needed to plan what foods they were to have, and what they would all be wearing.

"Since we both want to be married and I did say after I'm walking again, that we would marry. What if we make it for next month on Saturday August twenty sixth, is that too soon?"

"Are you kidding me?" Levi said as he picked Yvonne up, and swung her around in a circle. "I would marry you tomorrow, if I could. But the twenty sixth will be fine. We have the rest of our lives, to spend with each other." He was so excited, that the date to get married was finally set. "We have to call your folks up, and let them know that we picked a date. Their, probably going to wish, that they never went back to Florida so soon."

"I know, at first they were going to stay all summer, they thought that I would need them, to help me more than I did. But after them seeing that you were there for me, they decided to go back home. They could see that Van, and I were all taken care of. Now if they want to make it for our wedding, they will have to come back within a month again."

"I'll send them money to catch a plane here. I think that will be better than driving, all this way again."

"Oh, I'm so excited, I can hardly wait. I'm going to call them now, what you think?" she asked Levi.

"I think that we should have a talk, with Van first. But it's your call, whatever you want to do."

"Your right, will we talk with him first. I need to go wake him up then, because we have a lot to do today." With those words, Yvonne started up the stairs slowly, after her walking again she was still a little shaky at times. But she knew that, she was going to start coming up the stairs, or use the elevator after she was married anyways. So, she just might start to get used to it now.

Levi watched her closely, to make sure that she would not lose her balance. He didn't want to take any chance, in her falling by her legs getting weak, so he followed close behind. He was proud of how far she came by pushing herself, to walk again. He knew that it was hard work, watching her cry at times because the pain she would feel, after walking. She was determined to walk, so she never let anything, stand in her way.

Yvonne and Levi, walked in Vans room, leaning on his bed, she spoke softly in his ears. "Van, we have a surprise for you, get up honey. Levi and I, have something very important to tell you."

Van rolled over, and looked at the two of them standing there. "Mom did you walk up the stairs, or take the elevator?"

"I walked, but Levi followed close behind me, so nothing would happen to me. Will you sit up bud, we have something to tell you."

Van sat up rubbing, his eyes so he could focus looking at the two of them. "Okay I'm up, what's the surprise? Did I get a puppy?" He spoke quietly, with the sound of tiredness still in his voice.

"No, but we set a date, for Levi and I to marry. We will marry on August the 26 th. What do you think?"

"I'm happy for you mama, and you to Levi. Now you really are going to be my step dad, aren't you?"

"Yes, I am, and I'd like if you would be my best man."

"Really, Wow I get to be the best man. What is the best man mama?"

Yvonne and Levi looked at each other, and started to laugh. "I'll let Levi tell you since he's the one that asked you okay?"

"Aha!" he spoke shaking his head up and down.

Levi explained to Van what it was all about, and Van said that he understood. He was proud that Levi picked him to be his best man, when he was going to be his son.

"When do you want to go look at wedding cakes?" Yvonne asked directing her attention towards Levi.

"Why don't we stop by some places that make cakes today? We can do that before we go to the court house, or after we get our marriage license.

"Okay that sounds very good. I know you will need a wedding dress also, maybe Mable will want to help you with that."

"Yes, I will ask her."

Levi and Yvonne went down stairs, to wait for Van to come down, and eat some breakfast. "Did you see the look on Vans face, when I asked him to be my best man?"

"Yes, I did, I could tell that he was very touched by you asking him. Thank you for that Levi. I know it means the world to him."

"I wouldn't have it any other way. To me I feel somehow it was him that took a big part in the two of us getting together."

"Really that's great."

"I felt the attraction for you, the first time we met. But when I brought Van home with me, and he would talk of you, and him the way that he did. I don't know how to explain it really, but I somehow didn't ever want to lose touch with either of you. Then the more, I began to talk to you at the hospital, I could see all these wonderful things Van would tell me about you. I'll tell you one thing, that young man upstairs sure loves him mommy." he spoke with a chuckle.

"Oh, I just know that the three of us will be happy. I know that we haven't really known each other, for a long time. But we have spent countless hours getting to know one another, over these past few months. I must say, I sure am glad that we did meet."

"I know it seems as though I have known you for a long time. You know, I dated Roxie for two years, and never did I ever feel close to her as I do you. If I had I would have married her a long time ago."

"I believe God was saving us, for each other. No wonder I never cared to date anyone else, over the last couple years." she spoke giving a wink of her eye.

"Oh, here he comes, our big best man, coming down the stairs now." Levi spoke watching Van come down the stairs.

"Are you hungry, little man?" Yvonne asked.

"Yeah are you going to cook something, or is Mable?" "What difference does it make?"

"I like Mable's waffles. And you don't make the real ones."

"Van now we aren't going to bother Mable, with something like that. Now that I'm walking again, and able to do more work around here, I'm going to be doing that."

"Did I hear someone say, they want some of my waffles?" Mable asked coming in from the other room.

"Yes, I did." said Van. "But that's okay, mom said we don't want to bother you, with something like that."

Mable looked at Yvonne. "It's really no bother, I was going to offer anyway. I know that the two of you, have many plans to make for the wedding within a month. I could make up a big enough batch for all of us, if you don't mind."

"If you don't mind, then it's okay with me. Levi and I are talking about, our wedding plans. And Mable if you could, would you mind going to town with me this week to help me in finding a dress?"

"Really, you are asking me to help you with that. It would be an honor to do that with you. Thank you for asking." She spoke with tears coming to her eyes.

"I wouldn't want anyone else to take that part but you." Stated Yvonne.

"Okay then its settled. I'll go in the kitchen and get it started then."

After breakfast, Levi and Yvonne went into town, to take care of all that needed done. The hour was getting late in the afternoon, so they took a break between places, and got a bite to eat.

"I really think the second place we looked, made the prettiest cakes. What do you think?" Yvonne asked Levi, over their meal.

"Now was that at Martha's wedding cake decor?" "Yes."

"I was thinking the same thing, but I wanted you to be the one to pick it out. And I thought that the taste was the best too. I know it's always the women that do that sort of thing." he said giving her his famous wink.

"But I want you to be part of all the decisions. Well all accept my dress. And that will be Mable and I."

"Yes, of course, I think that is a very good idea. You just tell me how much money, you would like and it's yours."

Yvonne looked at Levi, with much love in her eyes. "I'm sorry that I don't have any money, to contribute to the wedding."

"Don't be silly, what's mine is yours. I don't even want you to think about you not having money. In fact, right after we are married, I will be adding you onto my checking account. I don't ever want you to feel, that whenever you want something that you have to come to me over it. We have plenty of money, for you to do what you feel you want to do."

Yvonne wrapped her arms around his neck. "It's going to take some time, for me to get used to that way of thinking. I worked from pay check to pay check, and never had enough to buy my son, and myself new clothes. So, this will take time for me, to get used to."

"Mama, did you pick out your cake?" asked Van as Levi and Yvonne arrived back home.

"We did honey, and it's very beautiful. We also picked out what kind of tux, the both of you will wear."

"What's a tux?"

"It's a man's suit that we rent, for the wedding." answered Levi.

"Why we don't buy them?"

"Because honey, there not just a suit that you would where to church, or something like that. This kind is a special suit." Yvonne tried to answer, but felt she was doing it the wrong way. She looked at Levi for help.

"If you think that you would like us to buy our tux, then we will." he wasn't sure how to answer, Van and all the questions he had either.

"Levi, you really don't need to do that. I know they cost a lot of money, and this will probably be the only time, that Van will where it."

"I know honey, but it's not like we don't have it."

Yvonne just looked at Levi, and then she said. "Van honey not always does the parents know how to answer their children, especially when they ask too many question. But we will not be buying you the tux. Now I know that you don't understand, but this kind of suit is just not one that you will ever wear again, more than likely. Okay do you understand?"

"Yes ma'am." he said as he headed down the hallway towards the game room.

"I'm sorry to say something different then you did to him. I know you're not used to ever saying no to him. But honey, although we will be having more money than we had before we got with you, I don't want Van to think, he can have whatever he wants, when he doesn't even need it. To me it's just a waste of money. Are you disappointed in me?"

"No not at all, you are his mother. I'm sure you know what you're doing, with him more than me. You have raised him, to be who he is. I see no reason to change that. It will just take me some time, to get used to the idea, that just because I have it, that it doesn't mean I need whatever I want either. So, this is a lesson for me also."

"Thanks for letting me teach you to." she spoke jokingly

"We will teach each other, and learn together." spoke Levi.

"Honey, I have a big court case coming up in just a couple of days. This one is my biggest case this year so far. I have been preparing for it, for weeks now. Tomorrow I will be going over things with my clients the better part of the day. I won't be able to be home till night is that alright?"

"Honey, this is your work. Of course, you take all the time that you need to take. I know that you have never lost a case so far, and I would not want you to start now, on the count of me."

"Thank you, my love, my sweet. I knew that you would understand."

The next day Mable and Yvonne went into town for dress shopping. She tried on so many dresses, that by the end of the day she had worn herself out. But with much help from Mable, she went home with the prettiest bride's dress she had ever seen before. She could not wait for the day she was to wear it for her wedding day. Mable had picked out a beautiful dress as well.

The wedding day was near, and that back yard was all set up but the chairs. Yvonne's folks had flown in a few days before the wedding. Levi had won his case in court, making it a one point two million dollar win for him. He took Yvonne and her parents out to celebrate.

The wedding day had finally arrived, and Yvonne was the prettiest picture of a magazine. Levi was gone all day, not being able to see her. Between Mable and Marilyn, the two kept her well hid from Levi until she was to walk down the aisle. Although they knew it was just a saying, never let the groom see the bride before the wedding was just silliness; they still wanted the first look that Levi was to see his bride, to be a memorable one. Her gown was white, with the look of silver trim around the sleeves, and the neck line. Her bouquet was white roses, with silver trim around them. Her long dark hair had curls all over, while it hung over her shoulders. Her shoes were white heels. The necklace she wore was one that Levi had bought for her a month after the two had met for the first time. It was one that he said reminded him of her, a diamond to behold the beauty of the one who wears it.

"Mom I'm so excited, but very nervous." Yvonne spoke, before heading out the door to go into the back yard where her groom awaited her entrance.

"You have nothing to be nervous about. You have the love of a man that God has chosen for you. I know that the two of you will have a good life together, just as you, and Mark did."

"Yes, we did, and I love Levi so much, like I did Mark. But I feel different, then I did with Mark."

"That's the way you should feel, no two love can be the same. Levi is a different man then Mark was. He was just as good of a man, but yet so different. Now come on your groom is going to wonder if you changed your mind. Let's get out there. Mable and I will go, and find our seat then you come." Marilyn scolded just a little, knowing it would be hard for Mable to come in and sit.

Yvonne knew that she better get out there, and meet her man in front of the Reverend. "Are you ready dad?" she asked walking out of the room.

"Yep take my arm, let's get out there, and get this wedding moving along. I must say, you are so very beautiful honey. You look much like your mama did at your age."

The people stood up, as Yvonne walked down the aisle, down to the front. Levi could not believe how beautiful Yvonne was at this very moment. He had always thought that she was ever so pretty, but this was amazing to him. He had never seen anyone in all his life, be this pretty. He could not wait, for the wedding to be over. All he could picture was their honeymoon that he would be taking her on. He was finally going to have this beautiful woman all to himself, at the Bahamas. The two decided that it would be a great place to spend some time alone, away from everything, and everyone they knew. Yvonne had never really been away from Van before the car accident. But she knew that he would be in good hands, with her folks for the two weeks that she and Levi would be gone.

Yvonne looked at Levi's cufflinks to see which ones he had on. For she was reminded of her dream, she had about her wedding. Yes, he indeed was wearing the diamond ones, she seen in her dream.

Yvonne took Levi's hand in front of everyone there. It was though she could feel their eyes watching her every move. Levi was the man of her dreams, in every way. She could hardly wait to leave on their private airplane that will take them far away from everything, for a couple of weeks.

When the preacher asked the two to say their vows, on which they wrote for each other, neither of them knowing what the other had written. They were going to hear it for the very first time.

"Levi, you were my light, when things seemed dark. You have given me hope, when I felt it was all gone. You've picked me up, when I've fallen. You held my hand, when I needed a friend. I will cherish our life together, today and forever. You and me forever we shall be with love and respect from me to you. I accept your hand in marriage, as my husband, my spouse, my love." Yvonne could barely get the words out of her mouth, standing there in front of everyone she began to cry.

"Until I met you, and Van. I used to think that life was all about me. You have taught me so much, in the past couple of months, that I never have learned in my whole life time. You are my joy, when I get up in the morning. You bring me laughter, where before it was all in vain. You gave me a new meaning, of living. Since meeting you, I no longer have to wonder when the darkness will leave. It's gone, forever. I take you, to be my bride, my wife and companion forever. I love you Yvonne with all of my heart, and I just want to thank you for pulling out in front of me, that day that we met."

Levi had tears in his eyes, as he said those last couple of words. While the crowd of people looked at each other, the crowd began to laugh. The Reverend spoke, I give to you for the very first time, Mr. and Mrs. Levi Ubani.

Everyone stood up and began to clap. Van walked behind the two, as they began to walk towards the back. Yvonne's maid of honor Shelly Bright was considerably taller than Van, and much older. But the two stood next to the bride and groom, for all others to come and shake their hands.

"I can finally call you my wife. I loved the vow you wrote for me. It meant so much, all those kind words."

"I feel the same, thank you Levi. I wondered if I was going to ever get through the ceremony when listening to you talk. I wanted to just wrap my arms around you, and kiss you ever so much."

"We will have plenty of time for all that, when we get to the Bahamas."

"Yes, we will, I can hardly wait. It's been hard, at times living here and not being able to love you, as a wife. But to-night honey you are all mine." she spoke raising her eye brows up and down.

"Come on the two of you, if you waited this long, you can wait a few more hours. Unless you feel the need to go in the house right now, I will just let the folks all know there was an urgency." Mack Dyer, Levi's lifetime friend spoke.

"Mack, let's keep it down, a bit huh. We don't need people hear you talking foolish. I think my bride and I are fine. Don't you honey?" he spoke looking at Yvonne.

"Yes, Mack we are fine, no need to be getting foolish, about things."

"Is Mack running his mouth, again?" asked Joyce a friend of Levi and Yvonne's.

"Oh, just a little, you know Mack. Always has to be the center of attention." stated Levi.

"Oh, come on, everyone is so serious all the time. You have to have some fun, in life." said Mack trying to ease tension that he caused.

"Everyone, we can head over to the tent to our right, there is lots of food for everyone. Shall we go?" Spoke Levi trying to get out of a sticky situation with Mack.

The wedding cake was beautiful it was a three layer that had a fountain at the top with the bride and groom. It had white with silver trim, and little silver beads that wrapped around it. Yvonne had never seen a prettier cake in all her life. Levi and Yvonne each gave each other a small bite of the cake. Mack and his foolishness, wanted Levi to shove a piece in Yvonne's face, But being the gentleman that he is, told Yvonne what Mack wanted him to do. So, to give Mack a piece of his own medicine, the two decided that Levi would put a piece of cake in Mack's face, just as soon as he had the opportunity to. He didn't have to wait too long. Levi watched as Mack came up to Yvonne, and asked her why she didn't marry him instead of Levi. Right when the words left Mack's mouth, a big piece of cake entered it, and some on his face. Yvonne started to laugh, for she knew he would get it before the day was over. Mack jumped back hoping to have missed what he now, was wearing.

"Why did you do that? Man, I can't believe you my brother."

"Now just maybe, you will stop with all the foolish talk, and be my friend."

"I am your friend man, I was just having some fun is all. I don't know why everyone has to be so serious. This is a party isn't it?" he asked disgusted that he was the one that got the cake, in his face and not Yvonne.

"I don't know why you're so mad, brother." Levi said. "You're the one that wanted my lovely wife to wear the cake, I just decide it would look better if you were the one to wear it not her, so lighten up, after all like you said it's a party, and I'm just celebrating."

"Yeah, yeah okay. I'll go bother someone else." Mack walked away shaking his head.

"The soft music began to play and Levi took his bride in his arms and led her out to the dance floor. "Honey I'll go easy on you, although your walking now, I can see at times, where it looks to me that your legs get shaky. Am I right?"

"Yes, you are, but they are getting better every day. I like it when you hold me tight like this anyway."

"Yes, they are getting stronger, I can see that just in the last week, how much better there doing." The two danced two songs, then Levi noticed Jack coming towards them.

"Can I have my daughter for a dance, do you mind?"

"No not at all, just as long as I can have her back." he gave Yvonne's hand over to her dads.

"Now honey, I haven't danced in years. So, you may have to show me just what to do."

"Aw dad, that's sweet. Although I knew that I would get my legs to walk again, at times I wondered if I would ever get to dance again. I have always liked to slow dance. And I love to dance at church, I'm so very thankful that I can now do that again, during praise and worship."

"When you were just a little girl, you liked to dance when your mother and I would take you to church."

"I remember that, mom was always pulling my dress down for me. She said that when I danced it would show too much off."

"Yes, I remember when she said that she would have to make you longer dresses."

"That's funny you remembered that, and she did make them longer. I know because she stopped pulling them down all the time for me."

"Here we are still standing here and the music stopped." said Jack.

"Oh, my I never even noticed. I was so caught up in dancing with my dad. That's something that I haven't done in about twenty years." She started looking around for Levi.

"Maybe it's been longer, then twenty years." "Dad I better go find my husband."

"Go on honey, I just wanted to have a dance with you, and tell you how much that I love you."

"I love you too dad."

Yvonne was looking all around, for Levi. When she walked out of the tent, she could see that he was talking with someone. She decided to walk up to them.

"Levi honey is everything alright?" she asked after seeing Roxie standing there.

"Everything is fine honey, I was just telling Roxie that she shouldn't be here. I didn't want her to ruin our wedding.

"I see, so what are you doing here Roxie, I know that you were never invited. I know this because I'm the one that sent out all the invitations. I'm sorry, I'm being very rude and that is not who I am. But whatever you may or may not have had with my husband, that is over, he is a married man. Would you kindly leave our home, and not come back? My husband and I have to be getting ready, to leave for our honeymoon." Yvonne felt ashamed, for how she talked to Roxie, she just wanted her and Levi to have a good marriage without her coming around trying to cause trouble.

Levi put his arm around Yvonne. "Honey I couldn't have said that any better if I would have said that myself. Roxie please move on with your life, as you can see, I did." The two walked away, with their arms embraced around each other's back.

Roxie stood there watching them as they walked back under the tent. So, she's not a crippled after all. And she's very pretty, but we'll see how long this marriage will last. If I can help it, it won't last as long as they think it will. I will get you back one way or the other. She spoke in a low tone, but Van stood close enough by to hear what she had to say.

After they ate and danced, Levi and Yvonne wanted to head for their honeymoon. They told everyone there thanks for joining them on their wedding day. Thy invited them to stay, eat and have fun. But they were headed out, and would be back in two weeks.

"Van now you listen to your grandparents, okay. I will miss you so much honey, and when we get back, we will all do something fun together. I think that the fair will be going just about the time we get home. Maybe we will go there, would you like that?"

"Yes mama, but I have something very important that I have to tell you, before you go." stated Van all excited.

"What is it Van?"

"I was standing outside the tent, when I heard you talking loud to someone. So, I went closer to hear you, and I see it was that one lady that came here that was mean to us."

"Yes, honey that was Roxie."

"Mama please just let me finish. She stood there after you, and Levi walked back to the tent. She was talking to herself, I heard her say that she would do whatever it took, to get Levi back."

"WHAT! You heard that, are you sure?"

"Yes, that's what I've been trying to tell you. She said well let's just see how long your marriage will last. Mama you won't let her break up your marriage, will you?"

"No of course not, and don't you worry about a thing. Van nothing is going to happen to Levi and I. We are a family now, and nothing is going to take that away from any of us okay."

"Your mom's right Van, there is no way that I will ever let the likes of Roxie come between us. And when your mom and I get back, from our honeymoon I will put an end to all that Roxie has been saying."

"We better get going, I love you all bye, we'll see you in two weeks, now remember Van be on your best behavior."

Levi and Yvonne were gone, ready to load the plane. When Yvonne could feel that she was getting all upset. "Oh, the thoughts of that woman saying that she will break our marriage up. Levi I never knew that I could get so angry until I met Roxie. First, she calls me homeless, then a cripple. Now her plan is to break up our marriage."

"I didn't know you had it in you, until I heard you at the house." he laughed. "Come on honey, let's enjoy our time together. I'll take care of her when we come back, you don't have to worry about that."

"Your right, this is what she would want, to ruin our honeymoon. Well I just won't let that happen, I am forever yours and you are forever mine.

"Now that's my girl." he said grabbing her and taking her close to him.

The two found their hotel, and got to their room. Yvonne was so nervous that she asked him, if he thought that he could wait another day, to be intimate with her the next day. She felt like she needed to break free from the nervousness first. Although Levi wanted nothing more than to be close with her in every way, he agreed to give her time. After the two of them laid down together, and began to kiss, it was Yvonne that asked him if the two of them could get in the hot tub together.

"Mrs. Ubani, you are asking a lot from a husband. Can we undress to get in there?"

Yvonne knew that she was being silly about the whole thing, the two were married now, and there was no shame, in her and her husband being intimate with each other. She agreed that they should indeed, come together, as a husband and wife. It was a night of passion, and dreams come true for the both of them. The two enjoyed each other's company, in way that only the two together could. And before they knew it, there time was up, and they were headed back to the states.

"Levi. I just wanted to say, I had the best of time with you in these last two weeks, then I could have ever dreamt of having. You are the most generous man that I have ever known. I miss my Van, and I will be very happy to see him. But on the other hand, I hate to see this come to an end."

"Honey trust me when I say, our honeymoon has not come to an end. It's only started, there will be many more vacations that we will take, some with Van, and some just the two of us."

"Thank you honey."

On the flight home, Yvonne wondered if Roxie was going to stop back over and be a bother to them again. She prayed quietly to herself so Levi would not hear her concerns. *"Lord, please bless my marriage, help Roxie not come between my husband and I. Help us to be strong in all that we face from here on out. Amen."*

"Mama, Van came running up to her, all excited as the car pulled in the driveway.

Yvonne opened the door, to embrace her son with both arms.

"I missed you, so much."

"It's so good to see you, did you miss me at all, maybe just a little huh?" she asked showing about an inch between her fingers.

"I missed you this much." He said with his arms held open as wide, as he could get them. "I'm so glad your home."

"Well what about me there sport?" asked Levi smiling at Van.

Van ran around to Levi's side, and hugged him tight. "I missed you and mama."

"We both missed you to, and glad to be home with you. Where is your grandma, and grandpa at?"

"They're in the house. Are you guys coming in, or are you just going to go home?"

"We'll come in for a while." stated Yvonne, then, we have to be getting home. I'm very tired, and need to unpack and get some sleep."

They went into Yvonne's house, to see her parents. And to find out any last bit of news, before going back home.

"Hi mom and dad how did everything go watching your grandson, for a couple of weeks?"

"It was great, no problems at all, and how was your time with each other. Did you enjoy yourselves?"

"We had a blast, I finally was able to do things, that I've always just dreamt of doing."

"I have heard most all my life about the Bahamas, and always wondered how it would be for me, if I ever got the chance to go. Now I can say it was wonderful we had so much fun, I hated to come back, so soon. But I missed my little guy, so much." she spoke squeezing Van lightly.

"If the two of you, ever want to go there some time, just let me know. I can make arrangements at work, and we can all go together sometime. I had forgotten how nice it is there. It's been a number of years since the last time I had gone." Levi told them.

"You mean to tell me that you would really pay are way there, cause that's the only way we could take a trip like that." asked Jack.

"Anytime you're ready, just let me know, if it's alright with my wife, that is. Then we can go."

"That's very nice of you Levi, and I would love to go there again. I'm just not for sure when, after just getting back, from there."

"Will I go next time?" asked Van.

"You sure will, little guy. We would have taken you this time, but your mom and I really needed that time together. But next time I will make sure you are right with us, okay."

"Okay."

16

O h, it's nice to be back home, but now that we are. There are so many
things that have to be done."

"Like what, Mrs. Ubani."

"I love it when you call me that, it just reminds me how good God is,
for bringing you in my life. I never want to forget that, when I was in my
darkest of times, he sent you, to help bring me through." Yvonne spoke
giving her husband a big hug.

"Now tell me, what we have so much to do?"

"Well for one thing, all my clothes will have to come up stairs, to your
bedroom, I mean our bedroom."

"Honey, I didn't want you to worry about that, when you came home,
so I asked Roman and Mable to bring your things up stairs, is that okay?"

"Really, you mean I don't have to do all of that. I'm going to have to
thank them."

The hour was getting late, and Yvonne was very tired from her trip.
She knew that sleep was calling for her. She spent some time with her folks,
and then the three of them headed back to her new home.

Levi spent some time talking with, Roman and Mable, just to find out that Roxie, came back to the house, and was at the gate trying to get them to let her come in.

"What do you mean, she was trying to talk you into letting her come in? For what can she possibly want, she knows that I'm married. I don't want to mention this to Yvonne. I don't want her to worry, she doesn't need this at all. I'll go talk with her tomorrow on my way to work, and see what it's going to take for her to leave my wife and I alone. I'm glad to hear that besides her coming over here, that everything else went well. I'm tired, and I think I'll go join my wife, and get some sleep. Good night."

"Good night Levi." they both replied.

Levi lay in bed wondering what he will say to Roxie, when he would see her the following day. *Why doesn't she just take a hint, and leave us alone. I'm going to have to make it real clear to her, that she better just leave us alone, or I will call the authorities on her.*

He fell to sleep thinking, about what he would say.

"Good morning handsome how was your sleep?"

"I slept very good lying next to you, in our own bed." said Levi.

"How was your sleep? Do you think this bed is comfortable to you?"

"Oh yes, I didn't think that I could be any more comfortable then the one down stairs, but this one is just as nice, maybe better, because I have you in here with me."

"Do you mind if I go into work today? I haven't been around much at all, and I just want to make sure everything is running smoothly with my business. I know that I can trust the men I've trained, to care for everything, and keep my business flowing well. But if I don't check in with them, and do my share of work, they will think they own the company." He laughed.

"Levi that is your business, and I would never want you to just stay home with me and forget about your work. You go and do whatever it is that you do there. Are you going to eat first?"

"I'll get some breakfast with you, if you're coming down • stairs. But if you wanted to sleep in longer, then I'll grab a bite, on the road."

"Would it bother you, if I slept in for a while longer? I just am feeling very lazy; it feels like I still have jet flight."

"Then you stay here and get some rest. I'll be home later on, this afternoon." Levi bent down and gave her a kiss goodbye.

Yvonne slept half the morning away, and Van came to wake her up.

"Mama are you ever going to get up? You were sleeping for a long time. Why you so tired, will you get up with me now?"

"What time is it?" she asked looking at the clock on her wall? Seeing it was eleven thirty. Oh, my, I'm sleeping my life away. I'm getting up right now I'm sorry honey that I've been sleeping for so long. I just feel so tired, let me jump in the shower to wake me up, then I'll be right down stairs okay."

"Okay mama."

Van went down stairs waiting for his mother, to come down. While he waited, he asked Mable if she could make him some of her famous waffles that he loved so much. Since she was so fond of Van, and his mother, she didn't mind making them at the spare of the moment.

"I don't know why, my mom has been sleeping in so long." Van sat watching Mable, stirring up her waffle mix. With his head in his hands, acting like he was so bored.

"It will be ready in just a few minutes okay?"

"Yeah, I just feel so bored with Levi being gone, when he just got home yesterday. And my mom seems to just want to sleep."

"Speaking of your mother, here she comes now So pick your chin up, and give her a big hug huh."

"Okay." he replied as he stood up, and wrapped his arms around his mother.

"Wow! What's that for?"

"I missed you mama, and wanted you to come down stairs."

"I missed you to buddy, I'm glad to be home with you, maybe if you would like, you and I can go for a walk today. Would you like that?"

"Sure, but where do you want to walk?"

"Here Van, your waffle is ready." said Mable. "Would you like me to make you one?" she asked Yvonne.

"I can do it, why don't you sit down, and let me make you one.

"Thank you, but Roman and I have already eaten four hours ago. It's almost time for me to be getting his lunch ready."

"Lunch; oh, my I don't know what's got into me, sleeping in this late. I never sleep this long. I need to stop being so tired. Maybe I will go into town today, and pick me up some good vitamins. By the way, thank you and Roman so much for all the work that you both have done, getting all my things up stairs while I was gone.

"Not a problem, was glad to do it. You might be low, on iron. You might want to get checked out by the doctor, if this keeps going." Mable said in a low tone, trying not to seem too pushy.

"Yeah, maybe I will." she said looking at Mable. "When is Levi coming home mama?"

"I'm not sure, I told him to take his time. He hasn't been spending much time at work, since we moved in here. I think he needs to be there a little more often. Beside's I thought that today, you and I could go for a walk, and go see your grandparents."

"Yah, I want to go see them."

"Okay after we finish eating, we will go for our walk then go see them. Does that sound alright with you?"

"Yes ma'am."

"I'm going to give Levi a call, and see how things are going now that he's back to work." Yvonne picked up the phone, and tried to get a hold of him, but his phone went right to his voice mail.

"Didn't he answer, you mama?"

"No, maybe he's gone to lunch at this time. It is about that time." She spoke looking at the watch on her wrist. "Mable I thank you, again for all the work you do around here. You do so much for all of us all the time and I never hear you complain."

"That's my job, and besides that, I enjoy, doing for others. But thank you, for letting me know that you care, and appreciate me."

Yvonne and Van went for a walk just like she had promised him they would. They talked about their new life, with Levi, Mable and Roman. What a difference it is then just a few months ago. Yvonne talked to Van, about her and Levi's time that they spent, in the Bahamas. Then they decided that they would take a drive into town, and go to a vitamin store, and then go out for an ice cream cone. The whole time that Yvonne and Van went about their day, Levi was busy trying to get a hold of Roxie. He wanted to tell her that she better not come out to his home, ever again stirring up trouble. He knocked at her door, several times, but no answer. He walked around to the back of the house, and knocked, but still no answer. *I know she's here, why won't she just come to the door, and let me tell her off.* He thought to himself. He walked over to look inside the garage door window. Her car was there, but yet she refuses to answer. *I might as well just get back to work; I should have come on my way, like I planned. Maybe someone stopped over and picked her up. I'll just try later.* As Levi was headed back to his car, he noticed a blue Chevy truck, older model parked a crossed the street. Not thinking too much about it, until he was driving down the road. *I wonder way that old truck, was in that neighborhood. I can't believe that someone in that suburb would own an old thing like that. Why would it be parked right out in front of Roxie's I've never seen it around these parts before.*

Just as he was trying to figure out why an old truck would just be sitting there, he got a phone call from Yvonne.

"Hi honey, how's your day going so far?" she asked him.

"Van and I are in town right now, I was wondering if you have already eaten your lunch?"

Levi looked at the time in his car, "A matter of fact, I'm in town right now, and I haven't had a bite, all day. I never even stopped to grab me a bite for breakfast. Where would the two of you, like to meet for lunch?"

"Van said that he wanted some tacos at taco bell. Is that alright with you?"

"Sure, that sounds good to me; I haven't had them in a long time. I'll meet you there in about five minutes."

"We'll be there." she hung up with him, and focused her attention, on Van. "He said that would be fine, so we're going to have tacos for lunch. Although it was not that long ago that we ate waffle's.'

"Alright, I know, but I miss having them mama. Mable never makes them, and you used to do that a lot. Now that you're walking, and driving again, do you think that we can have them again at home like we used to. Maybe Roman and Mable will like them too."

"Sure, I don't see why not. I'll mention it to her and see if they even like them. And if they don't I can just tell her, that for that night I will cook, for you and Levi." she said looking at Van's face, as he had a big smile come across it.

The three were eating, when Levi noticed an ambulance, flying real fast with its sirens on, going towards the way he just came from. He never seen any car accident, on his back from Roxie's, it must have just happened, he thought. The three finished up, their meal, and Levi told them that he would be home by four o'clock.

"That was a nice meal, I ate a lot more than I thought that I would." spoke Yvonne.

"Me too mama, but I knew that I would, because I never get them anymore." he spoke so serious, that Yvonne couldn't help but laugh.

Later that evening, when Levi and Yvonne were sitting back on the deck as a nice warm breeze was blowing, Mable came out to tell him that there were two cops at the gate wanting to see him.

"Cops, I wondered why." he said, as he and Yvonne got up and came in the house.

"I didn't have them come up without you talking to them."

Levi walked over to the camera, to see what they needed. "Can I help you, officers?"

"Are you Levi Ubani?"

"Well yes, I am, how can I help you?"

"Sir we would like to come up, and talk with you, would you mind opening up the gate."

"Sure, come on up." He looked over at Yvonne. "I can't imagine what they would want with me."

They heard a knock at the door, Levi opened the door. "Hello, you wanted to talk with me."

"Sir we need to know, if you know a woman by the name of Roxie Stratton that lives in the suburbs on twenty-five?"

"Yes, why you ask?"

"Do you drive a black corvette?"

"Yes, what's this all about?" He asked getting all worked up. "Did she call you, and say that I threw her out of my home?"

"Sir were you at 1138 Morgan lane today, around one o'clock?"

Levi looked over at Yvonne, as she now was staring at him. "Levi what's going on?"

"I'm not sure, honey. I'll find out. Yes, I was there, but when I went to her door, no one answered it, and then I looked in her garage to see if I could see her car, and when I seen it still at home. I just figured that someone had come and picked her up." He looked over at Yvonne, to see the look on her face. He could see, sadness written all over it. "Could you please tell me what this is all about?"

"We received a call at our office, that there was a black corvette at Roxie's residents, and the man who was there was trying to break in her place. This person said that you walked around her home, and was trying to open up her windows."

"I did walk around to the back, in case she couldn't hear me knocking at the front door, but I never tried to break in, or open up her windows. Who told you this?"

"Levi Ubani, I am placing you under arrest, for the murder." before they could continue, Levi screamed out "Murder, murder. I never murdered anyone, you saying that Roxie is dead. I can't believe it, dead." Levi looked at Yvonne, as the officer was placing the hand cuffs on his wrist. "Yvonne honey, I'm sorry I never told you that I went over to her home, I was just going to tell her that I didn't want her coming over here anymore bothering us. I swear honey I'm telling you the truth."

Yvonne stood there, not able to speak. Levi looked at her then at Roman, and Mable.

"I don't know what they're talking about, I never killed Roxie. Roman will you go call my lawyer, tell him to get down to the police station?"

"I will son, right away. And I know that you could never have done anything that their accusing you of." Spoke Roman.

The officers, took Levi out, and placed him in their back seat. All the while Yvonne watched from the front door, not knowing what to do. "I can't believe what just happened, I just can't believe it. Levi killed Roxie, this is Ludacris, and we will have to do something."

"Roman is calling his lawyer right now, as we speak. I don't know why someone would ever want to blame this on him. There is no way, that he could ever have killed her or anyone else."

"This is a nightmare; we just got married, and come home from our honeymoon. And this happens, now I don't believe for one minute that he could do something like this. Someone had to of seen something. I'm going to find out, by some neighbors, if someone seen something to help us out. We need to get to the bottom of this, and soon."

"Now you really need to wait, until we can find out more. Roman is talking to Mr. Allen Levi's lawyer right now, let's see what he has to say, before getting to excited, and do something that will hurt us in the long run." Mable said to Yvonne, trying to keep her calm.

"Mama, what's going to happen to Levi?" asked Van getting scared that he won't be seeing him anymore.

"I'm not sure honey, we need to just begin to pray right now for him." Yvonne and Van bowed their heads in prayer. "Dear Lord Jesus, we come to you right now, Lord you see Levi at this moment in time. You see ahead of time what is about to take place, and you know that he did not do what he is being accused of. So, God right now, I'm asking that you help the truth come out, and let the guilty be caught, in the name of Jesus, Amen."

"Amen." Van replied.

"Mr. Allen is on his way down to the jail, right now He's going to see if he can post bail. But he said he might not be able to, until tomorrow. Levi might have to go to court first, but he did say that they have no real evidence, against him. It's just a matter of proven that he only did what he said that he did."

"How are we going to find that out?" asked Yvonne.

"I'm sure Levi will hire someone to do their own investigation he has never been in trouble with the law, in all his life. They will prove that, someone else did this and is trying to put blame on him. He has always been an upstanding law-abiding man, and lawyer, and will be found not guilty."

"I sure hope so." as soon as those words left Yvonne's mouth, she regretted them. "I shouldn't have said that, what I mean to say is I believe that God is on our side. I know that Levi will not be found guilty. He will come home to his family, and soon. She spoke looking down at Van.

17

"Can I speak with Yvonne, please?" Was a strange voice over the phone?

"This is she, how can I help you."

"Yes, Mrs. Ubani. This is Mr. Allen, Levi's lawyer."

"Yes, I've been waiting for your call. Can you tell me what's going on with my husband? Is he able to get out, and come home?"

"Not at this time, he will be going to court, at nine in the morning. He would like you to be there. Then I will try to post bail, so he can come home."

"Thank you, for going to the jail to see him, I will be there at the court house tomorrow."

"Mrs. Ubani, I'd like to ask you a couple of questions, if you have some time?"

"Okay,"

"Could you think of anyone that would do this, and try to frame Levi?"

"No, I've been trying to think how this could even be possible. It's like a nightmare."

"Levi had told me, that right after the two of you were married, that Roxie came to the wedding. Is that true?"

"Yes, she showed up, at the reception."

"Can you tell me, what took place at that time?"

"I was dancing with my father, then after that. I didn't see Levi anywhere, I went out of the tent to look for him, and he was talking with Roxie."

"Do you know what they were talking about?"

"Why all the questions, aren't you supposed to be his lawyer? Did you ask him all these questions?" she asked getting all worked up.

"Yes, I did ask him these questions. But I'm trying to get to the bottom, of all this mess. And Levi told me that you were there to witness, what transpired between him, and her."

"I'm sorry, I just can't believe what has happened. What is it that you need to know?"

"What were the two of them talking about, when you arrive where they were?"

Yvonne took a moment to think, about the talk that took place that time she seen Roxie. "Levi was asking her why she was there at our wedding; he had asked her to leave."

"So, did she leave, after that?"

"No not right away I told her that she was not going to come between, Levi, and myself. I had said that we were married, and she needed to leave us be."

"Is there anything else that you think could help the case?"

"No that's all I know. Then Levi and I turned around, and went back into the tent. We never saw her again, the rest of the night."

"Did he tell you, that when the two of you were gone, on your honeymoon. That she came by, and seen Mable and Roman?"

"NO!"

"Well then, I'll leave it at that, and let him, tell you, when you see him tomorrow. Good night and I'll see you in the morning."

"Good night." Yvonne couldn't believe that he withheld something like that from her. Why would he do that, then he goes over to her house today, and don't say a thing the whole time we sat there and ate at taco bell, he never said a word.

"Was that his lawyer?" asked Mable.

"Yes, he was asking a lot of questions. But I don't know how, he thinks what he asked me will help Levi in anyway."

"What did he say, about getting him out?"

"He has to go to court tomorrow morning, and then he's going to try to get bail for him, so he can come home."

"I sure hope that he can, this is probably so terrifying to him. He's never been in jail a day in his life. I can't imagine what he's going through right now."

"I know, this is so wrong I can't believe that Roxie's dead, and how? I mean just like that she's dead. Something isn't making any sense to me."

"I know I can't believe it either. She was just here causing trouble for everyone, now she's gone. I wonder how she died."

"Mable, did you tell Levi that she stopped over here?"

"Yes, I did."

"Why didn't anyone tell me? Why would he withhold that from me? Was he trying to hide something?"

"Oh no, it's nothing like that. Levi didn't want you to worry; he was only trying to protect you."

"Protect me from what?"

"He asked Roman and me, not to tell you that Roxie came by, because he said that she was going to try and come between you and him. He didn't want you to fall for her junk, and be worried whenever he would leave the house."

"He should have told me, I am his wife. I should have known. Now he's being accused, of killing her. I just don't know what to think about all of this."

"Believe Levi honey, I know that he is not capable of doing this to anyone."

Roman walked out of the room, hanging his head down. His heart went out to Levi. What he must be going through was tearing Roman up. He needed to be alone now, and think.

After going to the den, he sat down on the sofa, with head in hands. He began to weep, and uncontrollable sobs. God why, why did you allow this to happen to him? How can you say that you love us, and this happens? Before Levi gave his life for you, he never went to jail, now that he's been going to church, you turn your back on him. Sobs were the beginning of a hard cry. Roman was trying to gain his wits, when it seemed as if someone else had come in the door. He heard a voice, that said just trust me. He turned his head to see who that was, that came in the door. To his amazement, there was no one there. *I must be hearing things.* He thought. God, I know that I have been to church, with my wife and Levi's family. And I know that I have never truly asked you in my heart although I went to the front with Levi and my wife, but I'm asking you tonight. If you are who they say you are at church. Then please help Levi, he needs more then what any of us can give him here. He believes in you, so make a believer out of me too. Get him out of jail amen. Roman sat there for a few more minutes, before going out of the room.

"Yvonne, have you seen where Roman went, I have looked all over for him." Asked Mable.

"No, I haven't. Maybe he went away for a while to think."

"His truck is still here." Right at that time Roman came out of the den, and walked back into the living room. "Where have you been? I've been looking all over for you." stated Mable.

"I went to pray."

"You went to pray." her response was like she was in shock. She had never known Roman to be a praying man, even though at times, he would attend going to church with her.

"That's good, I'm glad to hear that."

"I figured there's not a whole lot that we can do for him, so I know that Levi is a believer in prayer, he's been talking to me a lot about it. So, I just thought that I would go do some talking to God, for myself."

Mable walked over to Roman, and wrapped her arms around him, as though never to let him go. "We'll get through this, as well as Levi will."

Yvonne was sitting down next to Van, on the couch, with her head in her hands. She looked up hearing Roman and Mable talking about how they will make it through. "Maybe I should call the Reverend, and start a prayer chain for Levi. I feel so useless, for him right now I just can't imagine, what is going through his mind, right now." She walked over to the phone, and made her call to the Reverend.

"I think that we all should go down to court house in the morning, to support Levi." stated Yvonne after she hung up with the Reverend. "Both the Reverend, and Patsy are going to be there. Could the two of you come too?" she asked.

"Yes, of course, I wouldn't have it any other way. There's nothing here, that can't wait. And Mr. Walker, he can go out to the pond, and work on the bridge without me being here."

It was settled, they were all going to be at the court house for Levi come the following day. Somehow Yvonne, and her love for him, felt like the more support there for him, the better chances he has, of being found innocent. All she wanted was for this nightmare, to be over. She couldn't believe what was happening, how this kind of thing can even happen. Yeah, she's heard about people getting arrested, for crimes that they said they never committed. But this was different, she never knew those other folks, but now it was happening to a man, she just promised to love, and be with until death do them part.

When going to bed that evening, she began to question, herself. Did I jump into marriage way too fast, could Levi have done this sort of thing? Why was he at her home and failed to tell me that he even went to her house? Now she's dead, what did I do, getting married to a man that I hardly even knew.

She began to feel so over whelmed, that this has taken place in her life that she broke down and cried. Before she knew it, morning had arrived, and the light was shining, through the windows. She jumped up, from her bed. She was in a hurry to shower, before going to court. Forgetting all the doubts that fluttered her mind the night before, she quickly showered, and got Van up to dress and eat, so they could be at the court house to see Levi. Yvonne not being one to take the elevator much decided that today was the time to take it.

"Good morning, you look very nice." Mable told Yvonne.

"Thank you, this is one of the outfits that Levi bought for me, when we were at the Bahamas. I thought that today would be a good day, to wear it. You look very nice too Mable." she replied.

"Oh, this old thing, it's been forever since I went to the store to buy myself anything."

"Then we will just have to change that. How would you like the two of us going shopping together when this is all settled and Levi comes home?"

"I would love that, it's been too long. The only place I go, it seems is to church and back home."

"Oh my, all this time I never even called my parents to let them know, what's going on with Levi." Yvonne spoke picking up the phone, to call before leaving.

"Yes, you might want to tell them to be praying for him also. We really need people that know how to pray." Spoken from a woman, that just not too long ago, learned how to pray.

Yvonne talked to her dad, knowing that a time like this, he would be more understanding then her mother would be. By the time she got off the phone, she didn't even get the chance to eat any breakfast. She was glad, that Van had taken the time to eat. She wasn't sure how long; it would be for them at the court today. Is everyone ready to go?" she asked walking towards the door.

"Did you and Van want to drive with us?" asked Roman. "There's really no sense in taking two cars."

"Yes, that might be best, I'm really nervous right now, and don't feel like I should be driving."

They loaded up together in one car, with little talking all the way to the court house. When arriving to court, they sat in the court room waiting for Levi's arrival. Yvonne was looking around, when she seen him being escorted, by a police officer. He had hand cuffs on, and chains around his ankles. She couldn't believe her eyes; she placed a hand over her mouth, as she was afraid to yell at the officers for treating him like a criminal. To Yvonne, he didn't even fit the criminal look. She had always pictured a killer, long hair, dirty clothes, unshaven, and missing teeth. Levi didn't fit that picture, he was always very clean, and he always shaved. And he didn't have any missing teeth. She wanted to run up to him, and hug him. But the officer sat him down, on a chair meant for the criminals. She couldn't take her eyes off of him, she would move her mouth, as to speak to him, but nothing would come out.

"All arise, your honorable Judge Wilder, presiding. This is the case, for Levi Ubani."

The officer took him over to stand before the judge. "Are you Levi Ubani?"

"Yes, I am your honor."

Yvonne listened; very close to hear what kind of evidence that was against him.

"Your Honor, Levi Ubani, has been accused of this terrible crime, which in time you will see, that he did not commit." spoke Levi's lawyer Mr. Allen.

"This is not a trail, Mr. Allen. And you will be able to tell your side when its time."

"Yes, your Honor."

The judge continued to talk, about things that Yvonne didn't even understand. All she wanted was for Levi to come home, and be with her. She wanted all this to just go away. She could here Levi telling his side of the story, then she seen where the judge then looked straight at her. After Levi talked, his lawyer asked that he would get released, without bail for lack of evidence. The judge set bail, at a hundred thousand dollars. After posting bail, Levi was on his way home to be with his family.

On their ride home, he hugged Yvonne and Van all the way. "Honey can you ever forgive me, for going over to Roxie's house, and not letting you know about it. I am so sorry, I think that God is trying to punish me, for not telling you my wife what I was going to do, before I did it."

"I do forgive you, and I don't believe, not for one minute that its God punishing you. I believe that the devil is mad, because you gave your life to the Lord, so he is trying to make you think, that by doing that, it was a mistake. But don't you ever feel that way, because I believe that you will be found innocent."

"I think that this has got to be the second, most-scariest, time in all my life."

"You mean to tell me that there was another, that was scarier, then this is?" asked Yvonne.

"Yes, when I hit into you, the day we met. That was even more terrible. You see when I hit you; I couldn't tell if you were still alive, I couldn't see if you were breathing. That was so scary, to me. But this case, I know that I never did, what their accusing me of doing. Now Mr. Allen, he's a good lawyer, I'm sure that the truth will come out. At least I pray that it does."

"When do you go back to court Levi?" asked Roman from the front seat.

"I go back on the twentieth of September. That only leaves us a little time, for the truth to come out."

"You have a private investigator looking into thing, don't you?" asked Yvonne.

"Yes, I do, and I need to call him, when I get home. I'm hoping that he found something out, from her neighbors."

"Like what?"

"Like someone hanging around her place or someone that might have stopped over there, besides me."

When arriving home, Levi was glad to see the inside of the home he had built for himself, eleven years ago. He never thought that he would ever see the inside, of a jail before. It was a place that he would try with everything that he had, to never go there again.

"I'm going down to my office; I have to make some phone calls." Levi looks at Yvonne, when he was talking. But after seeing the way she looked at him, he asks her if she would like to come to the office with him.

"Yes, I would like to come. Van will you help Mable with making the lunch?" she looked at Mable and gave her a wink. She wanted something to distract him, from coming down to the office, with her and Levi.

"Honey," spoke Levi as they walked down the hallway that led to his office. "I'm sorry for everything that has happened. I hope that you believe me, when I say that I didn't kill Roxie."

"I do believe you; I didn't get much sleep, last night. My mind was playing tricks, on me."

"Like what?"

"I'm ashamed to admit, I had some doubts come across my mind."

Levi sat down behind his desk, not saying anything at first. Then he placed his hand on her hand and looked up at her and said. "If I was you, I probably would have done the same thing. I know that we didn't know each other for long when we married. Then what I did, about going to her house, and not telling you. Yeah I could understand why you would have doubts."

"Thanks for understanding; I tried to push the thoughts away. I prayed really hard, to find peace. I fell to sleep, praying. Then I woke up, not feeling the same way, at all. I'm behind you, one hundred percent. We will get to the bottom of this together."

"I knew that when I fell in love with you, that I had made a right choice. I'm going to call, the private investigator now, to see if he has some good news for me."

"Yes, that's what we need is good news."

"Hello, am I speaking with Ron Cutler?" Levi asked the voice, on the phone. "This is Levi Ubani, I spoke with you, yesterday, about doing some checking, on a case for me."

Yvonne sat very quiet, so not to interrupt what Levi was trying to find out. She listened, and tried to put words to what she could not hear from the other end of the phone.

"That's good news, please keep me informed, to what you find out. Thank you, very much."

"There's some good news, I hear huh?" She asked.

"Yes, He talked with some of the neighbors there, and two of them said, they seen an old blue pickup, that was there for more than an hour. A man was seen coming from Yvonne's driveway. Honey there's something that I need to tell you, before I call up Mr. Allen."

"Okay, I'm listening." she said as she sat back down.

"Oh, it's nothing bad, its good news. I think that I saw the same truck. There was an old blue Chevy that sat across the lane in front of Yvonne's, when I was there. But I didn't see anyone inside of it. I thought it funny, the old truck. I never remember ever seeing it there before."

"Did you tell your lawyer about it?"

"No, like I said it was weird for me to see it, but I'm sure there are some family that lives there that might have a friend, or family member, with an older truck. I'm going to call Mr. Allen right now."

Yvonne waited, for him to get done talking to his lawyer. Then she said now that he was out of jail, she thought that it would be a good idea, if the two of them went to see their Pastor, and his wife. "I believe that talking with the two of them, could help us. Many times, the Lord shows, The Reverend, things that are going to happen. I believe that we need to hear a good word, today don't you agree?"

"Yes, honey I do. Can we get something to eat first, I feel very hungry, I don't know how someone can live on the food they serve you in the jail. It was horrible."

"I never ate anything today; I could use a bite myself. I'm getting hungry."

"You should have eaten something, before coming down to the court house, today. Let's go see what Mable made up for lunch."

18

Levi and Yvonne went to see their Pastor, in hopes of getting a strong word from God, through him.

"I'll first start out to say, that when you first decided to withhold, anything from your wife, especially something that has to do with a woman, that was causing trouble for the both of you. It was just plain wrong."

"I know that now, at the time that I did that, I was trying to protect Yvonne, from Roxie's meanness. I never knew that she could be so mean, and cold hearted, until I met Yvonne, then all of her true colors came to arise really quick. I ask my wife to forgive me from not telling her that."

"Good, now that you have done that, I am sure that she forgave you, otherwise, I don't think that she would be here right now." He spoke looking at Yvonne. "Now we will talk to God, and ask Him to help the authorities, to find the person, that took that young lady's life. Shall we pray?"

With their heads bowed, and praying, asking God to help them in their time of need. Levi couldn't help but feel like the Pastor was upset with him. He thought that he got a little too personal, maybe that's what they do, when someone would come to see them. He thought. Then he realized, he wasn't even praying for himself, he was too busy thinking, about what the Pastor said that bothered him.

"Son I feel the Lord, saying that everything will be alright. Levi, now that don't mean, that it's all over. But what it does mean is trust Him, through all of this. He will make away where there seems to be no way. I believe that whoever did this, will be caught. And you will be able to return home to your family that God has blessed you with." he said as he squeezed Yvonne's hand.

"Thank you, sir, that's a good word, and the key word, is trust. I know that it may take a little time, for the truth to come out. But I cannot help but think, that it was God that brought Yvonne, and Van into my life. And if that is true, then I just can't believe it would have been for such a short time."

"I don't believe that is the case either. I know what I heard, and that was everything is going to be alright. Now I'm not trying to scare you, or Yvonne. But there are times, when Gods people went to prison, for crimes that they never committed. God had a bigger plan and purpose for them. Just look at Paul and Silas. They went to prison, and prayed and prayed. But you see why they were there, they were telling others about Jesus."

"But I can do that, out here. Why would I have to leave my family, and go to prison, to tell someone about the Lord?"

"Now dear boy, don't get yourself all worked up, it probably won't come down to that. I'm praying that it doesn't, and I know that the two of you are doing the same thing. Just put all your trust and hopes, in Him. He will see you through, all these darkest moments of your life."

"Thank you Reverend, we won't take up any more of your time. Patsy thank you for allowing us to come into your home, for some prayer." spoke Yvonne.

"That is quite alright child. Just like God seen you through in your darkest hours, when you couldn't walk, or even really knew that you would again. He was there with you through it all, he'll be there through this too. I'll see the two of you at church on Sunday. If you need anything, we're just a phone call away." she gave Yvonne a hug good bye, and told Levi just to trust and pray.

The two sat quietly, for a while on their way home, and then Yvonne spoke. "Do you feel any better about things, now? Or is it about the same, to you?"

"I think in some ways, I felt better before he went on to talk about, Paul and Silas."

"I was watching the look on your face, as he began to tell you the story of the two men in the bible. I don't think that he meant to cause you to be more frightened or anything like that."

"No, I don't think that he did either, but just what if by the time I go to court, and they haven't found the person, that did this. What if I have to take the fall, for someone else?"

"Do you really believe that God, will allow that to happen, to you?"

"I don't know anymore, I don't want to believe that."

"Then don't, that's just what the devil wants you to believe. It's a lie, to bring you down to where he wants you, not trusting in God. First of all, honey, you have to remember what God showed the Pastor, and that is everything, is going to be alright. So, from this point on, I want us to remember those words, and hold on to them. Because when God gives a word, we can take it to the bank. No more talking doubt and unbelief."

"Thank you honey, right now you are bringing strength to me. I will trust God at His word. And no more doubt."

"Good, I'm glad. If there's one thing that I learned, when Mark died I had to trust God, that He would care for Van and I. And I had many hard days, where I felt like I just could die. But God and His love reached down, and picked me up, time and time, again. I just have to let Him reach His loving arms around all of us, and take care of us now."

He listened to his wife talk, about losing her husband at the time. He knew that she was speaking from experience, of some hard times in her life. Now he was facing one of the hardest times, of his life. And he to, would trust that everything would turn out alright.

That night, Levi and Yvonne hung on to each other, so tight, as to never let each other go. "I wish that we could just hold each other, like this forever." spoke Yvonne.

"I know, honey, I do too. But morning will be here all too soon."

"I know, but for now, just keep holding me, will you. At least until I fall to sleep?"

"Yes unless, I fall to sleep first, and turn over on my other side. But I will try, not to okay?"

"If you do, that's okay. I know that you couldn't have gotten much sleep, at that place last night at all."

"No, I didn't. I wouldn't even call them beds. There so hard, and uncomfortable, I might have gotten two hours of sleep the whole night."

"I'm sorry honey; I won't keep you up any longer, by talking. I love you, and talk to you in the morning, good night."

"I love you to, good night, honey."

Morning came, with a ray of sunlight shining through the light drapes that hung on the windows. Yvonne lay in bed, hearing Levi breathing heavier then she heard from him before. She knew that he was still tired. She was trying to get out from underneath the covers, and not to wake him. Just as she got one of her legs out, and facing the floor. She felt his arm, wrap around her again. She lay still, so not to wake him, as she tried to move his hand lightly. If she didn't feel the need, to go down and be with Van, she would have rather just lay there with him for a while longer. After carefully removing his hand, she was able to slip out of the bed.

"You must have slept very hard last night?" Asked Roman.

"Yes, I did, I don't even remember, Yvonne getting out of bed today. I slept like a rock."

"Would you like something to eat?"

"Anything that you want to make is fine with me. Did Yvonne eat, before going out back?"

"No, she never did, in fact she walked back there with her robe still on."

"Really, well that's a new one. I'll be back in a few minutes." Levi was out the door, looking for Yvonne. But he didn't have to go far, when he noticed her, walking up the trail.

"What are you doing?" she asked.

"Coming to look for my lovely wife, that is still in her house robe."

"You know I had forgotten all about having this on me still. No wonder, I was getting some funny looks. I thought that it was because I had no makeup on."

"You are beautiful with no makeup, I have always told you that. Nope my guess, would be because you still had your house robe on. Are you coming up to the house right now?"

"Yes, I just came to check up on Van mainly. Now I was headed back to the house, to come see you. How are you doing today, did you get some good sleep?"

"Yes, I did, I never even felt you slip out of bed."

"I had to be very sneaky about it. Are you hungry, at all?"

"Yes, I am, Mable said that she would make us something to eat."

"Good because I feel hungry. How about us go back up to the house, and eat. Then we can figure out what we could do for the rest of the day."

"That sounds good to me."

19

"How about we go out for some four-wheel driven, we haven't done that in a while." asked Levi.

"Okay, that sounds like it could be some fun. Then after that can we, lay out and get some sun, by the pool?"

"Why don't I believe you, when you say that could be fun? By the look you gave me, said that you don't really want to go out on the four-wheeler, is that right, do you?"

"To be quite honest with you, I'm not feeling the best. My stomach feels a little upset."

"Do you think that is because, you waited so long to eat?"

"No that can't be it I went just about all day yesterday, before I ate when I was at the court house. It's different, but it's not that bad, it will pass. If you want to go riding then we can, I'll be fine."

"Oh no you don't, I won't have my wife, go riding when she doesn't feel up to it. I think that laying around the pool, is what we both need. I called into work, and let them know that I won't be coming in. By the way, when was the last time, you seen your parents?"

"It's been a few days ago, but I did call them, and asked them to be praying for you."

"Maybe tomorrow if you're up to it. We'll take Van over there with us and visit with them. Do you think that's something that you would want to do?"

"Yes, that will be fine. I know they plan on staying, for the fair that starts next week. But they said they want to go back to Florida, right after that."

"Then it's settled, we will spend the day with them tomorrow. Should we have them come here, or do you think that they would rather us go to your place?"

"I'll ask my dad, if they can come here. There's so much more to do here, we have the pool, and the game room. Not to mention, all the toys that we could go riding on. Beside I wanted, my parents to see, just how much the bridge is done before they head back."

"The bridge how is that looking?" "Beautiful, he's close to being done."

"Really, I'm going to have to get out there, and take a look at it."

"If you don't feel like laying out right now, walk back there and take a look at it."

"I told you, that I will lay out with you. Right now, with all that's been going on in our lives, I would like to be with you every minute that I can. Is that alright with you?"

"Of course, that's alright. I just don't want you to feel, that you have to be next to me, if there's something that you want to do."

"I won't I promise. Shall we get in a swimwear, so we can get a tan while laying out?"

"Yes, I'd like to wear the new one that you bought me, on our honeymoon."

"Please do, I haven't got to see you wear it yet, I know that you are going to look so sexy with it on."

Levi and Yvonne sat out in the sun, to where they felt so hot, that they needed to dip in the pool to cool off.

"Oh, that feels so cold after sitting in the sun, for so long." Yvonne scolded lightly, when Levi threw water on her as she went to dip in the pool.

"I'm sorry honey, I was just trying to help you cool off, you looked so hot." he said laughing at her, as she tried to return the favor.

The two began to swim, after both getting all wet. Levi wanted to try and show off, in front of Yvonne. He went to the tallest of his diving boards and as he jumped off of it, he did three complete roll over's.

"Wow, I'm impressed, that was great. I didn't know that you could do that. You never told me that you did that sort of stuff."

"I have always loved to swim; it's been one of my passions. I will have to say, that is the first time in a long time that I have done that. At first, I wasn't going to try it, and then at the last minute, I just told myself to get up there, and go for it."

"I'd love to do that, it looked so fun. Could you show Van, that sometime? I'd love for him to be able to learn how to do that."

"Sure, if you would like, that is if I get the nerve again." he was laughing. "Where is he now? Did you say he's out back watching the men build the bridge?"

"Yes, he likes to watch them work."

"You stay on your float, I have my phone here, and I'll call Roman, and see if Van wants to come up here."

"Okay, unless you want to take a walk with me, and we can see the bridge together."

"Are you feeling up to it, I know you said a while ago, that your stomach didn't feel the best, after your walk?"

"I feel fine now, I think that I can handle it. And if I start to feel sick again, then you can carry me, you're such a strong man." she was now teasing.

"Then we need to get dressed, and out of these wet clothes. I guess it is time for me to see how that bridge is coming along."

"It very well might be all done, by the time we get out there. It was close to being done, earlier when I was there." Yvonne stated as she was drying herself off, with a beach towel.

"Let's get changed now, and go see if that's were Van is still. I think he's either there with Roman, or he's playing some game, in the game room."

"I'm sure there's nothing to worry about, I just want him to know that I'm here for him if he needs me."

"I'm sure that he does, and I'm here to, however long that may be."

"Levi, why would you say that like that?"

"I don't know I've been really trying not to think about everything, that's been going on, these last couple of days. I've really been trying to focus, on God and not fear, of what can happen. But every once in a while, I just get a feeling, that I could be going to prison, for a crime that I didn't commit."

"I get scared at times and try not to think on what could happen. But I try to remember what God said, that everything will be alright. When I think on that, it gives me great peace, and hope. Whenever my mind begins to think, that there's a chance of you being found guilty, it takes all my hopes and joy away."

Levi didn't say anything he just kept his arm around Yvonne, as the two walked back to the pond. She could see, that Van was sitting there watching everything, that was going on with the bridge.

"Hi mom and Levi, the bridge is all done, now their working on the gazebo. Isn't it cool, Roman and I got to walk across, it already, and it didn't even fall."

"I sure hope not, that would have been terrible, if you would have fallen in." Levi said giving Yvonne a wink.

"This sure is pretty, and you already walked a crossed it huh?" asked Yvonne.

"Yep, do you want to go across, it now mama?"

"No honey, that's alright, I'll wait until the gentleman are gone, then I will take a walk across it. It sure is a nice bridge, they did an awesome job building it. What you think Levi?"

"I think it's great, I love it. I knew that he could do it, when I saw what a great job, he was doing at that home up town."

Levi talked with the men, while Yvonne chatted with Van. She wanted to make sure that he wasn't feeling left out, her not spending as much time with him, as she used to before getting married to Levi.

"I know that you love me mama, but I just like watching, these men build stuff. I would like to do this when I get big."

"You would huh. Well one never quite knows, when there young as you are, do they. God may have something completely different, for you to do. But if not, then this would be a fine job, working with wood, and building things."

"Are you ready to go back up to the house?" asked Levi.

"Sure, if you're ready, then I am." Then Yvonne focused her attention, towards Van. "You should have seen what Levi did, when we went swimming today."

"What!"

"He went to the highest, diving board, and jumped off it. And when he did, he did three summer saults, before hitting the water. It was so cool, to see that."

"Wow really, I want to see you do that too, can I see you do that Levi?" Van asked so excited.

Levi looked over at Yvonne, "Oh thanks honey." Then looking over at Van as he was waiting for an answer. "Sure, I'll do it for you, little man." he said ruffling up his hair. "I think that your mom, likes putting me on the spot. When I did that earlier, it was just on the spare of the moment type of thing. That was the first time I did anything like that, in a very long time."

"I'm sorry honey." Yvonne said all playful acting. "I really didn't mean to put you on the spot."

"Oh, I'm sure that you didn't." He smiled looking at Van. "If you would like buddy, I could teach you, while you're young how to do summer saults."

"You will really!" Van said all excited. "I would love to learn to do summer saults."

"Really my son doing that in water, isn't that dangerous?"

"Come on mama, it will be alright. You said how cool it looks for Levi to do that. So why would it be cool, for him and not me?"

"Oh boy, I think you got something started there, honey, anyway it was you that said you would like Van to learn to do this."

"I think that you're right, if Levi wants to teach you, how to do that. Then I won't stand in the way, of you learning something, that can be very good for your future. I guess I did ask him earlier if he could teach you how too."

"How would that help me, in the future mama?"

"It may be of some help, to your future. Remember when I was just telling you, that you don't know right now what you will do for a living when you get older?"

"Yes."

179

"When you get into high school, you may want to join the swim team. And if that be the case, then by you learning, how to jump off the diving board and doing summer saults, that may help you in the future, do you understand?"

"I think, but can I just learn how to without the future thing?"

Levi stood there laughing at him. "I think that might be just a little much for him to understand."

"I think that your right. Maybe for now, we will just focus on the now no need to confuse him any longer."

"We'll see you buddy, when you come back to the house." stated Levi.

"Okay, I will do that later Okay?"

"That's fine honey, but I don't want you going into the water here okay?"

"I know mama, I won't."

Levi and Yvonne walked back to the house, talking of their conversation with Van. "I think it was a little hard for him to understand this whole future thing. I think at times, I attend to forget he's only eight. You seem pretty good, at remembering that."

"I don't know how young girls, think. Whenever when I talk to Van, I try to remember what I knew at his age. And what I could understand, that's what I go by for the most part of it."

"So, you think that your pretty clever huh." she said jokingly.

"No, I'm just smart." he teased back, wrapping his arms around her, for the rest of their walk back to the house.

"What do you feel like doing, for the rest of the day?" asked Yvonne.

"One thing that I need to do is call up, Ron Cutler. I haven't talked with him today, and I need to know if he's found out anything else, from Roxie's neighbors."

"Yes, that does need to get done, it's only a few more days and you have to go back to court gain. Has your lawyer called you at all, today?"

"No not yet, I'll call Ron first, and see what he has to say. Then I'll call Mr. Allen.

Ron told Levi, that he found a woman that lives next to where Roxie lived. And she was willing, to come to court, and testify that she seen a man, that drove a blue pickup truck, snooping around Roxie's place, the day of the murder."

"That's great news, I wonder if she told the cops anything."

"I don't know, but I'm sure glad that she's willing to come to court, and tell what she seen. He could be the guy that killed, her."

"What I want to know is why someone wanted to kill her. What could she have done, that was so terrible, that someone would want her dead?"

"I don't know, that same question has gone through my head, at least a thousand times or more. All I wanted when I went there was to ask her to leave us alone, and if she didn't I would take a restraining order, out, on her. Or call the police if that didn't help."

"You know when you told me, about Roxie. I had a completely different picture, of her in my mind. Because you are so sweet and caring I just thought that since you were seeing her, that she would be the same way. Boy was I ever wrong, she was so mean, and had a very nasty attitude."

"Your right, and I never seen that in her, until she came back from her vacation. Then she became someone that I didn't even know anymore. How people can seem to change, so fast is beyond me."

"Did you ever think, after all this has happened? That she was really, that nasty way all along. Maybe she was just letting you see, one side of her this whole time?"

"But for two years, don't you think that it would be hard for someone to act sweet, for that long. It seems if it was just an act, that the cat inside of her would be just a ripping, the insides of her to get out."

"Maybe that's what happened, when she seen Van and I here. Her true colors finally came out. And that's what we all got to see."

The two discussed all the what if's, before Van came back up to the house for the rest of the day.

After Supper, Van reminded Levi about teaching him how to do summer saults. Levi chuckled at Van, for the last bite of food, in his mouth wasn't even gone, when he asked about it.

"Did you ever hear the old saying; about never go swimming, right after you eat? They say it could give you craps, in your stomach."

"I never heard that, but me and my mom, never had a pool before. So, we never knew that."

"Speak for yourself, young man. I did know that, but I may have not told you before, because we didn't have a pool, to worry about that. And when talking to others, the proper way you should talk would be, my mom and I, not me and my mom. Okay?"

"Yes ma'am, I just forgot."

The rest of the afternoon, went as planned. Levi did a triple summer sault off the tallest diving board. Van watched with amazement, and pure joy. He couldn't wait, for Levi to show him how it was done. Van quickly forgot about going back to the pond, with Roman to watch the men work and finish what they were doing. Now he had a whole new meaning, of hanging out with Levi. Three days have passed, and Van had learned, to do a summer sault under water. He kept Levi very occupied, with teaching him what he knew. When Levi wasn't in the pool to help, Jack was there helping him learn to turn over better, under water. Yvonne told him, that before he was allowed to jump off the diving board, he would have to know how to master it first under water.

"MOM, MAMA!" A loud scream was heard, coming from the outside."

Yvonne went running outside, to see what had happened, that caused such a ruckus. "Van what is the matter?"

"I did it, I really did it.

"You really did what?"

"Grandpa's been helping me master the summer sault. And I did, I finally did. Now can I do that from the diving board?"

"Van, you mean to tell me, that you did all that yelling, so you could tell me that you mastered the summer sault. I am happy for you Van, but there is a better way to tell your mother something like that. You about scared me to death, is that what you were trying to do?"

Van put his head down; he knew that his mother sounded upset. "I'm sorry mama, I was just so excited, that I can finally do that, after all my practicing. I just thought that you would be happy for me."

"Oh Van, I am happy for you. When Levi is able to be out here with you, I'll let him see how good you do that, and if he thinks that you're ready, then you can try it okay?"

"Okay mama." he said turning his back, and hanging his head down.

"Yvonne, I think when you came out here, and then you yelled at him it disappointed him pretty bad. I think that he thought that you would be a lot more excited for him, then you acted." stated Marilyn.

Yvonne was now feeling sad, for the way she acted towards Van. She never meant to hurt him, it was the way that he yelled. She knew that she needed to go ask him, to forgive her.

Van was sitting by the pool, when Yvonne asked if she could talk to him.

He walked over to his mom, with his head still lowered. "Yes mama."

"Van, I'm sorry honey, for raising my voice at you. I really didn't mean to, it was just the way you screamed, when I was in the house. I didn't know if something bad had happened. I guess when I saw that nothing bad took place, I was relieved in some way, but then in another way, it upset me to think that you yelled so loud, to get me to see what you could do. You see son, the kind of scream that you did come's when something bad had happened, not something good. I do want you to know, that I am proud that you didn't give up, and you kept working with it until you mastered it."

"I forgive you, mama." he said as he hugged her as tight as he could. "Can I show Levi now how good I can do? Momma, I will try never to scream like something is wrong again."

"Thank you, Van." She said with a smile. "Levi is in his office right now, talking with his lawyer. I'll go and see how much longer he's going to be."

"Okay, I hope that he can come out now, so I can show him."

"I'll go see right now." Yvonne knew that just by Vans actions, that he was so excited to show Levi just what he had learned, she too had hoped that he was all done talking, so he could come and watch Van.

"Levi are you almost done, in here?" she asked.

"Yes honey, I'm just saying that I'll see him tomorrow at court."

Yvonne sat down on the couch, in Levi's office. She really hated to bother him, at a time like this. But she also knew that he would want to see what Van has accomplished.

"How can I help you honey, you look very tired to me. Is something wrong?"

"No not really, I hated to even bother you with this, but I thought that you might want to see, how much Van has picked up with doing his summer sault. He said that he's ready, for the diving board now."

"Oh really, well then I will just have to see the little guy. Where is he at?"

"Outside with my father, the two of them, has been working on it for quite a while now but Van wants you to see."

"Then let's get out there, so we can watch what he can do." Levi looked over at Yvonne, as she stood up. "Honey are you feeling okay? You look like your either not feeling so good, or you are very tired. Which one is it?"

"Maybe a little of both, I do think that I need to rest a little. I don't know what it is, I've just been feeling so tired lately."

"Why don't you go lay down for a while, and I'll tell everyone that you aren't feeling the best, and went to lay down for a while."

"Are you sure that you don't mind. But what about Van, he is so much looking to show us what he can do."

"He can show me, and I'll let him know that you will watch him, at another time."

"Okay honey, but if you need me, just give me a holler." she said then she was gone, up the stairs and off to bed, for a nap. When lying down, Yvonne was thinking about how she's been feeling lately, for the past weeks. Did I catch the flu, why all of a sudden, have I been getting so sick? She drifted off, into a dream that she was having baby, a baby girl.

She woke from her dream. Oh no, she thought. Can it be that I am pregnant? She lay in bed until she fell into a deep sleep. She went back into the same dream, of her and Levi having a baby girl. This time she was able to see, that the baby had black curly hair, and dark brown eyes. She has a dark complexion like her father. Yvonne woke up rubbing her belly. She had to tell Levi her dream, but she thought that it might be better to wait, until after court. Then she thought that she better, go buy a home pregnancy test, to see if she test positive. Why let Levi carry this on his shoulders, when he has court to worry about. Lord God, please help Levi tomorrow in court. Let him be found innocent in Jesus name amen. How can I already be having the feeling of pregnancy this soon if I am pregnant? She thought to herself.

"You're up, did you manage to get a little rest?" asked Levi coming back into the house.

"Yes, I did a little." she said without going into any other detail. "So how did Van make out on his summer sault?"

"Oh honey, you would be so proud of him. He did an awesome job, I believe he's ready."

"Really, did he jump off the diving board then?"

"No, I asked him to wait for you, so you would be able to see him do that."

"Thank you honey, and yes I would really like to see him, but are you really sure that he won't get hurt by jumping?"

"Honey, whenever you do anything like jumping from a tall place. There's always a chance, of getting hurt. That's why I made sure that he could do it over and over again. Honey he is ready, I made sure before telling him that I will allow him to jump."

"Is he going to be jumping from the top, like you did?"

"Oh no, he's only going to be on the six-foot board. I would never have him go that far up, when he's so young."

"Okay, when do you want to do this?"

"I think that he's ready now, he's been waiting for you to get up. He's been staying right close to the pool." Levi laughed about Van and his persistence."

"Okay let's do this, before I change my mind, and not want him to."

"He'll be fine honey, he's doing a really great job under water. I told him, and showed him over, and over how's it's done."

"You showed him?"

"Yes, I did. I went to the smallest one then the second one, then the tallest one. And I did that several times."

"Good, then I will watch him."

Levi and Yvonne walked outside, to tell Van it's time to show them, what he can do. Van got up on the smallest board, so proud to be able to do summer saults.

"Be careful Van." Yvonne said as she sat there, praying quietly to herself.

They sat there watching closely, as he bent his knees, as to get up to jump. Then Yvonne sat there holding her breath, as he jumped, and did a perfect summer sault. She stood up clapping her hands, so proud of his accomplishment.

"You did an awesome job honey. I am so proud of you."

"Thanks mama. That was so much fun, can I do that again."

"Van, you really did make me proud son, you did a very good job. Too bad that your grandparents went back home so soon, they could have seen this for their self."

"When did they leave?" asked Yvonne.

"Right after you went upstairs, to take your nap."

"I felt bad, about going up stairs like that, I was just so tired."

"How are you feeling now?"

"I still feel a little tired, but better than before. Do you care if I go over to see, my parents, for a while?"

"Would you like me to go with you?"

"I'd like to go see them by myself, if you don't mind. I would really like to talk with them alone. Do you mind?"

"No not really, if you feel that you need to talk to them, then I will stay here with Van."

Yvonne told Van that she was going away for a while, but would be back in about an hour or two. She left still feeling very tired, she knew that when she was pregnant with Van, she got tired a lot. But this was different, she seemed to be more tired, then when she was before. She heard before, that every pregnancy was different. She needed to go to the store, and pick up a pregnancy test, before alarming Levi that he was to be a father. Feeling bad, for not being up front with him, as to why she didn't want him to go. She would go to the store first to get the test. Then she would take it once getting to her other home, to find out the results.

"Hi mom hi dad, how are you?" Yvonne asked when she arrived at her home. "I'm sorry about earlier, going up to take a nap, like I did. I just felt so tired."

"Well I'm glad to see that you're doing okay honey, you had me a little worried." said her dad.

"I'm sorry to worry the both of you, I think that Levi's been a little worried to. I have to use the restroom. Then I'll come out and visit with the two of you."

"Did you come here all by yourself?" asked her mother.

"Yes." she raised her voice a little, so they could hear her from the bathroom.

Yvonne opened the box up, and pulled out the pregnancy test. She read what she was to do, and then she did what the instructions said to do.

Standing next to the sink, in the bathroom, she watched as she could see the first line show up, and then she began to see the next line which led her to believe that she was indeed pregnant. I can't believe it, I'm pregnant, it must have happened on my honeymoon. How can I tell Levi, when he has so much on his plate right now, she thought walking out of the bathroom, and into the living room. "I think I know why, I've been so tired, and not feeling the best." she said to her parents.

"And why is that, do you think that it's because of what's been going on with Levi?"

"That's what I thought at first, now I believe it's because, I'm pregnant."

"PREGNANT!" and when did you find that out?" asked the mother, surprised by what Yvonne had said.

"I just found out a minute ago, in the bathroom. I took a home pregnancy test. And it said that I was."

"Are you going to go home and tell Levi?"

"I don't know what to do, he's got so much going on right now with this whole court thing, it's been hard on the both of us."

"I know honey, but it's his baby as well as yours, you need to go home, and tell him that he is going to be a daddy." Jack told her.

"Your right dad, I'm going to do that right now. I'll be back tomorrow, to visit the both of you." she gave them both a kiss, and then she left.

Yvonne came home sooner than Levi had thought that she would. "Is everything okay?"

"I think so, I found out some news, today. I was wondering how you would feel, about being a daddy?"

"A daddy?" he asked, then it hit him what she was talking about. "What, are you serious?"

"That's why I wanted to go to my parents, by myself. I wanted to take a pregnancy test, to make sure before I told you anything. I didn't want to get your hopes up, if I wasn't."

Levi picked her up gently, giving her a kiss. I am so happy, are you happy?"

"I am, I just want this court stuff to be over with and done. How long does something like this take? You know a murder trial?"

"I couldn't tell you, I have no idea. Every case is different, I pray that it won't take too long. I want to be with my family, more now than I ever have. And I didn't think that could be possible. I love you so much honey."

Yvonne could tell that he was very excited about the pregnancy. She wanted him to be glad about it, now she was just waiting for that same excitement to fall on her. Thoughts would come to her, what if he was found guilty, and had to go to prison right when the two married, and found out that they are going to be having a baby.

20

The following day came, for Levi to appear in court. He was nervous and scared. Yvonne was right at his side, praying that the real killer would be found, if he hadn't been already. When they walked in the court room, Yvonne noticed a woman that looked to be in her twenties, sitting there as she and Levi walked through the door. The woman seemed to be staring at Levi, like she might know him. But when Yvonne looked at him, it didn't seem to her that he knew who that woman was.

"Do you want to sit here, he asked pointing to the back row."

"That will be fine."

The two sat down waiting for the judge to walk in and begin. Their hands were held together so tight, that when Levi's lawyer entered, and asked him to come and sit with him at the table. It was hard for Yvonne to release her hand from him. Then he was called to take a stand. Levi told his side of the story, then the woman that Yvonne seen looking at him was called to testify.

"Could you tell the court, your full name?" asked Mr. Allen Levi's lawyer.

"Rachael Ann Miller."

"I'd like you to tell the court, what you seen on the day of September the third two thousand, and eighteen. At the address of where the murder of Roxy Stratton took place?"

"I saw a blue pickup truck pull up in front of the place parked across the road!'

"Did you see anyone get out of that truck?"

"Yes, I seen a man, get out and walk up Roxie's driveway. I watched him for a bit, then I saw her let him in."

"You are telling this court, that you saw Roxie open up her door, and let a man driving a blue pickup, come into her home?"

"Yes, that's what I've seen."

"Can you tell us anything else, about that day?"

"I saw when Mr. Ubani, came by."

"What can you tell the court, about that?"

"I saw as he pulled in the driveway, and walked up to the door."

"What else can you tell us, about that day?"

"Roxie never opened her door, so I watched as he walked around to the back of her house. Then I saw as he looked inside of her garage. Then he walked back to his car, and took off."

"Then what did you see?"

"I saw that man that drove the pickup, come out of her house, and get in his truck and leave."

"Did you see anyone come by her place after that?"

"No, I had a feeling, you know when you get a feeling that something is just not right?"

"Yes, I know, so what did you do when you got that feeling?"

"I first tried to call Roxie, but when she didn't answer her phone, I went over there, and knocked on her door. When she didn't answer, I knew that something was really wrong. So, I peaked in her window, and that's when I could see she was just laying right there, on the floor."

"Then what did you do?"

"I was tapping on her window, trying to see if she would get up. But when she didn't I called the police."

"Let me get this straight. You're sitting here, telling the court that when you saw Levi Ubani, he never even went into Roxie's home, nor did he get to see Roxie?"

"That is correct, he never did."

Did you see Roxie that day at all before, the man in the pickup truck came by?"

"Yes, I did, she was outside watering her plants." "Your honor, I am done with this witness."

Yvonne sat there, feeling happy that things had to be looking good for Levi. She was thanking God, for someone coming forth to tell what they had seen."

"Your honor, I don't see the need, to keep this court waiting to see if Levi is a murderer, any longer. It's clear to say, that he is not the man that we are looking for. I would like to think, with this new line of evidence, which the court has just heard that they will throw this case out of court."

"Mr. Allen, I hear what the witness has said, but we still don't have the other person, if there is another person. I will allow Mr. Ubani, to stay out of jail on his bond. However, we need to find, our killer."

"Thank you, your honor; we are working with the police, on that."

Levi stood up and walked back to Yvonne, after the judge set another court date. "Did you hear that honey, I knew that I had a bad feeling about, that blue truck? Now I have to come back, in October again. I sure hope that the police will find this guy, before then."

"I'm so happy, that you're coming home with Me." she said hugging him.

"Let's go home honey, and tell Roman and Mable to keep their prayers a coming."

"I want to tell them and Van about the Baby, I never told Van yet. But Now I feel some kind of new joy, and I can't wait to tell him, that he's going to be a big brother."

"Me too, I wish that my mother would have lived, to see her first grandchild." after Levi said that, he regretted it right away. "I'm sorry, honey I should never have said that, I wasn't thinking. I do consider Van just like he was my own son."

"I know that you do, and I wish that she could have been here to. My mother and father live so far away, it's not like the baby will have close grandparents."

"Maybe not, but we will be what she needs. We are a family, and we are strong and will teach her in the ways of the Lord."

"You said her, what made you say that?"

"Did I, I didn't even know that I did."

"I find that kind of neat, because yesterday when I went upstairs, and took a nap. I had a dream that I was pregnant. And it was a girl, in my dream."

"You're kidding me, really?"

"I'm telling you the truth; I think that is pretty cool, that you would say that."

Levi and Yvonne told the rest of the house hold, about the baby. Van didn't seem to say much, Yvonne questioned him as to why, he seemed to be disappointed.

"I don't want you and Levi to love the baby more." he stated.

"Oh, honey do you really think that I could love this baby, more then you. I could never love the baby more. You will both be my children, and I will love the both of you, the same."

Levi pulled Van close to his side. "And I feel the same way that your mom does. I know that I am not your birth father, but I love you just like, if I was. If you remember, it was you that I fell for first before your mom."

"I know, you told me that you wanted us to always be close."

"Yes, I did, and I meant it. I cared for you from the very beginning. And if you and your mom would let me, I'd like to adopt you, and then you would have our last name."

Van opened his eyes really big, "Really you will adopt me, and then you will be my real dad."

Levi looked over at Yvonne, not quite knowing what to say. "Van if your mom allows me to adopt you, then I will be your legal father. But you will always have a natural birth father."

"But you will be my dad, now right?"

"Van that will be something that Levi and I will talk about. After our talk, we will let you know what we come up with okay."

"Okay mama."

Later that night, as Levi and Yvonne were going to bed. She knew that she needed to address the issue of adoption. Do you really know what you're saying, when you're talking about adopting Van?"

"Yes, this is something that I have thought about, before we even married. I love Van as my very own. And I know that he had a father, that I'm sure loved him. But don't you think that it would be nice if he could call me dad, and have our last name as well. I hate for him to be the older brother, and have a different last name. I know that it's really up to you, what we decide about this, but I want Van to know that we having our baby won't change how I feel for him."

"If this is something that you feel this strong about, then I will support you all the way. I just want you to know, that if you were to adopt him, then whatever future he has will involve you. Rather it will be when he gets older, and gets in any kind of trouble. Which I pray will never happen. I just want you to know everything, and really think it over."

"Honey, I have. I know that if we ever divorced, I would have to pay child support, to him as well as the other child. I know that we won't divorce, I'm just saying I've thought it all through."

"It sounds to me, like you have been thinking about this for a while." she lay in bed, not knowing what would be the best thing to do.

"Honey, do you not really want this, because when you were married to Mark, he was a good dad?"

"I had a very good marriage with him, and yes he was a good father to Van. I just don't want to take his father away from him. Do you know what I mean?"

"Yes, I do. I think that you might feel that you would be dishonoring him."

"Yes, I guess in a way I do feel that way. And Van is so young, he doesn't know what he would be giving up. He would be getting our last name, which is always a nice thing. But what about his birth name. I just don't want him, when he's older to ask why he doesn't still have his birth name."

"Okay, I am so sorry that I ever brought this up in the first place. I should have talked to you first, before I opened up my big mouth."

"Honey, don't say that about yourself. I understand why, you would feel the way that you do. But please understand where I'm coming from."

"I guess tomorrow we need to talk with Van, and get him to understand. He seemed to like the idea, of having our last name, so much. I hate to disappoint him. But since I'm the one to open up the whole can of worms, I'd like to be the one to tell him why it can't happen."

"Okay, honey. You talk to him, and try to get him to understand. Then if you would like, I will talk to him."

"I can't say that I'm happy about this, but I can say, that I understand. Good night honey, I love you."

"Good night babe." Yvonne said as she rolled over to her other side.

Morning came, and Levi knew that he needed to clear up the mess, he had caused the night before. When he went down stairs, Van was eating his breakfast, with Mable. "Good morning, how was everyone's sleep?"

"Very good, how was yours?" asked Mable.

"It was okay, I need to have a talk with Van, just as soon as he is done eating."

"Are we going to talk about you adopting me?"

"Yes, buddy we are." he said sounding so disappointed.

"Why you so sad, don't you want to adopt me now?"

"Oh Van, it's nothing like that at all. I'd adopt you today, if I could."

"What is this about Levi?" asked Mable.

"I don't know if that's something, that I should really say, right now."

"Okay whatever it is, I hate to see you so disappointed. I know that all morning long, that's what this boy, has been talking about."

"What has he been talking about?" asked Yvonne, as she walked into the dining room.

Levi turns to see, her walking in the room. "I was telling Van that after he's done eating that we needed to have a talk. Mable was letting me know that all morning, Vans been talking about getting adopted."

"Oh, I see, so this is something that you really want to happen huh?"

"Oh yes mama. I want you, and Levi's last name. I think if my real dad was alive, I wouldn't want it changed, but I want Levi to be my dad now, because my real dads not with us anymore.

"It sounds to me, like you know what you want. I know that Levi really wants to be your dad too. I have been thinking, and I think that would be a very good idea. Levi you should call up your lawyer, and ask him what steps need to be done, to have this happen."

"Really, are you saying that I can adopt him now?"

"Yes honey, please forgive me, for how I acted last night. I was just thinking, of everything, but you and Van. I believe that this is something that should happen."

"I will go call him right now, and see what it's going to take, to get this done" Levi gave Yvonne a kiss, and he was gone to make a very important phone call.

Yvonne stood there looking at Mable, and Van. "He must really want this bad."

"So, do I mama, really, really bad. I don't want a different name then you have."

"Let's wait and see what Levi finds out, from his lawyer."

Within a few minutes, he was out to tell everyone the exciting news. "You won't believe how simple it really is, for me to be able to adopt Van."

"What did he say, he must have said that it can be done?"

"There will be a couple things that we will need to do. Then after that is done, it will only take a few weeks, and he can be adopted."

"Okay, what are the couple things that need to be done?"

Levi walked over to Yvonne, to whisper in her ear. "I don't want to mention it in front of Van. Can we talk alone?"

"Van, Levi and I are going to talk, for a minute. We'll be back in a few minutes."

"Is everything alright mama?" "Yes, its fine honey."

"What's the matter, I thought that you said that he could be adopted?"

"I did, that's true, but I didn't want to mention in front of Van, about Marks death certificate. The court will have to see that, before I can adopt Van. Then it's just a matter of signing paper work, and the judge will ask Van, if this is something that he wants."

"That seems simple enough, I have that at my home in town. We can go there today, if you would like. Then we can get your lawyer, to give us whatever paper work that we need to move this along."

"Why don't we eat, and then go do that. I'd like to have him be my son, before I go back to court."

"Do you think that it will be done in time, for that?"

"Yes, honey I do, my court date is about a month away. If we get this thing going today, and have all the papers filed, then I don't see any reason why, it shouldn't be done. I'll go call Allen up again, and tell him to get the paper work started."

"Why you go do that, I'll go see, what's for breakfast!' said Yvonne.

Levi did ask his lawyer, to get all the paper work drawn up. He and Yvonne had signed all the papers that needed to be signed. They had a court date set for the beginning part, of October.

"That's going to happen faster, then I thought that it would." Levi stated.

"I know, I thought for sure that you would have to come back to court, before we would get in there about the adoption. I know Van will be happy, about this."

"We have a little more than two weeks, and he will be my son. Can we have him start calling me dad now, if he wants to?"

"Sure, why don't we talk to him about it?"

Van was glad to know that he could start to call Levi his dad. He wanted to do that for a while, but was always too scared to ask him if he could. Now he wasn't going to waste, anytime doing it. The first time Levi heard Van call him dad, was so thrilling to him. He knew that he wanted to be a father, sometime in life. He just didn't know that it would come from an eight year old. Van would slip up, from time to time, and call him Levi. Then he would turn around and say sorry I mean dad.

After a couple weeks have past, Levi and Yvonne took a drive into town. When Levi happened to notice, a blue pickup truck that seemed to look much like the one, that was at Roxie's house, the day she was killed.

"Look! He was pointing. "I can almost swear, that truck right there, pulling out is the same truck that I saw at Roxie's. I'm going to follow it, you write down the licenses plate number."

"Maybe we should just call the cops, and let them come check it out. What if it is the killer, then what if they try to kill us?"

"I won't get that close, are you writing down the plate?"

"I'm trying to, but you need to get a little closer. But not to close, I don't want him to see us."

"Is this close enough?" asked Levi, trying to get a look at the driver.

"Yes, I got it now, does it still look like the same truck to you?"

"Yes, it does, I am sure it's the same one. But this is what I can't tell for sure." He said looking at the driver, the best he could.

"What?"

"The driver looks like, Mack Dryer. You know the one that came to our wedding. But why would he be driving an old piece of junk, like this. I have never, known him to drive something like this before."

"Are you sure, that's him?"

"I'm pretty sure, the thing is, if this is him. He sure looks rough. The Mack I know has always kept himself clean cut, and when I see this guy through his mirror, he looks very unclean."

"Should I call the cops?"

"Yes, you better, before he gets suspicious, of us following him. Tell them were we are at right now, and tell them that we are following, the truck that they been looking for."

Levi and Yvonne stayed close enough, to see when the cops would come along side of them. They slowed down enough to give room, for the cops to pull over the truck.

"I'm going to go past them slow. I want to see, for sure if it is Mack." Levi spoke getting in the other lane. "I was right, it is Mack. Why would he want to hurt Roxie, I just can't believe what I am seeing right now. I always thought that the two of them were friends. I wonder if they're going to do a police lineup. You know have that woman, that said she seen that truck and the driver go into Roxie's house."

"Don't you think that you should call your lawyer up, and tell him what's going on right now?"

"First before I do that, I want to make sure that their arresting him first. I'm going to turn around right here, in the taco bell, parking lot. I want to go back by them slow, to see what they're going to do."

He drove by slowly, so he could see, just what the police where doing. "Yep they are arresting him, their putting the hand cuffs on him right now They must have seen something, for them to be taking him to jail. I'm going to call Allen up right now."

"Do you think that they found something, in his truck?"

"They must have, otherwise why would they be putting him in the back of their car. Hello Allen, this is Levi Ubani. Hey do I ever have some news, at least I think I do."

Yvonne sat there listening to Levi talk, as he explained to Allen about Mack getting arrested. Allen told Levi that he was going to call down to the police station, to see if they will agree to a line up. Levi would have to wait to hear back from Mr. Allen. While he and Yvonne sat in the car praying, that if Mack was the one that did this horrible act, as to kill Roxie, that he be found guilty.

"You know Yvonne, as much as I want to be free, from this ugly thing that is being held over me, about Roxie. I hate to see, that Mack is the one that did this. Why would he ever want to kill her, I don't understand that, for the life of me. What could she of ever done to him, that would make him want her dead?"

"I don't know maybe there's a lot more to this, than you even know about. If he is the one, are you going to see if you can go to the jail, and see him?"

"I don't know yet. I guess it all depends on, what comes out in court."

The phone rang, and Levi looked on his caller id, to see whose name was on it. "It's Allen. Yes, Allen what did you find out? Okay thanks, for checking into it for me."

"Well what did he find out?"

"He said that they are going to do a police lineup, and as soon as they do, he will call me to let me know what the woman said."

"When are they going to do the line up?" "Tomorrow Allen said."

"Well we will just have to wait, but this could be it. We may get a phone call, saying that she picked him out, and you will be able to go free, right?"

"I'm sure of it, that's something that I will need to talk to Allen about. But first things first let's see if she even picks him out first."

"I'll keep my fingers crossed."

"Oh honey, I really don't want it to be Mack, I have been friends with him, sense we were just kids in school."

"I know honey, I'm sorry, but someone is the killer, and I don't want you to take the fall, because someone wanted to kill her."

"We'll just have to wait for the call we get from Allen tomorrow. He promised to call right after the lineup was done."

"It was a long night, for Levi and Yvonne. The two hardly talked the whole night, there seemed to be something in the atmosphere that made them not want to say much to each other. It was like they were thinking if they said too much to each other, then Levi would be the one to be found guilty even when he's wasn't.

Morning came, and Levi was pacing the floors, waiting for Allen to call with the news.

"If you're not careful, you will be buying new carpet." said Yvonne

"Whys that?" he asked.

"Your pacing so much, that you're going to wear a spot in the carpet." Just as she has said that, the phone rang.

He grabbed the phone, so fast, and answered. "Please just tell me is Mack the one that did this to Roxie?"

Yvonne watched as she seen Levi break down, and drop down to his knees. "Why, did he do that why?" Levi hung up the phone, with his face full of tears. Yvonne couldn't help but feel for him. Although she was grateful, that the killer was caught, she could tell that this was tearing her husband up. She held on to him, as they sat on the carpet and Levi wept for his friend until he couldn't weep no more.

Levi was found innocent, when returning to court. His lifelong friend Mack was found guilty of killing Roxie. In court Mack told about what took place, the day that Roxie died. He had told about how he and Roxie had been using and selling drugs. Mack told of how Roxie had stolen all the drug money and had no plans on giving him his part of the money. Mack told about how he took several different drugs before going to see Roxie. And when he got over to her place, the two of them got into a big fight and that is what ultimately led to her death. After Levi got over the shock of what happened, he later went to the jail to visit with Mack, and he told him about Jesus and His unfailing love, and forgiveness. Levi told Mack that God was a God of second chances, but it's our choice if we decide to live for him. That day, Mack accepted the Lord Jesus Christ, in his heart. Months later Yvonne had given birth to a beautiful baby girl, name Queeneth Marie Ubani. The proud parents decided after the birth of their daughter, that they would try for one more. And this time around, they had Levi Junior. The two began to sing in church together, and Levi got his minister licenses, and became to co-pastor at the church he and Yvonne belonged to. Often times when the Reverend was out of town, he would have Levi preach at church. Levi and Yvonne were known to be one of the happiest and well-loved couples in town.

THE END

199

Printed in the United States
By Bookmasters